Karen McDavid

Karen McDavid was born and raised in the hills of eastern Kentucky. She still resides there with her husband, two married children and three beautiful grandchildren. Having always been a homemaker, the drawing to write Under Heaven seemed too far reaching for the longest time. So by faith, but above all God's help, these words were written.

It is my hope that you laugh, you cry and yes, feel drawn to "look up".

Sincerely,

Karen McDavid

Under Heaven is inspired by Ecclesiastes 3:1.
"To everything there is a season, and a time to every purpose under the heaven." (KJV)

Heart to Heart Publishing, Inc.
528 Mud Creek Road * Morgantown, KY 42261
(270) 526-5589
www.hearttoheartpublishinginc.com

Copyright ©2016
Publishing Rights: Heart to Heart Publishing, Inc..
Publishing Date February 14, 2017

Library of Congress Control No. 2016954459

ISBN_978-1-937008-49-9

Senior Editor: L.J. Gill
Editor: Susan J. Mitchell
Cover Design & Illustration: Beth Walker
Layout: Beth Walker

Printed in United States of America

First Edition
10 9 8 7 6 5 4 3 2

Heart to Heart Publishing, Inc. books are available at a special discount for bulk purchase in the US by corporations, institutions and other organizations. For more information, please contact
Special Sales at (270) 526-5589

ϕ

This book is dedicated to my Husband whose unwavering encouragement lent determination to my pen.

Also many thanks to Heart to Heart Publishing and to Linda for the patience and knowledge willingly given.

ϕ

CHAPTER 1

A gray veil of moisture floated upon the morning air. The thick blanketing fog dampened Hannah's hair. She made her way down the narrow path that led to the creek behind her house. The dirt path, made smooth over time, was cool beneath her bare feet. Hannah felt a shiver run through her as she walked down the bank that gently sloped to the water's edge.

"It must be the morning dampness," Hannah thought out loud. But still there was a strange sense of foreboding that stirred within her.

Hannah preferred beginning her day with some time alone. The crisp running water was soothing to her ear. While sitting upon her favorite large rock which extended slightly into the rippling current, she noticed a strange silence. Even the birds seem to be unwilling to make their music on this mid-summer's day. Scooting closer, she dangled her feet into the therapeutic motion that gently lapped against her calves, wetting the hem of her everyday dress.

Reaching up to tie her long, waist-length, sable brown hair into a thick braid, Hannah thought of what lay ahead for the day's chores. She knew her mother would need help with the baking and preparing the berries to make jelly for canning from this year's abundant supply. Hannah could hear her father and brother working out by the barn. They were getting ready for the first cutting of hay. Hannah quickly splashed some of the cool water on her face. Standing to straighten her coolest, cotton dress, she knew the warm air would soon dry the edges of her sleeves and hem.

Turning to make her way back to help her mother, there was a very loud and terrible cry from her father. Feeling sick, Hannah ran as fast as she could around to the front of the house and toward the barn. Her mother was already out the front door and close to where her father and Toby were. Roman was kneeling over his son who lay motionless.

Hannah heard her father say to her mother, "Toby had a very bad fall from the barn loft door. "

Hannah ran to open the front door of the house. She rushed into Toby's room and folded down the quilts of his bed which her mother had already made up before starting breakfast that morning. Roman and Sophie lay their son tenderly down on his bed, both whispering prayers that their only son would be ok.

Time stood still for Hannah. Thoughts that her brother may be seriously injured because of his shallow breathing and his bluish, ashen face kept all other thoughts in the background.

Roman announced that he was going into town to get Doctor Hayes. The very small town of Sundance, Wyoming was only about three miles away. Hannah could tell her mother was trying to be strong while tending to Toby. Hannah looked up and asked God to allow her brother to live. She couldn't imagine life without her gentle and compassionate younger brother.

At a very early age they saw that Toby had a way with animals. His sensitivity to their needs made taking care of the horses and cows an easier job for their father. Now at fourteen years of age, he was becoming quite the young man. Hannah being five years older was a very protective sister.

A sobbing cry turned her attention back to her mother who sat holding Toby's hand. "Mama," Hannah said. "Dad will be right back with Doctor Hayes. It will be a quick trip to town if the doctor is not out on call."

Sophie turned her emerald-green eyes, that shined with unshed tears, upon her daughter. "Toby has to live! He just has to!" Sophie said as she grabbed a hold of her daughter's hand while still hanging on to her son's.

Hannah knew her mother must be drawing on every ounce of faith that she had. As they were both knelt beside the bed, Hannah began to recite the Lord's Prayer. After that, the only sound in the room was that of Toby's raspy breathing.

"It seems like an eternity since Father had left to fetch the doctor," Hannah thought to herself. She could tell by her

brother's pale skin and motionless body that he was in a very bad way.

After what had felt like hours, she heard the beating of horse's hooves outside. Rushing into the room with Dr. Hayes, Roman stood beside his wife while the doctor examined Toby. Hannah watched the doctor's face for any sign of hope. His expression remained emotionless while he listened to Toby's restricted and shallow breathing. *"I suppose they are trained to conceal their thoughts in order not to unnecessarily alarm the loved ones looking on. I sure do hope that is not the case here,"* Hannah told herself.

Hannah continued to watch as the doctor felt for injuries on Toby's head. Turning his head, he revealed a purplish bump just behind Toby's right ear. By this time, his breathing and pulse was almost non-existent.

Dr. Hayes straightened and said, "Roman and Sophie, you must prepare for the worst. Your son has internal injuries to his head and lungs and I am afraid it is only a matter of time. I'm so very sorry."

Roman and Sophie each knelt on either side of the bed and took Toby's hands in theirs. Shock and despair were evident upon their faces. Wrenching cries of remorse, disbelief and utter anguish filled the room. Hannah kept watching for the rise and fall of Toby's chest. Just as Toby drew his final breath, his eyes opened with a look of wonder and a countenance of peace and then he was gone.

In the following days they would all draw strength and hope from that last moment. Hannah knew that would be just as dear, sweet Toby would have wanted it. Dr. Hayes excused himself and went into the kitchen to give the family some time alone. Roman, Sophie and Hannah sat in silence except for the involuntary, heart-wrenching sobs that said what they themselves could not. Hannah was the first to leave the room. She walked to the kitchen table and sat down by the doctor. Words seemed to be unworthy of the feelings that lay like a heavy burden upon her chest. There was one word that seemed to press its awareness, "Why?"

Dr. Hayes rose and expressed his sympathies and said that he would drop by later this evening to see if they needed anything. Hannah decided to put on a fresh pot of coffee and walked outside. It was a beautiful clear day which was a great contrast to the gloomy cloud that now hung over the Jamison family. Walking back into the small house that had always felt like a sanctuary, now lent no comfort from the turmoil that took up residence in their hearts, Hannah stepped quietly into her room.

℘

Roman sat with a coffee cup tightly gripped in his large hands. Sophie sat with a grief stricken look upon her face as she absent-mindedly traced the pattern of a handmade quilt with her fingertip. The quilt that she now used as a tablecloth was one of the few things she had left of her mother's. The mantle clock chimed the two o'clock hour when a knocking at the front door startled them out of their mind's dwelling of deep thoughts. Hannah came out of her room to see who had arrived. Dr. Hayes and Preacher Carson were there to offer their condolences and to help with tomorrow's arrangements.

Preacher Carson removed his black hat before speaking. "The good doctor and I stopped by and let your brother and the rest of the family know what has happened. Jacob said he and your mother would be here shortly."

Roman motioned for them to come further into the room after clasping both of their hands.

Roman looked at Sophie before requesting prayer from Preacher Carson. "It would be of great comfort to us," he told him.

Everyone knelt and bowed their heads. "Dear Lord, we humbly ask you to bless this family who are so dear to my heart. Bless them with comfort to ease their pain. Bless them with strength through the lonely hours and may they lay their head upon your breast and allow themselves to grieve. When their season of mourning is passed, may their faith abound that much more. We thank you Lord for the time that you allowed us all to have down here on earth with Toby. He is resting in paradise now and amen."

On shaky legs, Sophie embraced them and walked them to the door as they said their goodbyes. She then turned to her husband and said, "Roman, would you help me to prepare Toby for his burial tomorrow before Jacob and your mother come?"

"Yes, we will take care of him together. Hannah, would you please fix a little bite to eat? Do not go to a lot of trouble because we are not very hungry."

Turning slowly, they went into their son's bedroom. Hannah could hear her parents working in quietness with an occasional sob coming from the room. She knew the days ahead would be difficult ones. She stood stirring last night's supper of left-over beans when her parents reentered the kitchen. Sophie went to her daughter and held her as though she might disappear. Roman had stepped outside to get some fresh air.

"Oh Hannah, we will need each other very much in the days ahead. Even though we do not understand why this has happened, we know where our help comes from. Let's go and sit down and wait for your father to come back inside," Sophie told her daughter as they took a seat.

❧

The rhythmic beat of horse's hooves and the clatter of a carriage sounded as it drew up to the front of the house. The familiar voices of Grandma Rose and Uncle Jacob were a welcoming sound. Roman's younger brother, Jacob and his wife Sarah, lived only about a half an hour's walk towards town. Their only child, Mandy was a close friend and cousin of Hannah's. A very wise and spirited Grandma Rose has lived with them since the death of Grandpa a few years ago.

"Oh Rose! It is so good to have you here. Your wisdom and grace are a much needed blessing to us all," Sophie said through an emotionally strained voice. Hannah also hugged her grandmother and led her to a seat at the table.

Removing a worn scarf from her snowy, white head, Grandma Rose said, "Where is Roman? Jacob and I did not see him when we pulled up. How are all of you all holding up?" Sophie pulled out a chair next to Grandma Rose.

"We are still so very much in shock. It is as if all of this is a bad dream. It doesn't seem real. I'm also worried that Roman is blaming himself for the accident."

"Jacob is outside. I'm sure he will find Roman and will try to calm his fears. We will all be there for each other."

"Sarah and Mandy send their love and condolences and said they will be here early tomorrow," explained Grandma Rose.

The Jamison family was small, consisting of Grandma Rose, her two sons and their wives and daughters. Sophie was an only child and her parents passed away of influenza only a few years after moving to Wyoming from Ohio. Sophie and Roman had been married a short while before they passed on. The only other relative of Sophie's was an Aunt Dianne who still resided in Ohio, if still alive. The small town of Sundance, Wyoming lay nestled in a valley on the edge of the Great Black Hills. The settlement remained unnamed until a few short years ago. The big gold rush brought many passersby but the town itself was still largely unsettled and quiet. While Roman and Sophie carved out their own piece of land having acquired some from the Homestead Act of 1862, as well as gaining the land that Sophie's parents left behind, Jacob stayed on the home place just a couple of miles away. There were a few neighboring farms on the outskirts of town but there had still been very little change since Roman and Sophie's marriage.

Roman and Jacob entered moments later. Grandma Rose took her eldest son and in silence just held him. There were no words that could heal such a deep wound. Time would act as a salve to soothe their broken hearts. A scar would be left as a reminder of their great loss. Memories would be held to like precious gems to be taken out and treasured from time to time. Jacob announced that it was getting late. He would finish doing what needed done and he would return with the family for the burial tomorrow. Grandma Rose insisted on staying the night.

That night, they all sat quietly, each reminiscing about special times with Toby. After everyone had gone to bed, Hannah wondered what thoughts lay behind the expressions on her parent's faces. Underneath the sadness that was so obviously displayed, there was regret in her father's eyes and a far-away look in her mother's. Hannah could not help but be curious as to what was on her mother's mind. She had seen this look before when her mother thought no one else was looking. It was a puzzle. Sleep was a long time coming to all that night.

℘

The next day dawned bright and sunny. It was a contradiction to the atmosphere in the hearts of the Jamison family. Shortly after a quick breakfast, Jacob arrived with Sarah and Mandy and with an abundance of food. The burial was to take place at noon along with a gathering of townspeople and nearby neighbors who came by to pay their respects. Roman and Sophie stood out on their front porch to greet those that came.

First to come were their closest neighbors, Jack and Ruth Johnson. They were a spry, elderly couple who was very fond of the family.

"Roman, you and Sophie know that Ruth and I are never far if you need anything. We are so sorry for your loss," Jack said as he and Ruth embraced them tightly. Some of the other visitors who came to pay their respects included Widow Barkley, who ran the town's only boarding house. Right behind her were Luke and Anna Calder. They were the proprietors of the general store. Paul and Emma Sullivan drove up in their small buck wagon. Paul quickly got down and helped Emma who was expecting their first child. Emma was the school teacher but was looking for a replacement because she was due in two months' time.

"We will miss dear Toby very much and so will his classmates," Emma said with unshed tears threatening to fall.

Of course Doctor Hayes and Preacher Carson were there also. They stood off to the side to allow those that came some time with the family. Hannah and Mandy accepted the many dishes of food that were brought.

With the sun signaling the noon hour, their beloved Toby was laid to rest. Preacher Carson's carefully spoken words were chosen with care. Hannah and Mandy had lovingly picked a bouquet of flowers and laid them next to the handmade wooden cross. The branches of the large bur oak tree acted as arms protectively sheltering the grave.

Hannah was the last to follow after the service. Turning to look back at the grave, she saw two doves light upon each side of the cross. Amazed at the sight, Hannah thought of the peaceful look upon her brother's face as he drew his last breath. *"God must have a purpose for taking my brother so soon. I wonder when it will be my time to die,"* Hannah mused.

CHAPTER 2

The next day came with an unwelcome sense of reality. Roman was preparing for a long day of gathering in the hay. He knew he would have to work extra hard in order to get it all taken care of. So as soon as breakfast was over, he excused himself. They had all been very quiet during breakfast. Maybe starting the day's work would be good therapy to keep their minds and hands busy. Sophie began collecting the jars and berries from the cellar to be canned. Roman had built a fire up outside for the canning process, to keep from heating up the house on such a warm summer's day. Soon Hannah and Sophie had several jars filled and ready for the large cooker that now simmered over the fire.

Some of the time would be spent waiting, so Hannah decided to take her father some cold water. She also grabbed a few cookies from one of the platters brought by a kind neighbor yesterday. She noticed that he hadn't eaten much breakfast and the extra energy would do him good.

As Hannah was on her way back to the house, she saw Emma Sullivan walking up the front porch steps. "Hello, Emma. What a nice surprise. Did you walk all this way?" Hannah inquired of the petite and curly, blonde haired school teacher.

"Yes. As you know, it is not such a long way. Paul drove out to meet the new neighbors while I came over here."

"Oh yes, we heard about the new neighbors but let's get you inside. Mama would skin me if I kept you on your feet longer than necessary. She will be so glad to see you." Hannah reached to open the door for Emma.

Sophie turned at the sound of the door opening and with a pleased expression she gave Emma a hug and motioned for her to take a chair at the table. "Emma please sit down. You look a little winded. Can I get you a cold glass of water or milk? I was just waiting on Hannah so we could take a break together," Sophie said as she pulled a handkerchief from her apron pocket and wiped her forehead.

"Some water would be nice. I hope it is not too soon to stop by. How are you all doing?" Emma asked with concern in her voice.

"We are just trying to stay busy. A person is never prepared to lose a loved one," Sophie said while setting a tall glass of water before Emma.

"So what brings you out this way? I am kind of surprised to see you. Is everything ok?" Hannah asked.

Emma took a drink of water and said, "Well, as you both know, I will be having my baby in a couple of months. Probably about the same time that school starts back up. Paul and I decided that it would be best if we went ahead and found someone to take over the teaching position for me. I immediately thought of you, Hannah." Pleasantly surprised, Hannah looked to her mother for approval.

Sophie gave her daughter an understanding look and replied. "I know nothing would please Hannah more but we must first ask her father for permission."

Emma explained that there were only sixteen children from the ages of six to thirteen. Hannah would have no problem managing by herself. Also when colder weather moved in, Mr.

Calder always went over to the schoolhouse and started a fire in the mornings. He would make sure there was plenty of wood supplied also.

The conversation then turned to the coming baby. "Emma, have you chosen a name for the baby yet?" Hannah asked.

"Paul and I like Elizabeth for a girl and Mathew for a boy. I'm finding myself getting very anxious. I am kind of excited and worried at the same time."

"You know, Emma, I was exactly the same way when I was pregnant with Hannah and Toby. It was always such a relief when they finally got here," Sophie told the nervous mother to be.

"I don't think I will ever get married and have children. Besides there certainly are not very many eligible bachelors that live around here," Hannah grumbled.

"I hear the new neighbors that Paul went to see today just so happen to have a son or two. Their last name is Daniels and according to Widow Barkley, they have two sons and a daughter. I am sure we will all be making their acquaintance," Emma informed them. Sophie stood to get some more oatmeal cookies when they heard Emma's husband pull up out front.

"Please no more of those delicious cookies for me. Paul will be ready to get back home," Emma said and then looked to Hannah.

"As soon as you have thought over the teaching position, please let me know." Paul was walking around the wagon to help his wife when she came out the front door. After saying their goodbyes, they drove slowly away.

The time went fast while visiting with Emma. The first batch of berries was already done. They would have time for one more before supper. Sophie hurriedly put together a small lunch for Roman. She was running behind by the time Emma left. "Hannah, while you are getting the next batch of jelly ready, I will take your father something to eat."

"Ok. Take your time, Mama, I can manage things here," Hannah said as her mind whirled with thoughts of the teaching proposition.

She was so pleased with the chance to be a teacher. She loved children and also enjoyed learning as a child. And try as she might, she could not help but wonder about the new neighbors that Emma had mentioned.

❧

Outside Sophie did not see Roman at first. It looked as if he was not out there until she caught a glimpse of his navy-blue clad leg bent at the knee. He was sitting on the ground leaning back against the wagon wheel.

"Roman, I almost didn't see you there," Sophie said. "I brought you something to eat. It's not much, just a ham sandwich, apple and cold water."

Roman patted the ground beside him. "Set with me a spell. It seems as though I can't get much work done today." He began to eat the food his wife had brought him.

"Roman I know that you are missing Toby very much. In a way it is probably harder on you than it is on us. You and Toby have spent every day together this summer."

"I can't help but feel that his death is my fault. If only I had not told him to go up to the barn loft and check the pulley system in order to store some of the hay up there. None of this would have happened."

"Roman we may never know the reason why God has chosen our son out of this world to be with Him. Our faith is the only thing that will see us through. We must allow time to soften the intense hurt that we now feel," Sophie expressed with more confidence than she actually felt.

"Sophie I will try and remember that in the difficult days ahead. You know that patience is not one of my strong suits." His wife only nodded her head in agreement.

After Roman finished his lunch and started back to work, Sophie walked back to the house to join her daughter. Sophie knew Hannah was grieving silently and hoped that she would want to talk.

❧

Upon entering the house, she saw that most of the work had already been done. Hannah was out back putting the jars into the cookers.

Sophie patted a chair beside her and said, "Come, let's sit for a spell. How are you doing? You have been very quiet for most of the morning. It does help to stay busy but our loss is so very fresh."

"I know, Mama. It was all I could think about until Emma came by. Then I felt guilty about feeling happy at the thought of being the teacher of our small town. Sometimes I feel like we are doing wrong by Toby for getting back to our normal routine. I feel like our lives should stop because Toby's life has stopped. I have many mixed emotions."

"I know, sweetheart. But we must ask God to make a way for us. Your father and I are having feelings of guilt and confusion also. We will just take one day at a time."

The evening sun was beginning to set when they were all able to finally sit down. Roman and Sophie each sat in a rocking chair placed before the fireplace. This morning they had not built a fire in the fireplace due to the warm mornings they were having. They had built up a fire in the kitchen cook stove for some coffee and they ate leftovers all day from yesterday. Hannah went to bed earlier than her usual time that night. She was physically and mentally exhausted.

The next morning Hannah was the first to rise so she quietly made her way down to her rock by the creek. She knelt upon the rock's surface and said a prayer before walking back up to the house. Her parents were at the table almost ready to eat breakfast. Hannah sat down and they all said a silent prayer of thanks before beginning to eat. The oats and honey hit the spot.

Roman looked to Hannah and said, "Your mother has told me about Emma asking you to take over the teaching position in town. What do you think about taking on such a large responsibility?"

Hannah swallowed the oats before saying, "I think that although it would be a large undertaking at first, it is something that I would enjoy very much. The one thing that worries me is that I do not want to cause Mama more work here at home."

Sophie sat down her coffee cup and looked at her daughter. "I suppose that most of the canning will be taken care of by the time school starts back up. We can get the root crops in when you are here. Your father and I feel we will manage just fine. If this is something you really want to do, then you should take the opportunity set before you."

"Now that you have brought up managing the harvest, there is more work than I will be able to handle on my own now that Toby is gone," Roman's sadness was visible on his face at the thought of not having his son by his side. "I am going to check around and see if there is anyone who could use a job for the next couple of months. The corn crop will need taken care of. There is also the second cutting of hay and plenty of fencing that needs mending. I would ask Jacob but he has more than he can handle already."

"So it's all settled then. Hannah you will teach and the next time we go into town we will stop by and tell Emma and your father can start asking around for someone to help on the farm," Sophie stated with a smile.

Hannah hugged both her parents and thanked them for being so understanding. "Maybe if we get caught up on things around here by the end of the week, we could all make that trip to town."

"Yes that would be nice," Sophie replied.

The week flew by and a lot was accomplished. Saturday dawned bright and much less humid. Hannah suggested they stop on their way to Sundance and invite Mandy along. So shortly after breakfast they made their way towards town. They made the turn to stop by Paul and Emma's place first. It was only a few minutes off the main road and Hannah was very anxious to let Emma know of her decision. Sophie stepped down from the wagon while Hannah climbed out the back. Roman saw Paul out by the barn and told them he would visit with Paul while they were inside.

Emma was opening the door before Sophie and Hannah had even reached the front porch. "What a pleasant surprise! Do come in. I was just doing some baking before the house gets too warm."

"We came by to let you know that I definitely will be taking that teaching job. If it is not too much trouble, I would like to come over sometime and ask you some questions so that I can be better prepared."

Emma clapped her hands together, "This is wonderful news! Of course, you can come any time. There are a few things that I will need to give you. Also we can discuss the children and at what level they will each be starting."

"Any help you can give me will be greatly appreciated."

Sophie inquired of how Emma had been feeling lately. "You should start slowing down and resting more. You will need your strength when the baby comes."

"I know you are right, Sophie. But there is always so much needing done. Soon most of the garden work will be done and things won't be so demanding after that."

Sophie rose to her feet. "Hannah and I must be going. We are going to stop by and see if Mandy would like to go to town with us. The girls haven't spent much time together this summer. Roman is waiting outside with Paul."

"Thanks again Emma for such a wonderful opportunity," Hannah said.

"You are very welcome. Remember to come by sometime. Have a good trip to town and we will see you soon."

"Bye," said Sophie and Hannah in unison. Roman saw them come out and tendered his goodbyes to Paul. He had learned from Paul that the new neighbors had a son that might be interested in doing some extra work around his farm.

After stopping and collecting Mandy, the drive to town seemed to go by swiftly. Hannah and Mandy were so excited to see each other that their chatter was non-stop. Coming over a rise, the town of Sundance came into view. The surrounding mountainous landscape seemed inspiring to those nestled in the valley below. Roman halted the horses in front of the general store. After helping Sophie down, he asked how long she and the girls would be shopping.

Sophie said, "We should be done in about an hour. Is that long enough for you to do your business?"

"It should be but take your time. We are in no hurry today."

"Ok, see you soon. Come along girls,"

Sophie led them into the store. As soon as Sophie and the girls stepped inside the store, they were greeted enthusiastically by a short and plump Anna Calder. Luke and Anna have been running the store for many years, almost one of the first buildings to make up the town.

"Sophie! What a nice surprise. Everyone has been so busy this summer that I haven't seen many people come into town, even for supplies. It is great to see you and the girls," Anna expressed excitedly.

"How have you and Luke been fairing? I haven't seen you at the last couple of Sunday meetings."

"We are just having trouble with these old bones. They don't work as well as they used to. We just stayed home to rest but we hope to make it tomorrow."

Sophie looked around and saw that the girls were looking at the yard goods. "I see you have a nice selection of material. I hope to have time to sew up a couple of dresses as soon as the summertime chores are under control. We are very thankful to have such a bounty this year."

"Yes, most of the neighbors have been blessed as well," Anna agreed. "Speaking of neighbors, have you met the new family? I have not but Katherine Barkley has told me that their names are Andrew and Alice Daniels. You know Katherine. She tries to keep up with everyone and everything around here."

"Yes but with this small community it is not a hard job to do. Well I think I will look around a bit before Roman gets back. I have a list of staples that you can put together for me, if you don't mind," Sophie said while giving Anna the paper.

Hannah and Mandy had already chosen some material for making a dress. Hannah held up a soft light-green which complicated her eyes that were flecked with gold. Mandy who was much fairer, admired a cornflower blue that went with her blond hair and blue eyes. Just as Sophie and the girls were taking care of paying for their purchases, Roman came inside the store.

"Hello, Anna. Where is Luke at today?"

"He had to go out of town to pick up some stuff for the store that we were running short on."

"Be sure and tell him hello. Maybe we will see you both tomorrow for church service."

"Yes if it is the Lord's will. It sure was good to talk to you all," Anna smiled.

They all said their goodbyes and left after loading up their purchases into the wagon. It would be dinner time by the time they arrived home.

℘

Roman wanted to say hello to his mother when they reached Mandy's house.

Grandma Rose was on the front porch swinging and singing an old gospel hymn. "I was wondering if you were going to have time to stop by for a few minutes. You have all been in our prayers." Grandma Rose motioned for them to sit down.

Sarah and Jacob came out of the house. "Would you all care for a cool glass of lemonade? I made some fresh just this morning," offered Sarah.

"That sounds wonderful. It has been a very warm ride," Sophie said. Mandy went inside with her mother and helped her with the lemonade. Hannah sat by Grandma Rose on the swing, appreciating the cool breeze that was a relief against her sun-warmed skin.

Grandma Rose turned to Hannah. "So what did you buy for yourself at the store? I'm sure you and Mandy did not come back empty handed," laughed Grandma Rose.

"Oh Grandma you know us so well. We both brought back some yard goods to make a new dress. I tried to get Mama to buy some, but she decided not to for some reason."

"I'm sure your mother is just not ready to do that sort of thing. It is a very deep wound that your mother carries. A mother's love for a child is something very special," Grandma Rose whispered for Hannah's ears only.

Hannah looked at her mother remembering the secret longing that would surface in her eyes when she thought no one was looking. Hannah had not thought anything of it until the passing of Toby. That look of deep loss was there before losing Toby. Maybe one day her mother would open up to her in her own time.

Everyone's attention turned to what Jacob was telling Roman. "Our new neighbors come from down south of us. Andrew has purchased a nice piece of property. He plans on growing wheat. Andrew and his wife, Alice, have two sons and a daughter. They seem like real nice and honest people. It's good to have decent neighbors that you can depend on after all the unrest of recent years."

"Do you know if one of their sons would be interested in helping me around the place for a while?" Roman asked.

"It wouldn't hurt to ask. I'm sure that they will be just settling in for it is too late to start working the land this year."

Sarah politely interrupted the men. "Would you all care to stay and have some dinner? We have fried chicken and there is more than enough."

Roman looked to Sophie for a reply. At her nod he said, "We would love to if you are sure it is no trouble."

"Great! Ladies let's all go in and finish up. We will leave the men to their talk."

Roman and Jacob continued to discuss the perilous times that came with settling the unpopulated areas of the west. There had been much change in the last few years and it was plain that much more was on its way and not for the good. They had had enough trouble over the years with the big ranchers and their free grazing tactics. They did not mind mending a few cut fences but hoped that they could manage in peace. Jacob even heard talk in town of a saloon taking up residence soon. They prayed not.

The rest of the day went by with much good conversation and soon it was time to leave. They said their farewells and would see each other tomorrow for church.

CHAPTER 3

The next day ushered in clear blue skies. Breakfast was a silent affair of sausage and eggs. Everyone seemed to be lost in their own thoughts. The table had an empty space just like the one that occupied their hearts. After cleaning up the breakfast dishes, Hannah made her way once again to the special spot beside the creek. Life seemed to be so uncertain. The future had no guarantees and this left Hannah afraid to hope, dream or make plans for her life. Leaning back to feel the sun's warm rays, she noticed a small, periwinkle butterfly circling just above her. As if the tiny creature decided it was safe, it lighted upon Hannah's hand. Hannah thought the butterfly must trust her not to hurt it.

Suddenly a voice inside her spoke three simple words. *"Trust in me."* The revelation both surprised and brought tears to Hannah's eyes.

She thanked God for the little miracle that helped to calm her fears. With a feeling of peace, Hannah walked back to the house to finish getting ready for church.

❦

Several people were already present when they pulled into the churchyard. Hannah was quick to notice the new family that was talking to Preacher Carson and a couple of young ministers just starting out. Amongst them stood a tall young man who looked to be about his early twenties. Next to him was a slightly younger man who was obviously his brother. There was also a young girl whom Hannah judged to be about twelve. The father and mother was a handsome couple and it appeared that they were going to be an asset to their community. Hannah's eyes kept straying to the older of the two young men. He had sandy, blond hair that had been touched by the sun and in need of a trim. His skin was darkened from spending many hours outside.

Hannah felt nervous, an emotion that was usually a stranger to her. She unconsciously stepped behind her mother, suddenly feeling self-conscious. Preacher Carson waved and motioned for them to come over. Hannah walked with eyes downcast and staying behind her parents. The preacher introduced them to each other. Roman and Sophie shook hands with Andrew and

Alice Daniels. Andrew introduced his sons, Isaac and Joshua and his daughter, Katie.

Roman introduced Hannah and then informed them that she would be the new school teacher this year. Katie would be very welcome as a new student this fall. Everyone soon started gathering into the small church house.

Hannah was very aware of Isaac as he walked up the steps behind her. *"What's wrong with me?"* Hannah thought to herself. *"You would think I have never seen a handsome young man before. Well come to think of it, not one this handsome anyway."*

Taking their seats, the congregation began to sing "Rock of Ages". Hannah found it hard to concentrate on what the young preacher was saying. The Daniels men sat directly across from her on the men's side. Hannah forced herself to pay more attention. The preacher was in the book of Job. She knew that the Lord did give and that He did take away for He had all power. It was a good scripture to remind her that He knew what was best. After Preacher Carson was blessed to uplift everyone's spirit, several songs were sung before church was dismissed. Roman and Sophie said their goodbyes to everyone.

Roman invited the new family home to have dinner with them. He assured them that they would be most welcome. Sophie was caught by surprise, so all the way home she thought about what to fix to eat. Thankfully she and Hannah had prepared extra chicken and vegetables yesterday. They had also baked an apple cake and berry cobbler. With a little more effort, they would manage just fine.

Hannah was caught completely off guard. Normally she would not think anything of someone coming over for dinner. They had done so numerous times. Even though she did not admit it, she knew why it was different this time. Isaac disturbed her. This was not something that she could control and control was something that she prided herself of having. She was always able to be slow to speak and always, always in control of her feelings.

Preparing the rest of the meal took several minutes. Sophie and Alice were getting along nicely. Katie also wanted to help so she was asked to set the table and pour everyone a glass of water and milk.

Hannah took the opportunity to get acquainted with Katie. "How old are you Katie?" Hannah asked the very slim and well mannered, young girl.

"I'm eleven but I will soon be twelve. My birthday is next month."

"Have you had much schooling? I'm going to be the new teacher and I will need to know what grade levels to prepare for."

"I am at the seventh grade level. They only taught up to the eighth grade where I went school," Katie proudly informed her.

"That's great, Katie! If you are willing, I may need some help with the smaller children."

Sophie announced that dinner was ready. "Hannah, go and tell the men folk to come inside."

"Yes, Mama," Hannah responded.

There was exactly enough room at the table for everyone. The table, made of sturdy oak, had benches along each side and two captain chairs at the ends. Roman and Andrew sat at the ends. Sophie and Alice sat across from each other, likewise Joshua and Katie. Much to Hannah's unease, she found herself directly across from Isaac. After a silent prayer, the eating and conversation begin. Hannah tried to look everywhere but right in front of her. She was so uncomfortable that she couldn't eat. Her stomach was in knots. Finally, she raised her head and looked into a pair of startling blue eyes. *"Was that laughter she saw?"* Isaac knew Hannah was uneasy. He saw it in those beautiful green eyes with tiny gold flecks. She couldn't hide the blush that tinted her cheek bones.

"So, Hannah, I hear you are about to become the new school teacher around these parts. If you don't mind my saying, you look barely out of school yourself."

"Well if you don't mind my saying, you don't have to be old to be responsible and capable. Besides I am nineteen and in a couple of months I will be twenty years old," Hannah returned.

"I meant it as a compliment. I didn't mean to get you all riled up." Isaac watched as Hannah's face turned even redder.

"Please forgive me. I guess I am more nervous about the teaching position than I thought. I usually don't jump to conclusions so easily. What do you plan on doing? Will you help your father or will you do something else?" Hannah purposely changed the subject.

"For now I am planning on helping Dad get started but eventually I would like to get into the cattle business. My father has always grown wheat and corn. If I could acquire enough land around here, I would like to start up a ranch," Isaac said with enthusiasm.

Roman could not help but to overhear their conversation. He thought it would be a good time to bring up his need for some help with his farm. "Isaac, I couldn't help but hear you say that you wanted to learn about cattle. I am going to hire someone to help me around here for a few months and if you would be interested, I'd be much obliged."

"Absolutely! That would be great. I did notice your cattle on our way in. It will allow me to learn more about them. I understand you also raise corn. Do you sell part of your corn crop as well?"

"Yes. There will also be some fence mending to take care of. Ever since they came out with this barbed wire fencing, there is always some in need of repairing."

"When would you like for me to start? I will need to stick close to home for at least another week, maybe longer, to help my parents get settled in," Isaac explained.

"That will be fine. Come when you can. I understand that there is much to be done on a new place," Roman expressed thankfully.

After dinner, all of the men went out on the porch to drink their coffee and to discuss their farms. Andrew informed Roman that he planned on growing wheat on most of his pasture and then maybe later he would like to include corn. Before winter set in, he wanted to repair the old barn and make the small house more livable for Alice and Katie. Sophie and Alice sat down in the rocking chairs before the fireplace while Hannah and Katie finished the dishes. Alice inquired about the townspeople, trying to learn a little about them beforehand. She had met most of them at church today but very little about where they lived or what they did.

Sophie laughed, "If you run into the Widow Barkley, who owns the town boarding house, you will have no problem catching up on the latest news. Bless her heart. I think that she just gets very lonely since her husband passed on a few years ago."

"I imagine a person would become very lonesome. Does she get very many boarders staying with her?"

"Most of the time there are usually a couple but at times there can be several. We still get a few prospectors from time to time in search of the Black Hills gold," Sophie said.

Hannah and Katie came in and sat down on the hearth in front of them. Katie chimed in. "Did people really strike it rich?"

"I think some did quite well but others mostly just wasted their time. Wealth can sometimes change a person if they are not careful. We must all be very thankful for what God has given us, both spiritually and naturally," Sophie gently instructed. *"Mama is such a light to people. I hope that I can grow in grace and knowledge like her,"* Hannah thought to herself.

Time is the predecessor of many lessons in life. It is not some empty space but has its own purposeful intent to make us evolve for the better. Hannah studied upon how a person can take the events in their life and with God's help have them work for the good to help us grow.

A short while later Alice announced that they needed to be going. She and Katie stepped out onto the front porch to see if Andrew was ready also. Andrew handed Sophie his coffee cup and thanked her for the wonderful dinner. "You all will have to come and have dinner with us one day soon." Hannah hung back as they all said their farewells.

She watched Isaac stand and stretch his tall body. His eyes caught hers and she quickly lowered hers in embarrassment. Then they were gone with a promise to see each other soon.

The next couple of weeks kept everyone busy. Isaac let Roman know that it would take longer for him to square things away than he had initially thought. Hannah was unconsciously looking forward to his presence. She had learned from Katie that Isaac was twenty-three years old and Joshua was twenty. Staying busy with storing what the climate offered them, did little to keep those blue eyes from coming before her.

The first of September was coming up fast. Hannah was becoming anxious about starting teaching. It was only two weeks away. With things being caught up around the house, Hannah thought she had better be paying Emma that visit. There was much preparing to be done. She let her mother know of her plans and invited her to come along. Sophie said she would stay home and see if Roman needed any help.

Hannah decided to walk to Emma's because it was such a beautiful day. She wore one of her cool, cotton dresses. The golden color matched the flecks in her eyes and went nicely with her dark, shining tresses. About half-way to Emma's, she saw someone traveling the road towards her. Her heart skipped a beat when she saw that it was Isaac.

As he drew closer, Isaac asked, "Where are you off to Hannah?"

"I was on my way to see Emma Sullivan. She is the one who handed the teaching job down to me. She is going to help me get things ready for school. Are you on your way to see my father?"

"Yes. I wanted to let him know that I can start helping him any time now." Hannah fingered the ruffle that adorned the waist of her dress as she talked.

"He will be glad to hear that. My dad has had a hard time since my brother died. It will do him good to have some company while he works. It is very kind of you to help him out."

"The feeling is mutual. To tell you the truth, I could use the extra income and it will also be a learning experience. I hope your Dad has a lot of patience. I know absolutely nothing about cattle but it is something that I find very interesting."

"I'm sure you will both get along well together. How is everyone doing at your place? I haven't really had a chance to see anyone lately," Hannah said as she swiped at an errant curl that had escaped its hold.

"Everyone is well. There is still much to do but nothing that Josh can't handle now that most of the pressing stuff has been taken care of," Isaac said as he watched Hannah shift nervously from one foot to another.

"I should probably get going to Emma's. There are a lot of things to go over. I guess I will be seeing you soon. You will be tired of seeing me once you start working for my father," Hannah laughed.

"Ok. I'll see you later but I won't get tired of seeing you," Isaac told her with a serious look in his eyes. Hannah let out a long pent up deep breath as she continued on down the dirt road towards Emma's house. Isaac definitely unsettled her.

Never having really spent much time around boys her age, Hannah was a little confused about the strange new feelings she had when she was around Isaac Daniels. He was very attractive but then so was his brother, Joshua. "I must tread carefully around him until I get to know him better." Hannah's cautious nature was making itself known.

Isaac was glad that he ran into Hannah. He liked being around her. She had an honest quality that he hadn't seen in other girls her age. Working for Mr. Jamison was going to be especially nice if he got to see Hannah every day. Then he remembered that soon she would be teaching and they might not see each other as much as he would like.

Roman was outside beside the barn when he strolled into the yard. He was working on some of his equipment that he used to gather his corn crop in with. Roman looked up when he saw Isaac and motioned for him to come on over. "I am glad that you are here. I was just passing some time on some of this old equipment that was in dire need of repair. I was out checking my cattle on the north hill when I saw that one of my youngest heifers is about to give birth. So if you could help with holding this, we will finish up here and head on out there to see how far along she has come," Roman said.

"Sure thing, I hope things go well. I've heard that sometimes first calves have a little trouble being born."

"You are right. We may have to help her a little. We will take along a rope just in case." Roman told Isaac.

They managed to repair the reaper and decided they had better head on out and check the cow. Roman informed Sophie of where they were going and that it may be a while before their return. Isaac was still amazed at the beauty of the land. He had come from all flat country to this majestic place where there were hills and valleys and beautiful pasture. Isaac inquired of Roman how much land he owned.

"I own about one hundred and fifty acres plus about that much more that we obtained from Sophie's parents when they passed away. Fortunately, there is enough flat land to grow hay and corn. There is also a good supply of water for the cattle running from these hills. It is a good life but also at times a difficult one."

"Dad and Mom acquired a modest amount of land but plenty for what he wants to raise on it. Dad will grow spring wheat and corn for his money crops. He will only grow enough hay necessary for the farm animals," Isaac said.

"I understand that you are interested in raising beef cattle yourself. What made you decide on cattle to make a living at?"

"I helped with a couple of cattle drives but I realize that I still have much to learn. Whatever a man decides to do there is always a risk involved when you depend on the land and nature for your living," Isaac said as he side stepped a cow patty in his path.

Roman agreed by shaking his head. "But it is a fulfilling life to be able to work with God's creation. There is nothing more satisfying than to see His hand in our everyday lives. This country is still very unsettled and when you are ready I don't see it being a problem to purchase land nearby."

"I hope you are right. I think I have already lost my heart to this beautiful landscape. It is something that I will try hard to obtain," Isaac said while gazing at the green hillside pasture.

Pointing towards a cow lying at the foot of the hill directly in front of them, Roman said, "Look, there she is and it appears that we are just in time. Let's hurry and see if she needs help." The young cow was in heavy labor. Roman saw that the calf was in the right position. Its front hooves and nose were showing.

"It looks as though they are doing fine. We will wait and let nature take its course," Roman said unable to hide the excitement in his voice.

Roman motioned for Isaac to follow him. They took a seat beneath a large ponderosa pine far enough away to keep from making the new mother nervous. After about twenty minutes, a new, little bull calf was born. Roman told Isaac that they would wait and make sure that the calf suckled before they left. It was very important for the calf to nurse within about one hour after being born. It took several attempts before the calf was finally able to stand upon shaking legs. As it became stronger, the calf went in search of its first meal. To Isaac, it was a sight to behold. To see how instinctively a mother and calf knew just what to do. While the calf was nursing, several of the other cows came to see the new addition to their herd.

As they walked back home, Roman and Isaac discussed matters about the farm and what needed to be done first. They would be very busy for the next few weeks and Roman asked Isaac again if he was sure he could be spared from home right now.

"Yes, my father and I have talked and things will be well under control with Josh there." Upon returning home, they decided to get started at seven o'clock in the morning.

Isaac thought about Hannah on his way back home. He had hoped that he would run into her again but knew that she probably had a lot to go over with Emma. *"That's ok,"* thought Isaac. *"Being able to work at the Jamison farm should present him with plenty of opportunities to see Hannah in the days to come."*

❧

Hannah was deep in thought as she walked the tree lined, dirt road that lead to Paul and Emma's home. Hearing a slight whining noise, Hannah turned to see a dog following her. The dog appeared to be lost. Cautiously, she held her hand out to the rather large and peculiar animal. Something inside her told her to be kind to him. Very warily, the dog slowly came close enough for Hannah to lightly pat him on the head. Then without warning, he turned and entered the woods again. Hannah continued her walk and was at Emma's in a few short minutes. Emma could be seen outside sweeping her porch off.

Hannah spoke a loud greeting so as not to startle Emma with her coming. "Hello, Hannah. You couldn't have come at a better time. I was fixing to have some lemonade and sit for a spell. Take a seat and I will go and fetch us some."

"That sounds heavenly. The day has grown to be very warm," Hannah said as she sat down on the swing. In a couple of minutes, they were discussing the school children. Emma told her of the general routine of how the day was laid out, the grade level of each child and any special circumstances that needed attention.

"The books are still at the school house along with many of the supplies that will be needed. Getting organized will save you a lot of time and as you get to know the children, you will learn the needs of each individual," explained Emma.

"I am starting to get very nervous as the first day fast approaches. I think that I will go into town in a couple of days and begin preparing the classroom."

Their conversation turned to the baby's eminent arrival and all the preparing that Emma had been doing herself. Emma told Hannah that Ruth Johnson would be there to help deliver the baby when the time came. She had delivered many babies in her time but the doctor would be close by just in case.

"I hope you will have an easy delivery and all goes well. You will be in our prayers," Hannah encouraged Emma.

"I must be getting back home for it will soon be time to help Mama with supper. I want to thank you again for all your help."

"Goodbye, Hannah," Emma said.

The walk home went by so fast that Hannah was there before she knew it. Her mind was whirling with many thoughts. It seemed like before that her life was uneventful. Now in a small space of time things had changed to become very interesting with many things to contemplate upon. She almost felt like dancing but her heart was still in mourning.

UNDER HEAVEN ❧ Karen McDavid

CHAPTER 4

The next day sailed in on clear skies and a cool breeze. After having several days of humid heat, the change would make a much more comfortable work day. Sophie told Hannah that days like this softened a body's temperament.

Roman was already outside working on his hay equipment while he waited for Isaac to arrive. Sophie was at the chicken house gathering some eggs when Isaac strolled into the yard. Isaac glanced toward the house but didn't see any sign of Hannah.

Sophie waved and greeted him with a smile. "Hello, Isaac. It's good to see you. Roman, as you can see, has already gotten started. I hope he doesn't work you too hard."

Isaac laughed, "I'm sure that I will be just fine. I'm thankful for the work. Well I had better get moving or your husband will think he made a mistake in asking me to work for him."

Sophie nodded and began walking back to the house. The thought of how she would sometimes look out the kitchen window and watch Toby and Roman work and sometimes play together made her heart heavy. Today she was having a hard time. Her mind was filled with regrets. Some days were worse than others and again she would need the Lord's help to see her through another day. Hannah had just stepped inside the back door after returning from her special place. She saw her mother wipe her eyes quickly with the back of her hand. Hannah walked over and gave her mother a hug. Hannah had thought to go into town and start cleaning the schoolhouse today but decided to put it off until tomorrow.

She didn't want to leave her mother alone today. "Mama, I thought it would be nice to have some fresh plum pie for supper today. Maybe after the chores are done we could go down by the creek and pick some of those big, juicy ones that I saw the other day. There may be enough to take to the dinner after church on Sunday." Hannah suggested.

"That sounds like a fine idea. I would hate to see all those plums go to waste. There should also be time later this week to make some plum jelly. While I tidy up inside and put a roast on to cook, you can go out to where your father is and ask him to get us a long shaking stick before they leave for the fields," Sophie said as she gathered the breakfast dishes into the sink.

Reluctantly Hannah walked out to where her father and Isaac were working. *"I hope Isaac doesn't think I made up some excuse to come out here and see him,"* Hannah grumbled to herself. Trying to act calm, she asked her father for the shaking stick.

"Sure Hannah, I think there is an old one that I tucked away in the barn corner. I'll go and fetch it," Roman said.

Isaac leaned his tall frame against the corral fence. With his arms folded across his chest, he looked at Hannah. She looked so uncomfortable standing there shifting from one foot to another.

He also noticed that when the sun shined upon her dark hair it almost turned red. "So what are your plans for today Hannah?"

"Mama and I are going to pick some plums for some pies. We will take some for after church and maybe enjoy one today as well. Will you and your family be staying for dinner after church Sunday?" Hannah asked.

"I assume we will be. It would be a shame to miss out on all that good food. Maybe you and I can take some time to talk and get to know each other better." It was more of a statement than a question.

Taken by surprise, Hannah could hear her heart beat pounding in her ears. "That would be nice," she said as matter of fact as she could.

"Here you go," Roman's voice broke into their thoughts. He handed her the long sturdy stick.

"Thanks Dad. I'll see you later." Hannah hurried back towards the house. Going around back, her mother was waiting for her. They gathered enough plums to make several pies not to mention many pints of jelly.

"Let's sit out here in the shade and prepare the plums. It is a nice day to enjoy the cool breeze," Sophie said and motioned for Hannah to take the seat beside her. They set the large pan between them to catch the plums as they cleaned them.

"Mama, what was it like back in Ohio where you lived when you were young?"

"It was so very different from here. Even though it was many years ago, the east was much more populated than it is here, your Grandfather Charles and Grandmother Clara ran a small store which meant that I grew up in town. The town was small at first then later it built up around us. The only other family we had close by was my Aunt Dianne. She is my mother's sister."

"Do you ever miss being back there?" Hannah asked.

"No. This is where I belong. Life out here, though we have to work harder, is more satisfying than being amongst all those people. A person can be more lonesome in a crowd than by oneself in this vast country. We left there and came out here and as far as I know, my parents were much happier here even if only for a few short years," Sophie told her daughter.

"I can't imagine living anywhere else. I hope our small town stays as peaceful as it is now," Hannah said as she grabbed another plum from the bucket. In short order they had prepared enough plums for the pies. Sophie stood and stretched her tall and still slim body. Hannah thought how beautiful her mother was. Her dark hair was showing just a sprinkling of gray which only emphasized her thoughtful and graceful ways.

❦

Hannah studied upon the upcoming church dinner. It would be the last one before colder weather set in. Most everyone would be there and she was anxious about seeing Isaac again. Then she immediately berated herself for putting such importance upon the occasion when the church service itself is of much greater importance. She would make it a point to pray for an enlightening meeting and that there would be an increase to the church family.

They went back inside and Sophie began gathering the ingredients for the pies. "I thought we would get started on the pies since the men have already taken their lunches with them. Your father thought they would get a lot more done if they didn't have to come back to the house to eat."

Hannah agreed. "If we get started now, we can be finished before the house heats up too much."

Eyebrows drawn together in thought, Hannah said, "Mama, I hope that you won't have too much of an extra burden placed on you when I start teaching."

"Nonsense, it will do us both good to stay busy. But not so busy that we don't take time out for prayer in good times and bad."

Hannah looked up from the dough that she had been kneading and said, "I wish that I had the faith that you have Mama. I feel so very weak."

"Faith and knowledge is something that you will grow in. The good Lord will help you along with precious miracles as you go through life. All you have to do is be wise enough to see them when He gives them to you. Trust Him Hannah, you must trust Him." Sophie paused when she saw a tear splash onto the table beside the bowl that she was stirring in. A whispered thank you in her heart went up to God for His many blessings.

The rest of the day went by fast as they worked and talked together. Hannah was so glad that she had stayed home instead of going into town.

℘

After supper everyone was exhausted from their hard day's labor. While Roman and Sophie sat out on the front porch swing, Hannah decided to walk down by the creek to do some praying before bedtime. It was still light enough outside that she made her way easily to the rock.

Words seem to come flooding forth and after she was done she felt as if she had been cleansed. The earth and the woods around her smelled pure. Hearing a noise to her left, she turned and saw the dog that she had met on her way to Emma's. The gray dog cautiously approached Hannah. Hannah felt no need to be alarmed and continued to sit still while the creature made its way closer. She had never seen this animal anywhere before, so the dog must be on his own.

Hannah noticed his eyes when he came closer. One was brown and the other blue. "What a unique feature," she said to the dog. Soon the animal was close enough for her to reach out and touch the top of his head. Then just as he had appeared out of the blue, he was gone. Puzzled as to what the dog's presence might mean, she knew the answer would come in due time. She could not deny the connection that she felt with the strange animal.

❦

That night before they turned in, Hannah chose to tell her parents about the gray dog that had mysteriously appeared to her on two occasions. "I feel as though he is a special dog with a cautiousness that makes him hold back," expressed Hannah with a puzzled look on her face.

"You must be very careful of an animal like that. You never know what they might do. Whatever you do, do not force yourself on him. Let the dog come to you," Roman said.

"I will try to make him feel safe and not threatened. I hope he will one day trust me enough to let me be his friend," Hannah told her parents.

"Well I think it is time that we all turned in. Tomorrow will be a busy day for us all. Hannah has decided to go and make ready the schoolhouse and I thought that maybe I will go and pay Grandma Rose a visit," Sophie informed them.

The next morning Hannah awoke with excitement for the day ahead. After breakfast she gathered some old rags and other cleaning supplies needed for the school. With any luck she should be able to finish the inside and go back later to do a little on the outside as well. Sophie joined Hannah for the walk that morning. Roman and Isaac were already getting started for the day's work. Isaac looked up to see Hannah and her mother and waved to them with a bright smile. Hannah found herself again looking forward to Sunday afternoon.

In a short time, the small road to Jacob's house came into view. Sophie told Hannah to take her time and to not worry about getting home in time to help with supper.

"Ok, I'll try not to be too long. Have a nice visit with the family," Hannah said.

About twenty minutes later the white-washed schoolhouse came into sight. Hannah could see the outside would need little attention. She hoped the inside faired just as well. Opening the front door, Hannah was pleased to find the inside in good condition. A little soap and water and a broom would do wonders. The windows would need shining as well. So after a few hours the whole room was tidied and in a state of preparedness. It had taken less time than she had planned to clean the inside so she walked outside to start knocking down cobwebs and shining windows. The outhouse was swept out along with the front and back porches.

With all the cleaning done, Hannah made a list of supplies that she would require. Things like chalk, pencils and paper were in the most shortage. After organizing the books and finding a new lesson planner, she looked around and was satisfied with her handiwork. Noticing that it was now becoming quite late, Hannah hurried over to the general store to purchase some of the items on her list. She would begin planning in advance to be better prepared.

§

"Hello, Hannah!", Anna exclaimed while rushing over and giving her a hug. A hug like she had always given her since she was a little girl. "It's so nice to see you. I trust everything is well with your parents?"

"Yes, they are doing as well as one would expect. We have all been very busy. Things should slow down for Mama and me since we have put away most of what we wanted to preserve. Dad is still working very hard. I worry that he works so hard in order to keep his mind busy. My brother's death has been especially hard on him."

"I am sure you are right. You all have been in our prayers. So what can I do for you? I saw you over there getting the school ready for the children. I know you will do an excellent job with them," Anna said with a smiling face.

Hannah smiled her thanks and said, "Here is my list. I hope that I didn't forget anything. Emma has been very helpful but I must admit that I am very nervous about getting started."

Anna handed Hannah a sack filled with the supplies she had requested. "Good luck dear and tell your parents hello for us."

"I will. Thank you and tell Mr. Calder hello for me also."

After leaving the supplies on the desk in the schoolhouse, Hannah walked slowly back home. She looked up into the heavens as she walked. According to the sun's position in the sky, she knew it was getting close to supper time. Taking in the beautiful surroundings, Hannah took time to notice the soft billowing clouds as they floated to the east. A tiny ground squirrel rustled the leaves beside her while a large black bird flew above with a trained eye on the ground below, looking for its next meal. The flowing creek beside the road helped to calm her thoughts, she listened to its gurgling sound as the water caressed each rock while making its way down stream. Hannah was deep in thought when she heard the crunch of dirt and rock beneath Isaac's feet. She didn't expect to run into him and became acutely aware of how disarrayed her appearance must look to him. She tucked her wayward hair back as best as she could. "Hello, Isaac, I didn't expect to run into you. I guess I thought that it was later in the day than it actually is," Hannah explained.

Isaac smiled and said, "I was hoping to run into you. I stayed a little longer to finish up what I was doing. I haven't seen you as much as I assumed I would. I was beginning to think that you might be avoiding me."

"I know. I have been very busy. My father seems to be keeping you pretty busy also. As a matter of fact, I am very much looking forward to Sunday when we can all relax and enjoy each other's company," Hannah said with her cheeks turning a soft pink. Isaac looked at her with those unsettling eyes of his. Hannah was unaware of how beautiful she was with her hair all loosed from its ribbon and her flawless skin smudged with dirt. Isaac knew he was making her uncomfortable standing there staring at her like this.

"Until Sunday then," Isaac said rubbing one of the smudges from her cheek with his thumb. He then continued toward his home in long strides. Hannah was shaken by his touch. She wondered if this could be the beginning of a relationship. Time would tell, as it did all things. She would pray for the Lord's will to be done in her life.

That evening everyone just rested. They sat on the front porch and told each other of their day. Mama had a nice visit with Grandma Rose, Sarah and Mandy. Dad had gotten a lot accomplished with the crop. Hannah told them how she had cleaned the schoolhouse inside and out. Of course, she didn't mention running into Isaac. She needed time to ponder about that herself.

CHAPTER 5

Hannah awoke very early Sunday morning. Sleep had eluded her until the early morning hours. She was so anxious that the few hours that she missed didn't bother her. There were many preparations to be made. She and her mother had cooked most of the food the day before. The last minute baking would be done this morning. The dinner after church was the last time everyone could get together, before cooler weather set in. Not only did those who attended church stay afterwards but all who wanted to come were invited.

School would start the following week so the farmers would use that time to get most of their harvest in. The children would be glad when school began because they had worked hard all summer long.

Hannah waited until she had helped her mother pack everything up and the breakfast dishes were washed and put away, before she went to get dressed. Hannah chose a buttercup, yellow dress to wear. She tied part of her thick tresses back with a wide silver-gray ribbon and let the rest fall down in a cascade of waves. She knew she shouldn't be so worried about her appearance but she wanted to look nice today. After tucking all of the food safely inside the wagon, they started to church with plenty of time to drive slowly so that nothing would spill.

There was already a larger crowd than usual gathered around the tables set up for the food. The men all stood around talking about various things, especially the weather and their crops. The women arranged their covered dishes on the tables which were placed in the shade to protect the food from the hot sun. Hannah and her parents went to follow the rest of the crowd into the church house. There were extra chairs setup along the aisles to accommodate everyone. Hannah noticed that Isaac was still standing until the elderly and women were all seated. He then took a seat in the back of the house. The singing began and was especially sweet this day with so many voices blended in harmony. The messages were delivered in spirit and held everyone's attention.

All too soon the meeting came to an end and everyone went outside to enjoy the beautiful day the Lord had given them. There was an abundance of good food and conversation with those they had not seen for a while. Hannah was sitting beside Mandy when Isaac strolled up and asked her if she would care to join him for a walk. Hannah could hear Mandy try to stifle a quiet giggle as she reached out to accept Isaac's offered hand to help her up. Hannah had already asked her parents for permission to take a short walk with Isaac.

℘

They were both silent for the first few minutes, as they walked towards an old bridge not far or out of sight from everyone else. Hannah sensed that Isaac had something on his mind. Isaac stopped and turned to look at her with serious eyes, not with the laughing eyes that she was used to seeing. Hannah was even more nervous now and wondered what he was thinking.

"Hannah, I would like to ask your father for permission to come calling on you. I know we haven't spent much time together but I've known since the first time that I saw you that I wanted to get to know you better," Isaac looked directly at her to see her reaction.

"I would like that very much. We have both been so busy lately that I don't know when we will find the time," Hannah said. She felt strangely uncomfortable standing so close while looking up into his eyes.

Taking her small hand into his large, work-roughened one, Isaac said, "We will find a little time because, anything is better than just running into you, or seeing you from afar."

"I had no idea you really felt that way. I thought it was just me," Hannah said as Isaac kept a hold of her hand. They continued walking towards the bridge. They were being sure to stay in plain sight of the on-lookers.

The area was surrounded with summer's late flowers. They walked onto the old covered bridge and sat down with their feet dangling over the side. The water was only a few feet below them as it flowed calmly, almost still in its decent downstream. It was perfect for the baptisms that came along, when God saw fit to give the increase. Isaac had not let loose of Hannah's hand as they sat there next to each other. *Am I falling in love with Isaac?* wondered Hannah. She knew that she was very inexperienced for she had never had a relationship before. Deep inside, she knew that this was something special. She hoped that this is what God wanted for her. She would pray for help in making wise decisions.

"Isaac, what are your future plans? I know that you are interested in raising beef cattle but how do you plan on going about it?"

"When I can save enough money to purchase some land, preferably some land close by, then I will get a few head of cattle and just start out small. As soon as we arrived in this part of the country, I immediately felt like I was at home. What about you? I know that right now you are teaching but do you want to have a family some day?" Isaac asked.

"Yes. Having a family is what I want most. But for now, teaching will be very rewarding and I believe that I will enjoy it. How long do you think that it will take before you are able to afford a place of your own?" Hannah asked, a bit too forwardly if she did say so herself.

"I think for maybe another year or so. I have been putting away extra money for a few years now. I have known for a long time what I wanted to make a living at."

Isaac absentmindedly stroked the top of her hand with his thumb. The gesture did not go unnoticed by Hannah as she continued the conversation.

"I wish you could have known my little brother, Toby. You would have liked him. He had a special gift with animals. I still miss him so very much." Isaac wrapped his arm around Hannah's shoulders.

"I'm so sorry Hannah. I wish that I could have been there for you." Hannah leaned into Isaac and accepted the comfort that his embrace offered. Hannah looked up into Isaac's eyes and knew that he wanted to kiss her, when his gaze traveled to her lips. But she also knew that he would refrain from doing so out of respect for her. Suddenly feeling very shy, Hannah pulled slightly away to look down at the moving water below. They sat there in content silence until they heard voices coming towards them.

It was Mandy and Joshua. "Hello, you two. We were about to give up on you coming back so we thought that we would come and get you ourselves," a breathless and excited Mandy told them.

"They are getting ready to play a game of skip rocks back this way. The creek is much wider up there. All of the young adults are playing. We thought that maybe you and Hannah would like to play also," Joshua said with a sheepish look on his face.

"What do you say Hannah? Do you want to show these two how it's done?" Isaac teased.

"Sure, why not. It is a rather calm activity and should not disturb anyone. I could also use the exercise after stuffing myself with all of that delicious food," Hannah said as her mind tried to process all of the emotions that she was feeling.

She felt as though they were growing closer with every encounter. She wondered if it showed all over her face.

They all made their way back to the churchyard. She could hear the singing becoming louder as she drew closer to the crowd. Many of the men and women were blending their voices in the old church hymns. A loud hallelujah would often grace the ear as well. They stopped far enough away, so as not to disturb the singing and they all found a good rock to throw. The rest of the afternoon went by far too quickly. By the time they helped clean up the food and tables, it was five o'clock before they pulled into their yard.

❧

When they had gotten their leftovers stored away, they all just sat and rested the rest of the evening. Hannah noticed that even her father had fallen asleep in the rocking chair.

Sophie lowered her voice when she asked Hannah about her walk with Isaac.

"It was very nice, Mama. We really enjoy spending time together. Although today, we were all too soon interrupted by Mandy and Joshua," laughed Hannah. "Do you think that they could be interested in each other?"

"I'm not really sure. They don't really seem to be but these things are sometimes hard to tell. Your father and I were taken with each other right off. My parents were not willing to give me up so soon but after they got to know Roman, they finally relented and allowed us to start seeing each other." Sophie said, as if it were only yesterday. Then just as quick as the happy memories appeared in her eyes, they were gone. It was as if a shutter had been pulled over her heart to hide what was inside.

Hannah chose to change the subject. "What are your plans for this week? Is there anything that you want to do this week before school begins?"

Sophie folded her hands in her lap. "I thought that we would make the dress that you bought material for. I have some yarn that would make a nice new shawl. The mornings are becoming quite cool now and before you know it, we will be dragging out our winter attire."

"I had almost forgotten about making that dress. I could use another dress, now that I will be teaching. I could also use your help with the sewing. Sewing is definitely not one of my strong suits," laughed Hannah.

"I know. You and your father are both lacking when it comes to patience." Sophie's love shined in her eyes as she gently nudged Roman's shoulder to wake him to go to bed.

The next morning, they awakened to a loud clap of thunder and hard pelting rain. Roman had already put on the coffee, when Sophie and Hannah came from their bedrooms.

Roman looked up and said, "I'm thankful that I went ahead and got that hay in a little earlier than I had planned. Much of it would have been lost, by the looks of things out there."

"What will you do today, since it is so bad outside? Hannah and I are planning on doing some sewing," Sophie said.

"I will just go out to the barn and take care of some things that I have been putting off for just such a day as this."

They sat eating a breakfast of eggs and bacon when a loud rap at the door was heard. Roman rose from the table to see who it was with a concerned look upon his face.

After a few long strides, he pulled open the door and a wet and worried Paul Sullivan stood there. "Emma is in labor and the pains are already close together and very hard. Sophie, you were the closest so I came here first," A very anxious and very upset Paul said without even coming in.

"Sophie, you and Hannah go with Paul. I will go and get Ruth Johnson. She will know what to do. If Jack can bring her, I will ride into town for the doctor, just in case," Roman said while slipping on his boots and a thin coat for the ride. Sophie and Hannah quickly changed their clothing and road with Paul to his home.

℘

They were all whispering prayers under their breath. Hannah had never witnessed a birth before and wasn't sure she wanted to now. They arrived at the Sullivan farm at record speed. When they entered the house, Sophie asked Hannah to wait in the kitchen until they checked on Emma. Emma was drenched in sweat and was in much pain by now. Sophie explained to Emma that Ruth Johnson was on her way. It was difficult to console Emma but Sophie tried as best as she could.

The contractions were very close together so Sophie instructed Paul to go and help Hannah to prepare some clean cloths and hot water. Sophie was calming Emma with soothing words of hope, when Hannah brought in the requested items. Hannah then went back to fetch some cool water for Emma's forehead. Ruth arrived a short time later. She checked Emma to make sure the baby's head was in position. "Emma, the baby's head is in the proper position but is having trouble moving down," Ruth said in a calm manner.

"Sophie, help me get Emma up into a squatting stance. Have Hannah help you hold her up. One on each arm," Ruth said with the knowledge of one who had done this many times before.

"Emma, you must push very hard when the next pain comes. The force of gravity will help you. I will be right here for the baby when it comes. Everything will be perfectly fine." Ruth told her with a voice of confidence.

After about four more contractions and pushes, the baby was born. It was a beautiful baby girl. She was a rather large baby for a first time mother. They were all relieved when the sound of a healthy cry filled the air. Hannah was amazed at what she had just witnessed. She asked Paul to come and see his beautiful baby girl.

Ruth and Sophie made the new mother and baby comfortable, before going and giving the new parents some privacy. Roman entered the door without Dr. Hayes. He explained that the doctor had left a note on his door saying that he was out attending an elderly man who suffered with pneumonia. Sophie informed him that everything went fine and all was well.

They all sat around the table with relieved expressions. Ruth told her husband, Jack, that she would remain here until tomorrow. She would help look after the baby so Emma could rest as much as possible.

ℰ

By the time Hannah and her parents got back home it was after lunchtime. It was still raining so they stuck to their original plans for the day. Hannah looked away from cutting the new material for her dress, to comment on the new baby. "Do all first time mothers have trouble giving birth?"

"No. It's always different. Some women never have any trouble or have trouble with one child and not the other. Emma had some trouble delivering but she also had her rather quickly and that is a blessing. You mustn't worry about these things. The moment a mother sees what a beautiful miracle is performed, the pain that she has endured seems to fade into the background."

"I guess it is up to me to provide you and Dad with grandchildren. I will try not to let you down."

Sophie dropped her knitting needle and when she looked up she had a small tear exit the corner of her eye. Hannah was confused and troubled by what she saw. Normally when her mother was upset about Toby, she didn't try to hide her hurt. Something just wasn't right. They continued to sew and knit until supper.

They would continue to work on their projects, as time allowed over the next few days. Time flew by and before Hannah knew it, school was starting the following day.

She hadn't seen much of Isaac and wondered if he had spoken to her father yet. She sure hoped so.

The great excitement of her first day of teaching could not even keep her mind off Isaac Daniels.

CHAPTER 6

Hannah chose one of her cooler dresses to wear, as it was still getting a little warm up in the day. She would wait and wear her new dress that she had made at a later time because it was made of a heavier material.

Hannah was not quite as tall as her mother but favored her very much. She twisted her long hair into a bun at the nape of her neck. She wanted to look presentable and wished to make a good impression on her first day. Many parents would bring their children in on the first day, especially the younger ones.

The walk to school would do her good and it would not be long before the harsh winds and cold temperatures, would persuade her to saddle up Goldie for the ride to the schoolhouse. She was informed by the town livery stable that she was welcome to shelter Goldie during school hours.

Katherine Barkley was also kind enough to offer her lodging at the boarding house, if for some reason the weather prevented her from traveling back home. The weather could be very unpredictable out here.

§

Isaac was outside helping Roman when he saw Hannah walking down the road towards school. He was planning on asking for permission to officially begin courting Hannah this morning. Isaac knew that Roman would be especially protective of Hannah. He did not blame him, but this made him very nervous about putting the question to him.

Today they would begin making some new fence posts, for many were deteriorating in the ground. They would first have to scout some trees that were the right size and were preferably hard wood. This would be a time consuming project but a necessary one. They had worked hard all morning long. Isaac thought that he would never see the dinner hour arrive. Roman led Isaac to a large alpine tree to take a seat on the ground to enjoy their lunch. The tree provided a rather cool retreat from the sun's rays which were warm for September but much welcomed. Roman knew, that not too far into the days ahead, a preview of cooler weather would usher in another Wyoming winter.

Sophie brought out a basket of bacon sandwiches for their lunch. She also placed oatmeal cookies and fresh squeezed lemonade into the basket. Roman was especially pleased with the corn crop this year because he wanted to be able to provide Sophie with a few extras that she so deserved. She never complained and she was always thankful for having the necessities in life.

Roman looked at Isaac who seemed to be preoccupied for some reason today. He hoped that nothing was wrong. Roman felt that the Lord had brought Isaac along to help fill the void that Toby left behind. In any case, he was grateful for Isaac's help and company.

"Are you ok, Isaac? You seem to have something on your mind. You are always welcome to speak your peace with me if you feel the need to," Roman said with sincerity.

"Thanks but I'm doing fine. But now that you have brought it up, I may as well get it off my chest," Isaac took a deep breath before continuing. "I would like to have your permission to start calling on Hannah. I have spoken to her and it is her wish also,"

Isaac said with a hint of determination but also with respect for Roman's authority.

"You can relax Isaac. This does not come as a surprise to me. Even though Sophie and I haven't mentioned it, I'm sure that she has expected it as well. So I will speak for us both and grant you permission to see my daughter."

"Thank you, sir," a relieved Isaac shook Roman's hand enthusiastically.

They finished their lunch while talking of the future tasks that lay ahead for the farm. With most of the crops close to being harvested, Isaac was looking forward to working more around the cattle. Soon they left their shaded haven to return to work.

❦

Hannah's morning was very challenging. Most of the time was spent separating the children into their appropriate grade levels. There were two very young students who were there for the first time. Emma had filled her in on the basics and to which children tended to be slower learners. So, Hannah did not always go by age but grouped the children together according to the lessons that were to be covered. She, of course, would not put them together if there was very much of an age difference.

She was careful to consider the children's feelings in all things. All of the sixteen students that Emma had enrolled were still present this year, along with Katie and the two young ones which made her nineteen.

Hannah already was familiar with most of the student's names. She decided to start the whole class with a simple assignment. Those who could, were asked to write a short paper about their summer vacation. The rest were told to write the alphabet as far as they were able to. The children, over all, appeared to be very well behaved. But then again, it was only the first day of school.

When it was time to be dismissed, Hannah told the students how pleased she was to be their teacher and was looking forward to tomorrow.

After the children were gone, Hannah let out a deep breath. *"I sure hope that I can handle this responsibility. I would hate to let everyone down. Maybe things will feel smoother in a few days when I can be in more of a routine,"* thought Hannah as she tidied up the room before leaving.

Hannah's thoughts again returned to Isaac as she walked home. She wondered if he had talked to her father yet. It seemed as though life was not as simple as it was prior to Toby's death. There were so many different emotions, such as sorrow and pain, excitement and uncertainty and most of all this uncontrollable longing to spend time with Isaac. All of these feelings came in such a short space of time that she didn't know whether to weep or to laugh, to mourn or to dance.

The rustle of fallen leaves caught her ear as she walked along the well-worn road towards home. Even after the heavy rain not long ago, the earth was unusually dry. She peered into the line of trees to see what had made a noise. For a fleeting second, she caught a glimpse of the gray dog who now seemed to be her quiet and distant companion.

When Hannah arrived home, she saw that Isaac was helping her father unload some fence posts from the wagon. She went over to say hello. "You are finished sooner than I expected. Things must have gone well or you didn't take time to rest. Which one was it?"

"You are right on both accounts, Hannah. Things went very well and we only stopped for lunch. Your dad is a real work horse," Isaac teased.

"I didn't hear any complaining on your part Isaac. But since we are done early, you may as well stay and have supper with us. I'm sure Hannah won't mind," Roman said with a twinkle in his eyes and a teasing grin.

"I don't mind at all. I had better go and tell Mama and see what I can do to help," an embarrassed and pleased Hannah replied.

❧

Hannah hurried to the house and was greeted with the smell of fresh baked molasses cake. Sophie said hello as she stirred the dough for chicken and dumplings. Setting her lunch pail and papers on a small table in the living room, Hannah gave her mother a quick peck on the cheek before going to wash up.

When Hannah returned she said, "Dad has invited Isaac to have supper with us. What can I do to help?"

Sophie saw the glow that still lingered upon her daughter's cheeks. A person would have to be blind not to notice the affection that was growing between Isaac and Hannah.

Sophie pointed to a jar of last year's corn and said, "You can get the corn started and then we will finish deboning the chicken for the dumplings."

"I didn't realize that I was so hungry until I walked in here and smelled all of these enticing aromas," exclaimed Hannah.

"How was your first day of teaching? You look a little tired this evening."

"Today was more trying than I expected it to be. But I think that after a few days we will be able to settle into more of a routine. The children are very well behaved for the most part but children will be children."

"Sit down and rest for a few minutes. We have plenty of time before the men will be here. I'm inclined to think that it is you who has taken on the load and it's not me that you have to worry about. Maybe you should ride Goldie to school in the morning if it will help," Sophie suggested.

"No at least not yet. I am more mentally tired than physically. I will become more used to teaching once I feel more comfortable with things and the children get settled back into learning. It is an adjustment for them also."

"You are probably right. I think that you will find that patience is a practice worth remembering when dealing with children," said Sophie while bringing the chicken to the table so that they could debone it together.

"Enough about my day, how was your day? I hope you haven't been doing too much. I can see that you have the house spotless," Hannah said as she glanced about the house.

"Actually, I just took my time and cleaned and then in the afternoon, I sat out back and took a small nap," laughed Sophie. She then rose and took the chicken and added it to the dumplings already cooking on the stove. Hannah collected the dinnerware and began to set the table. She was happy to be setting the extra plate for Isaac. By the look on her father's face, it seemed as though Isaac had taken care of getting permission to come calling on her. Hannah thought about how she had never really been involved with anyone. There was just no one she had ever been interested in not to mention that young men were in short supply around here.

Caught up in her thoughts, she didn't hear her father and Isaac enter the front door.

"Something sure smells good in here! I'm so hungry I could eat a bear," Roman reached out to give his loving wife a loving embrace. Laughing at Roman's exaggeration, "You are always hungry husband!"

The men took their seats at the table for they had washed up outside. Hannah poured everyone a tall glass of milk while Sophie brought the food to the table. It was good for Hannah to hear the banter between her parents again. Things seemed to be getting back to normal or at least closer. They all bowed their heads and whispered a silent prayer. When Hannah was smaller, she asked her father why they said their prayer in silence instead of out loud like most people.

Her father replied, "That way my children will begin to talk to God from their hearts and not just listen to one man's prayer."

As they ate, Roman and Isaac discussed how they would start building the fence the next day. Hannah watched how Isaac's face lit up at the prospect of working among the cattle again. She wondered when Isaac would want to spend some time together. The daylight hours were becoming shorter and there was not much left after he finished work.

Isaac turned his attention to Hannah. "How was your first day of teaching, Hannah?"

Swallowing her food before speaking, Hannah studied upon her response. She didn't want to sound incapable but she wanted to be truthful also. "I really loved being around the children but it was a little trying getting everything organized. I'm thinking of putting a test together to be more certain of what grade level each student is at."

"That sounds like a good idea. I wouldn't worry too much though. Things will fall into place and you will have them in a learning routine before you know it."

"I sure hope so, Isaac. Thanks for the encouragement." Hannah reached for her glass of milk while trying to act more composed and confident than she felt.

Sophie watched as the young couple interacted. There was no doubt that her daughter has chosen Isaac to be the one. The beginning of a relationship was as delicate as a rose petal. She would do much praying that the Lord's will is done in her precious daughter's life concerning Isaac.

Sophie waited until everyone had finished their supper before bringing the cake to the table. "Who's up for dessert?" All three said in unison, "Me!"

Almost too full to move, they all slowly rose from the table. Quickly before anyone spoke, Sophie said to Roman, "Would you mind helping me with the dishes? There aren't many and I am sure these two would like a moment alone."

"Sure thing sweetheart, I wouldn't want Isaac to think a man couldn't help his wife every now and then." Her father's joking had her blushing, so Hannah was glad when Isaac asked her if she wanted to take a short walk before he had to leave.

℘

Isaac thanked Sophie for the delicious meal and pleasant company. "You are very welcome," Sophie said with a smile.

Isaac opened the door for Hannah. Suddenly feeling nervous, Hannah wondered if it was because they were now considered an official couple. It was a scary and wonderful thought.

"I'd like to show you a place that is very special to me," said Hannah. She led Isaac around back and down the worn path to her favorite spot beside the creek. It was especially beautiful this time of year when all the bright colors of fall touched the trees. The whole area was fenced in for cattle which kept the surrounding landscape looking clean and well tamed.

"This is a lovely and secluded spot. You wouldn't have known that it was here because of the sloping bank. I'm happy that you wished to share it with me, Hannah."

"Right here upon this rock is where the Lord saved my soul. I've spent many hours here, especially to pray." She was hoping that Isaac would share with her an equal experience of his love for God. It was vital to her that they both are of the same mind concerning their faith. Isaac knew exactly what Hannah needed from him. She looked so lovely and serious standing there in front of him.

Taking her hand, they both stepped upon the large rock and sat down. "My parents lost just about everything before they moved here. There was a terrible storm with hail and a tornado. We lost the crop and much of the house and barn. But my parents did not hold a grudge against God. They took it as a sign that it was His will that they move. I didn't understand how they could not be angry. I was angry. I thought it so unfair. My parent's faith was so solid and I wondered at their sense of peace. After I saw that being angry didn't change anything, I wanted to seek after that which my parents had. It wasn't easy but on my journey here, I made a journey towards God."

Isaac brushed a tear from his cheek with the back of his hand. "I found what I was seeking for and the Lord saved my soul. So you need not worry my dear Hannah, we are equally yoked in our love for God."

Hannah raised tear-filled eyes up to Isaac. "I am so very thankful that you revealed unto me what's in your heart. I am so very thankful that God brought you and your family here, that He brought you to me." They just sat there for a time enjoying the moment that would long be remembered.

Isaac reached and raised Hannah's face to his and gently kissed her on the cheek. Hannah knew what had just passed between them was more than just special, it was sacred.

CHAPTER 7

The next couple of weeks went by quickly. Hannah had to stay after school to tutor two of the children for several days. Unfortunately, she did not get to see much of Isaac. Isaac's time had also been occupied at home, helping his father do some last minute repairs on their barn before cold and wet weather set in. It would be Saturday evening before she and Isaac could enjoy one another's company again. Today as Hannah sat at her desk, she thought of what she might wear come Saturday. The days were becoming a bit brisker, she thought about wearing the new wrap that her mother had made for her.

Tomorrow was Friday and she had to stay late with the children. The students were starting to settle into a routine and things were running more smoothly. She tried not to give them too much homework because many of the children had time consuming chores when they got home. They were all now reading close to their own grade level and the two younger students were busy writing their alphabet.

Hannah was having trouble concentrating on grading the papers laid out in front of her. She turned her head to look out the window that cast a view of the main street in the small town. She could see some of the regular townspeople going about their usual business. Luke Calder was sweeping off the boarded walk in front of his store. Dr. Hayes was in deep conversation with the town's blacksmith. Hannah also noticed Mrs. Barkley standing in front of her boarding house, which also served as a diner, talking to someone she did not recognize. The lady had her back towards her so she could not put a name to the face. Hannah had not been aware that anyone was expecting a family member or friend for a visit. Her curiosity was peeked.

Hannah pulled out the pocket watch that her father had given her. It was three o'clock. She announced to the children that it was time to go home. They hurriedly put their books away and said their goodbyes. Hannah stayed to finish grading the papers and afterwards she straightened up the schoolhouse so that everything would be in working order for the next day.

The walk home was surprisingly cooler than she had expected. The wind had picked up causing Hannah to pull her wrap more closely about her. No one was outside when she arrived home.

Sophie turned at the sound of the door opening. "Hello Hannah. I thought for a moment that it was your father coming back. He has been out on the hills checking on the cows that are close to birthing."

"Oh, I was wondering why I did not see him anywhere outside. How has your day been?" Hannah asked her mother.

"I have been catching up on some laundry and sewing. After I am finished mending some of the old clothes, I thought it would be nice to have some new warmer clothing for the winter," Sophie suggested. "Maybe we can sew together in the evenings. It will soon start to become dark earlier and it will give us something to do after supper."

Sophie saw the tired look in her daughter's eyes. "Why don't you sit down and rest while I finish up here. Supper is almost ready."

"I guess I am a little tired. I am still trying to get used to my job. Although I am not physically stressed, I am somewhat mentally exhausted," Hannah said as she sat down at the head of the table in her father's chair. After relaxing for a few moments Hannah asked, "Mama, do you know of anyone hereabouts who may be expecting a family member or a friend in to visit?"

"No, why do you ask?"

"I saw a lady talking to Mrs. Barkley outside the boarding house today. I didn't get to see her face because she had her back turned to me but she did not look familiar to me."

"I haven't heard anyone speak of anything such as that. So I really don't know for sure if anyone was supposed to arrive or not. Maybe we will learn more come Sunday at church."

"Yes. You are probably right," Hannah agreed.

"It has been a while since we had Grandma Rose and the rest of the family over for dinner. Maybe we should have them over after church for dinner and get caught up on some much needed time together," suggested Sophie as she left the stove to sit at the table with Hannah.

"I would like that very much. I have not seen Mandy lately and we have some catching up to do."

Hannah turned her head and looked out the small kitchen window to see her father ride into the yard. She rose to help her mother set the table for supper. They were having some vegetable soup, which would hit the spot, since she was still chilled from the walk home.

Roman walked in and hung his hat by the door. "Everything seems to be ok with the cattle. But there will be a lot of fence mending to do this winter. That soup sure smells good. Let's eat because I am starving!"

After dinner, Hannah asked her parents if it would be alright if she packed a small picnic lunch for Isaac and her on Saturday. They gave their permission as long as they weren't gone too far or too long. Hannah finished her chores and teaching duties soon after supper was over. Her mind then went to contemplate what she would fix to eat come Saturday morning. Roman and Sophie sat in front of the fire that had been built to keep the chill out through the night. Hannah turned in early to get a good night's sleep.

Hannah awoke just as daylight was breaking. Her parents were already up and sitting at the table with a cup of coffee. The house was still warm from the fire that had burnt slowly all night.

"Good morning. If it is alright, I would like to take some time this morning and walk down to the creek," Hannah asked.

"Go ahead honey. We are only having oatmeal this morning. It will be ready when you return," Sophie told her daughter.

The dew lay heavily on the ground and it looked as if the day was going to be a clear one. The sun was showing its magnificent power as it slowly rose to light the new day. Hannah felt the need to have some privacy and to pray for the help she knew that she would need in her life. She ended her petition, as always, with the Lord's Prayer. Rising to a sitting position, Hannah pulled a handkerchief from her pocket to wipe her eyes. When she looked up, she was surprised to see the dog sitting very close and very still.

"Hi there, where did you come from? Maybe I should give you a name since you seem to be my friend. Let's see, it has to be a very special name because I can see that you are a very special dog," Hannah spoke softly while holding her hand out to see if he wanted her to pet him. *"No not yet,"* Hannah thought.

Hannah studied for a minute and the thought suddenly came to her. "I will call him Spirit," Hannah said out loud. "For I know not whence he cometh, nor whither he goeth, like the spirit of God." Hannah looked up into the heavens once more to thank God for all of his goodness. When she looked back down, Spirit was gone.

§

After breakfast, she had put an extra biscuit into her pocket. She went out to her rock and placed the biscuit there. If Spirit was not already out there watching, she knew that he would be back.

§

Saturday morning finally came for Hannah. It had seemed an eternity since she had spent time with Isaac. She must have slept later than usual because the sun was shining brightly through her window. Roman had already eaten breakfast and gone out to do the necessary chores. Sophie had set aside some bacon and eggs for her daughter. She and Roman had trod lightly that morning in hopes of allowing their daughter to gain a little extra sleep.

"I'm sorry that I slept so late. I was more tired than I thought. I am going to help with the baking for tomorrow's dinner after church," Hannah said to her mother.

"Ok, but first eat your breakfast. We have plenty of time for that. You will also need to prepare your picnic lunch at the same time," Sophie reminded her daughter.

They were busy all morning. Sophie fried enough chicken for the dinner and for Hannah to take with her that afternoon. They prepared several desserts and baked three loaves of bread. Before they left for church in the morning, the rest of the vegetables would be cooked. Hannah filled her basket with chicken, bread, fried potatoes and plum cobbler.

Hannah glanced at the clock and was shocked to see that it was getting close to the time for Isaac to arrive. Hurriedly, she grabbed her clean dress and went to bathe in the small room that her father had built just for that purpose. She had left the door open all morning so the room would warm up. Hannah wore her long hair down with a ribbon holding it away from her face. Her dress was a dark lavender color that complimented her delicate, porcelain-like skin. A knock on the door caught Hannah's attention.

"Hannah is everything ok? Do you need anything?" Sophie asked.

"No, Mama, I'll be right out." Quickly grabbing her dirty clothes and putting them in the basket, she went into the kitchen.

"You look lovely. I think I heard Isaac drive up a moment ago," Sophie said while walking over to look out the kitchen window. "He is talking to your father now."

"You know that you don't have to worry about me. You and Dad raised me to have good judgment and to know right from wrong," Hannah consoled her mother. She could tell her mother worried but would not say so. Roman and Isaac finally entered the house. Isaac's eyes searched the room for Hannah. The look that he gave her told her all she needed to know.

He was pleased with her appearance. A little too pleased which made her cheeks turn red right there in front of her parents. "I'll have Hannah home safely and on time," said Isaac as he took the picnic basket from her hands. Hannah grabbed her hat and gave her parents a kiss goodbye.

After Isaac and Hannah had left, Roman took his wife's hands in his. "You need not fret over Hannah, my love, for Isaac is a man of God. We have talked about many things while working together over the past several days. We couldn't ask for a better man to entrust our precious Hannah with."

"I hope you are right, Roman. I just have this funny feeling that won't go away. Maybe I am just scared of losing Hannah when the loss of Toby is still so fresh."

"Sophie, I know just the thing to take your mind off those worries. In a couple of hours, when we finish up what needs doing, why don't we ride into town and see if we can find something special for Hannah's twentieth birthday? It will be here before you know it," Roman suggested.

"That's a wonderful idea! It might do me some good to get out of the house for a while," Sophie smiled gratefully at her husband. Roman and Sophie took the wagon into town a short while later.

℘

There were many people milling about town. Roman hitched the horses in front of Luke and Anna's store. Sophie eyed a beautiful warm winter wrap as soon as she entered. It was the color of Hannah's hair and had large ornate buttons down its front. It would look lovely on Hannah and it would also be useful on those long cold trips to school and back this winter. Sophie turned at the sound of the door opening. She had been so happy to find something for Hannah so quickly that she didn't get to speak to Mrs. Barkley before she left the store.

Anna walked over to where Sophie stood running her hand along the soft inner lining of the wrap. "Sophie, how are you doing? It is so nice to see you," Anna greeted her with sincerity.

"Very well," Sophie replied. "Who was that with Mrs. Barkley? I don't believe I have ever seen her around before."

"You haven't. She only arrived in town about a week ago. Her name is Bella White. She is a relative of Katherine's from Kentucky or Ohio, I'm not sure which. Her mother passed away and she has come to spend some time with Katherine and help her at the boarding house and diner."

"I'm sure the help and especially the company will be much welcomed by Mrs. Barkley."

"So, what can I help you find today? I see you are checking out that beautiful winter wrap. It is one of the nicest pieces of outerwear that we have for winter. Would you like to try it on?" offered Anna.

"No, thank you. I am actually thinking of purchasing it for Hannah's birthday. It looks to be about the right size for her. If Roman agrees, we will take it," Sophie said. Sophie handed Anna a small list of food items to gather for her while she waited for Roman. Sophie recalled Hannah telling her of the young lady she saw with Mrs. Barkley the other day. Maybe they would all get to meet her very soon. Roman agreed that the wrap would make the perfect gift for their daughter.

After talking some more with Luke and Anna, they collected their belongings and headed home. They enjoyed the clear day and comfortable temperature that the fall day granted them. Sophie wondered how her daughter's day was going.

Isaac and Hannah sat closely on the wagon seat as they made their way to a beautiful spot by the lake that bordered his parent's property.

Hannah was surprised to see a number of ducks floating aimlessly upon the water. "This is absolutely breathtaking. Thank you so much for bringing me here. Let's go set the food by the big alpine tree over there," Hannah said with appreciation for their surroundings written all over her face.

Isaac was pleased that Hannah was enjoying the scenery so much. "I am glad that you like it. I hope you will enjoy my company as much."

"I very much enjoy being with you most of all. Why don't we stretch our legs a bit before we eat?"

Isaac took Hannah's hand in his and they walked and talked of many things. While their conversation was only of light matters, they were strongly conscious of one another. They were finding that they had much in common. Hannah turned and looked up into Isaac's eyes. She could tell that he would rather talk of more serious matters but knew the time to be too soon. She felt his grip tighten on her hand instead. Isaac regretfully let Hannah's hand go when they had returned to the large tree in order to spread the blanket out for them to sit on.

He looked at Hannah and saw that her face was a little flushed. "How about we have some lunch now? I'm starving to death." Isaac said with mock exaggeration.

Hannah laughed, "Yes, I am getting a little hungry myself."

While they ate their lunch, Isaac told Hannah that there was land for sale that bordered the lake on the other side. It was connected to some of his parent's property which they now sat on.

"I hope to acquire a piece of this land. I can only hope that it is not already taken when I am finally able to afford it."

"If it is the Lord's will, it will be here. It would be a wonderful place to raise a family," Hannah said while taking in the area all around her.

Isaac pointed down to the water's edge. "There is a small boat with the paddle hidden behind the cattails, would you like to take a trip upon the still waters?"

"Oh, yes, let's go right now!" Hannah's eyes were bright with eagerness. The small boat rocked as they stepped in and sat down upon the flat boards for seats. The calm water mirrored the trees along the banks. Hannah could see several fish lazily swimming close to the water's surface. She had not expected such a treat as this. She looked up to see Isaac looking at her instead of at his surroundings. He looked very pleased that she was enjoying the day.

All too soon they were picking up their basket and journeying towards home. The afternoon went by way too quickly. But she knew that Isaac would not break his word to her parents. Hannah asked Isaac in but he declined saying he should be getting home. Isaac gave her a kiss on the cheek after he helped her down from the wagon. They said their goodbyes with thoughts of seeing each other again very soon.

CHAPTER 8

Hannah awoke to the smell of bacon frying and the rich aroma of coffee. She did not drink coffee but loved the smell of it in the mornings. Hannah could hear her mother singing "Amazing Grace" as she went about her kitchen duties. It looked as if it was going to be a gorgeous day for church and for having the family over. She was excited about seeing her cousin, Mandy. It had been a good spell since she and Mandy had some good light-hearted fun.

After helping her mother with the remainder of the dishes chosen for dinner, Hannah went to get ready for church. She had previously decided on what to wear, so she had time to relax a bit before leaving. Roman drove the wagon up to the porch. Sophie and Hannah both came out with hats on to help shield them from the sun's rays. Although the sun was not too hot, it was still very bright.

❧

Very soon they were arriving at the church grounds. Hannah glanced around in search of Isaac. She saw him standing by the church steps talking to Katherine Barkley and the young lady she saw the other day. She had completely forgotten about her. She noticed that she was close to her own age, maybe a little older. She appeared to be quite lovely from a distance. She had very black hair and was tall and thin. For some reason Hannah felt threatened when she saw Isaac talking to her. She had never experienced this feeling before but had to admit that she was plain old jealous. *"I must not get myself all worked up for nothing,"* thought Hannah to herself. *"Isaac is just being kind to the newcomer."* Roman helped Hannah and Sophie down from the wagon and escorted them over to where the crowd was gathering in front of the church. Isaac saw them and smiled and waved them over. The new lady turned toward them and looked each of them over as if she was looking for something in particular. Then she looked at them with brilliant green eyes and smiled.

Katherine was bubbling over with excitement when she said, "Hello, Roman and Sophie, I would like you to meet my cousin,

Bella White." Katherine then turned to Hannah and said, "This is their daughter, Hannah."

"It is very nice to make your acquaintance, Miss White. Welcome to our little town," said Roman as Sophie nodded her greeting in agreement. They all extended their hands to Bella in kind welcome.

"It is indeed very nice to meet you," Hannah said extending her hand also.

"Thank you all very much. Everyone that I have met has made me feel welcome indeed," Bella said while including Isaac with her eyes. Mrs. Barkley explained that Bella's mother had passed away just a few months ago. Since Bella was an only child, she wanted a chance to get to know some more of her relatives. Therefore, shortly after her mother's death she corresponded with Katherine informing her of her wish to come and visit.

Sophie politely said, "I hope your trip was pleasant and beautiful as well, Bella."

"The trip was very long but the scenery became more breathtaking the closer I got to the Black Hills. I am very glad that I came," Bella said looking directly into Sophie's eyes.

Roman placed his hand in the crook of his wife's arm. "Shall we go inside? Church is about to start."

Hannah had a hard time concentrating on what the preacher had to say as she sat behind Bella and her beautiful thick mane of black hair. *"I'm just being silly. Bella seems like a very nice young lady. I just need to get to know her better. I have never been suspicious of anyone else before I got to know them first,"* Hannah thought guiltily.

℘

After church was over, Hannah invited Isaac to dinner with the rest of the family. Isaac declined, saying that he had to help his father take care of something at home. Hannah was disappointed but told him that she understood. Hannah and Mandy rode in the same wagon and caught up on what each of them had been doing since they last saw each other. Mandy said she had been busy babysitting one of the neighbor's children because the mother had taken ill and would be a while recovering. Between there and work at home, she had very little spare time. "What did you think of Mrs. Barkley's cousin, Bella?" Mandy asked.

Hannah chose her words carefully. "She seems to be nice. She certainly is very lovely. Maybe we will have the opportunity to get to know her better," Hannah said.

"I wonder how long she will be visiting," Mandy said with her eyebrows slightly drawn together.

"Probably for a while, at least that is the impression I got from Mrs. Barkley," Hannah said as they pulled up in front of the house. Jacob was following close behind with Sarah and Grandma Rose.

℘

The men stayed outside and talked while the women prepared the food. Grandma Rose was telling Sophie that she thought we were going to have a bad winter this year. It is good that they were spending some time together now before old man winter arrived.

"Grandma Rose, what do you think of Katherine's cousin, Bella?" Mandy asked as she pinched a small bite of the stack cake that was placed in front of her.

"Well I expect that she has been a lonely girl for a quite some time. I got the feeling that she did not have much family back where she came from. It just takes time to really get to know a person if they will allow you to."

"You are right. Some people are like an open book while others are very guarded with their thoughts and dreams," Sophie joined in.

Hannah finished setting the table. "I think that is everything. I will tell Dad and Jacob that dinner is ready." Everyone around the dinner table enjoyed much light-hearted conversation.

The rest of the afternoon went by way too fast. When they said their goodbyes, they promised to see each other soon. It seemed to Hannah that their visits were becoming farther and farther apart. Hannah lay awake for several hours that night. Thoughts of the day kept running through her mind. She really didn't have anything bothering her in particular but something made her feel uneasy. She would pray for peace that would calm her heart.

CHAPTER 9

Waking to a beautiful October morning, Hannah looked forward to seeing the children for she had planned a special day for them. She quickly said her prayers and dressed before going into the kitchen. She could hear parents discussing what they would do with their day.

Sophie looked up from stirring the oatmeal when she heard her daughter come into the room. "Good morning, sweetheart, how did you sleep?"

"Not very well but I am certainly glad it is going to be a nice day outside for the students. It's hard to believe that October is here already."

Roman stood up and pushed his chair back. "I need to get going if Isaac and I are going to get any work done today. We will need to take advantage of all the good weather that comes our way."

"Here is your lunch. What time do you think that you will return?", Sophie handed him his hat and also his jacket.

"We won't be back until around four-thirty this afternoon."

"We will see you then," Sophie offered her cheek for his good-bye kiss that he always gives her.

After eating breakfast, Hannah made her lunch and got ready for the day. Hannah thought her mother looked rather tired this morning. She hoped nothing was wrong and her mother just had not slept well.

℘

The walk to school was refreshing to Hannah's mind. Even though the air was quite nippy, the clear blue sky and bright sunshine made up for it. The schoolhouse was already surrounded by children playing. Hannah wasted no time getting inside and to write some math problems on the chalkboard before she went to ring the bell.

When Hannah opened the back door, she was consumed with smoke. Coughing and unable to see, she quickly stepped back outside and took a deep breath of fresh air. Confused and shaken, Hannah thought about what could have caused the wood stove to smoke up the inside like that. *"It must be the pipe is clogged up,"* she thought. Hannah told the children to remain outside while she went to investigate the stove pipe. The pipe extended from the stove and straight through the wall to the outside. It was as she suspected. There was very little smoke coming out. Hannah found a long stick lying on the ground and stuck down the pipe. Only a few inches in she was prevented from going any further. She jabbed the stick back and forth until some of the obstruction broke loose. It was just a lot of sticks and leaves.

"How in the world did that get in there?" Hannah said in frustration. After several attempts at removing as much as she could of the debris, the smoke was soon starting to come through the pipe again. Hannah took her handkerchief and covered her mouth and nose. She went inside to open all of the windows and open both doors. Hannah led the students to a grassy spot and had them share their reading books while the smoke was clearing out. She pondered on how the pipe could have gotten plugged up like that in the first place. *"Maybe it was an animal"* was her first thought. After the children were finished reading, they all went inside. The smoke had cleared but the smell had not.

Now was a good time to tell the children of her plans for today. "Children put your books away. Today we are going to do a special project. It is one that you can all participate in. I am going to give you each a sack and I want you to put your name on it. When everyone is finished, we are going to go together into the woods along the road and gather as many types of leaves that we can each find," Hannah said and could see that she had stirred their interests. "When we come back we will label each leaf as to what type it is. I have a book that will help you identify them. Don't worry if they have turned a different color, we will figure it out. So if everyone is ready, we will spend most of the day outside."

Hannah enlisted the help of Katie and some of the other children to keep a watch on the younger ones. There was a gentle breeze that lightly rustled the leaves causing some of them to fall dancing towards the ground. The ground squirrels were chasing each other up and down the trees seemingly oblivious to those around. Hannah could hear the joyful ring of laughter being carried on the wind. She thought that the simplest things in life can be the greatest gifts because they give a pure tranquility that can soothe the soul.

Time passed so freely that it was soon time to call the children together and walk back to the schoolhouse. The younger students were getting tired, so after they all had their lunch Hannah suggested that they all had some quiet time. They could nap or read or do their homework, whichever they chose. Hannah was preparing tomorrow's lessons when she turned to look out the window towards town. A silhouette of someone standing in the upstairs window of the boarding house caught her attention. It looked as though they were just standing there staring at her. *"But that's just ridiculous,"* thought Hannah to herself. A chill shook her body. She straightened the papers on her desk and then slowly glanced back to see if they were still there. They were gone. She figured she was probably just being silly. It was someone looking out but not at her was the reasonable explanation, she reasoned.

Hannah checked the time. She told the students to leave their leaf sacks at school and they would study them tomorrow together. After dismissing the children, Hannah straightened up the room before leaving.

❧

For no exact reason, Hannah felt a little unsettled as she started out of town on her walk home. She thought of asking Luke if he had noticed anything peculiar when he built the fire this morning. On second thought, Luke wouldn't have left if he thought something was out of the ordinary. She knew him too well for that.

"Hey, Hannah!" yelled Josh coming up from behind her.

Startled from her train of thoughts, Hannah dropped her lunch bucket and books at the sound of Josh's voice. "Oh! Hello, Josh. I'm sorry that I wasn't paying any attention or I would have spoken."

"That's ok." Josh ran up quickly and helped Hannah pick up her belongings. "If it is ok with you, I will walk part of the way with you. I was just on my way back home after checking on an order for Dad."

"Sure, I would enjoy your company. It has been a while since I have talked to you. I'm guessing Katie is probably half way home by now. I always stay and straighten up before I leave."

"So how are things going with my brother? Is he behaving himself?"

"Of course but lately we haven't been able to see much of each other. Mostly only on weekends," Hannah said.

"Yeah, Dad has needed his help some too but not for much longer."

Hannah glanced Josh's way and smiled teasingly at him before saying, "How about you? Have you got your eye on anyone special yet?"

"Yes, but a lot of good it does me. It seems like every time I get around her I end up making her mad at me," Josh said with disappointment in his voice.

"You wouldn't happen to be talking about my dear cousin, Mandy, would you?"

"Yes, how did you know?"

"Well because there are not very many eligible women around these parts, also because Mandy is a very high strung individual who wears her heart on her sleeve. I believe that she must have feelings for you or she wouldn't bother with being mad at you at all."

"Do you really think so?"

"Just take things slow Josh. You will need the patience of Job with Mandy," laughed Hannah.

They continued to talk of small things until they reached Josh's road. "It was very nice talking to you Hannah. My brother sure is a lucky guy," Josh said as he handed her books back to her.

Hannah smiled her thanks. "I'll see you later, maybe over the weekend." Hannah waved and continued her walk home.

§◌

Hannah could see her mother in the side yard taking down clothes off the line. It appeared as if her father and Isaac had not returned from the pasture yet. She hurried to assist her mother. "Let me carry that for you, Mama." Hannah reached for the basket of laundry.

"How was your day at school?" Sophie asked her daughter as they went towards the house.

"To tell you the truth, it started out just horrible. When I got there the whole room was filled with smoke. I had to ask the children to stay outside while I investigated what the problem was," Hannah said somewhat winded as she sat the full basket down on the table.

"How could something like that have happened?" Concern was evident in Sophie's voice and expression.

"Well the only thing that I could think of to do was to see if the pipe was obstructed in some way, although I see no reason why it should have gotten that way all at once. Luke has always taken great care of all of that for the school. So I went out and I immediately saw that the smoke was not coming through the pipe.

"What did you do next?" asked Sophie.

"The only logical thing to do was to find a long stick and jam it down the pipe. Sure enough, the whole thing was plugged up with dirt, leaves and sticks. I am very thankful that nothing caught on fire."

"How do you suppose that all of that got in there in the first place, Hannah?" A puzzled Sophie asked her daughter.

"The only explanation that I could come up with is that it had to be an animal of some kind. When I get a chance, I will talk to Luke and see what he thinks."

"That's a good idea. Why don't you sit down and rest while I finish up supper? Your father will be here soon and we will also ask Isaac to stay and eat," Sophie said trying to cheer up her daughter.

Hannah went to wash her face and tidy her appearance before going out on the front porch and relaxing on the swing. She had almost fallen asleep when she heard Isaac and her father ride into the yard. Her heart never failed to quicken its pace whenever Isaac was near.

After stabling the horses, Roman and Isaac walked over to the porch where Hannah now stood by the steps. "Isaac, you may as well stay and eat a bite with us. You won't get home in time before supper to do anything today. I didn't realize that it was so late. Time just seemed to have gotten away from me," Roman said in an apologetic tone.

"I'd love to stay if it is no trouble."

"Not at all, I will let Sophie know you're staying. There is some soap and water out back so you can wash up."

"Thanks," Isaac told Roman. He then turned to Hannah and said, "I will be right back. Don't go anywhere." Hannah smiled and nodded her head. She sat back down in the swing and waited for Isaac. She was glad that she did not have to wait until the weekend to see Isaac again. Even for just a little while this evening was better than nothing.

Isaac came around the corner of the house a few minutes later. He sat down beside Hannah and took her hand in his. Hannah scooted closer. "I know that I have been busy lately but I need to work as much as I can. I was serious when I told you that I wanted to buy some property," Isaac looked at her closely to see her reaction.

"I understand and I want that too. I will try to be supportive. We will find time to be together."

"How are you doing Hannah? You looked a little tired when I walked up."

"I'm doing fine. It was just a trying day at school. You being here has more than made up for it," Hannah said. Isaac put his arm around Hannah's shoulders and he felt her relax against him. She let out a sigh of contentment. She could feel her love grow for Isaac with the passing of time.

All too soon, Roman announced that supper was on the table. They all gathered to enjoy a meal of fried chicken, mashed potatoes, turnips and cornbread. Sophie had made a jelly roll for dessert.

Roman turned his attention to his daughter. "Your mother has been telling me about what happened this morning at the schoolhouse. Do you suppose one of the children pulled a prank without realizing the dangerous consequences that could have resulted from such an action?"

"It honestly had never occurred to me that it could have been one of my students," Hannah answered. She saw the questioning look in Isaac's eyes and said, "This morning when I got to school the whole house was filled with smoke. The pipe had been packed full of sticks and other debris from outside."

A fleeting expression of anger flashed in Isaac's eyes. "Are you sure there was no harm done to you or any of the children?"

"Yes. All of the children were still outside playing when I arrived. I am just thankful that no one was hurt. Luckily Luke had only built a small fire otherwise things might have been much worse. The only way that I can figure the pipe got in that condition is that some animal made a nest in there," Hannah ventured at a guess.

Roman nodded his disagreement. "That's not very likely in my opinion. It has never happened here, especially when a fire is being kept rather often now that it has started getting cool in the mornings."

"I agree Roman. We should start paying close attention until we know it is safe again," Isaac stated.

Hannah hurriedly spoke. "There is no cause for everyone to worry needlessly. I will just leave a bit early for a while and check everything out before the children arrive. I will alert Luke so that he can inspect things before he builds a fire. So let's finish eating and enjoy our supper."

Sophie asked Roman how the cattle were fairing that grazed way out in the hill pasture. She hoped to change the subject to lighten matters for she could see that Isaac was getting far too worked up. Although she didn't mind seeing that the young man cared deeply for her daughter, she also knew her daughter was a little too independent for her own good sometimes. She was quite stubborn on occasion to boot.

"The pasture is holding out remarkably well for this time of year. I am concerned about the water supply. I may have to move them soon if it doesn't rain before long," Roman said as he stabbed another piece of fried chicken with his fork and placed it on his plate.

"It's hard to believe that it is already the middle of October. Where has the time gone?" Sophie exclaimed. "Hannah, your birthday is in just a few days. This Saturday is October the seventeenth. Is there anything special that you wish to do?"

"You know that I don't like to make a fuss. There is no need to go to any trouble."

Isaac turned a fake sad face toward Hannah and said, "You mean that I can't come and see my girl on her birthday?"

"Oh quit being silly Isaac. You know that I want you to come and see me," Hannah said consolingly in the same mocking voice.

❧

After dinner was finished and the dishes were cleaned, Hannah walked with Isaac part of the way home. The moon was full and bright and they had no trouble seeing because it was not completely dark yet. Isaac stopped before they had gone very far because he didn't want Hannah to have but a short walk back.

"I'm glad that you could stay for supper tonight. I hope your parents aren't too worried," Hannah said to Isaac.

"They will have already figured out that I stayed on to visit with you. Hannah, I have been thinking. I could leave early in the morning and walk you to school before going to work. What do you think?"

"There is no need, really. Besides I am going to go and talk with Luke first anyway. Please don't worry. I am sure that it was just some unusual thing that happened."

With concern still etched on Isaac's face, he saw that Hannah would not move on the matter. Isaac reached out and gathered Hannah close in a possessive embrace. Hannah was comforted and was in much more need of the safe feeling that his embrace provided than she cared to admit. Without words, they parted and went their separate ways, both thinking that one day they would have a home of their own. Hannah noticed the night air had turned much cooler in the last few minutes. She quickened her steps to reach home and its warmth.

That night Hannah's sleep was invaded with a dream of a cloaked figure chasing after her. She could never see who or what was behind her but it never did catch her. She awoke the next morning very disturbed and very tired from her restless night. While Hannah got ready for school that morning, she reflected back on the dream that had seemed so real that when she awakened, she was crying and standing beside the bed. Never had a dream affected her like that before. Hannah kept telling herself that it was just a dream. Hannah had only enough time to grab a biscuit on her way out the door. She did not allow herself time for breakfast because she had almost forgotten that she had to speak with Luke this morning before class began. Her mother handed her a packed lunch as she went out the door, a lunch which would have been sorely missed a few hours later.

Luke was just closing the schoolhouse door when Hannah walked into the yard. He smiled and said, "Well, hello, Hannah. You are bright and early this morning."

"Yes, I wanted to speak with you for a moment if that's alright," Hannah said a little out of breath from her brisk walk into town.

"What's on your mind? I hope everything is alright."

"Yes, everything is ok. At least I think it is. You see, yesterday morning when I got here, the schoolhouse was filled with smoke. I was wondering if you noticed anything out of the ordinary when you were here building the fire yesterday?"

"I didn't notice anything amiss. I have only been building up small fires so that you can add more to it if you need to. I had no problem getting the fire to draw. Did you find out what the trouble was?"

"The pipe outside was filled with sticks and leaves. The smoke could not escape. Let's take a look out back to be sure it is still clear today." Hannah and Luke walked around to see the smoke flowing freely from the pipe.

Luke scratched his bearded chin, "I can't understand how that could have happened without me knowing it. If the pipe had been like that when I had built the fire all of the smoke would have come in on me immediately. That's a peculiar thing to be sure."

"I agree with you and I thought you ought to know so we can both look out for it in the future. I won't keep you and please tell Anna hello for me."

"I will and don't you worry about it. We will keep an eye on things much closer," Luke patted Hannah's shoulder.

"Thank you," Hannah said with gratitude. Hannah went inside and began to prepare for the day ahead.

❦

Although she was tired from a restless night, the day went by quickly and enjoyably. Hannah had noticed that while grading some papers the wind had picked up and was blowing many of what was left of the leaves on the trees. It looked as if some weather was brewing. She glanced at her watch and decided to let the students leave a few minutes early in order to get home before the storm arrived. Hannah rushed to straighten the classroom. She made sure the fire had completely died down and that everything was securely shut before heading home.

The sky had darkened considerably since the children had left. She whispered a prayer that they all would make it home before the clouds opened up. Hannah could tell by the fast moving clouds that it would not be long before the storm passed through. She probably would be no more than half way home before getting a good soaking. Deciding to wait the storm out, Hannah went over to the boarding house to have a cup of tea to pass the time.

❦

There was no one in the small dining room where Mrs. Barkley served meals to her boarders and to the townspeople. It seemed as if everyone was in for the evening.

At the sound of the kitchen door opening, Hannah turned to see Bella's eyes searching the room to see who had entered from the street. "Good afternoon, Hannah," Bella said with a beautiful smile that did not quite reach her eyes.

"Hello. I hope it's alright that I came over. It looks like I am the only one here and I don't want to put you out," Hannah said while thinking that this might not have been such a good idea after all.

"Not at all, please have a seat. It's been dead in here all day. I'm glad for the company. Can I get you something to eat?" Bella offered.

"A cup of tea would be nice if it is no trouble. I thought I'd wait the storm out. They usually don't last too long. Where's Katherine? She's well I hope."

"She is doing fine. Right now she is lying down. We did a lot of cleaning this morning and I am afraid that she has just over done it a little," said Bella as she gracefully walked into the kitchen area. After sitting down, Hannah heard the rain start pelting hard against the window. She looked at the clock on the wall. The children should have all had time to get home before the rain started. Hannah had been so busy that she had not noticed how everyone from town had either left or gone indoors. She must be more cautious for the children's sake in the future.

Bella reentered the room with a tray of tea and a plate of cookies. "I hope you like oatmeal cookies. We saw that we were going to be slow today and didn't prepare much ahead," said Bella as she poured them both a cup of tea.

"Thank you and I love oatmeal cookies. My mother makes them quite often although not as much now that my brother, Toby, has passed away," said Hannah which brought certain memories to mind.

"I'm sorry to hear that. Was he your only sibling?"

"Yes and I miss him very much."

"I'm sure you do. I am an only child myself. Some people don't know how fortunate they are to have a family," Bella said with a hint of jealousy.

"You are right and I should be more thankful for the time that I was allowed to have with my brother. So how are you enjoying your stay in this part of the country," asked Hannah? She got a feeling that she should change the subject.

"It is different but very beautiful here. The people are all very welcoming. I haven't been out past the town limits yet but as soon as things are caught up here, I plan to do a little exploring."

Hannah looked outside and saw that the rain had almost stopped. "Well I should be getting home. I hope that one day very soon you will come and have dinner at our place. My parents would be very pleased if you would come."

"That would be great. Thank you and be careful. The storm may not be completely over yet." The screen door creaked as Bella opened it for Hannah. Hannah smiled and waved goodbye as she carefully made her way down the wet, wooden steps.

The sky was overcast with a dreary gray that seemed to impose its very presence into Hannah's own mood. *"There is something about Bella that I can't quite figure out. She seems very nice but just beneath her pleasant exterior there lies a contradiction of determination and vulnerability,"* thought Hannah.

❧

The walk home was made as swiftly as her small feet would carry her. Hannah did not like the uneasy feelings that seemed to be intruding upon the peaceful world that she had worked hard to find again after Toby's death. She would feel better once she got home. She would take time to go down to her special place. She would pray.

CHAPTER 10

Sophie worked quietly in the kitchen hoping not to awaken Hannah too early. Today was her daughter's twentieth birthday. Even though Hannah did not wish to make a big fuss, Sophie knew that there was a good chance that this would be Hannah's last birthday here at home. *"How quickly the years have flown by,"* Sophie spoke her thoughts in a whisper. She was icing the chocolate cake that she had baked the day before. They were having the rest of the family over as well as Isaac and his family. Sarah was helping with dinner and would arrive early to help.

Roman was out checking the animals before he set up the table outside for extra seating. It was a glorious fall day. The air had a bite but the sun's bright rays would add a touch of warmth to the body and soul. Sophie hoped that Hannah would relax and enjoy the day which the Lord had made. Hannah had looked very tired all week. Whatever was bothering her, maybe she could put it out of her mind for a few hours.

The sun spilled through Hannah's window and warmed her face, to gently awaken her from sleep. Unaccustomed to sleeping long enough to enjoy the sun's special attention, Hannah sunk deeper into her blankets to bask in the warmth for a while longer. She could hear her mother moving about the kitchen. Looking forward to seeing Isaac, she climbed out of bed in anticipation of the day ahead.

Sophie smiled when Hannah entered the kitchen. "Good morning Hannah. Did you sleep well?" Sophie set a plate of hot eggs and bacon on the table for her.

"Yes, I had a good nights' rest. I must have been very tired to have slept so late," said Hannah in an apologetic voice for staying in bed for so long.

"Don't be silly. You deserve to sleep in on your birthday. I know you said not to make a fuss but everyone wanted to come and spend the day with you," explained Sophie. The cooking that her mother had already done was enough to let her know that they would be having company.

"What time will everyone be arriving?" Hannah inquired. She didn't know how hungry she was until she sat down to eat her breakfast. She had eaten very little for super the night before.

"Sarah said they would be here around noon to help before Isaac and his family got here. I have already prepared most of the food so we can relax and enjoy each other's company."

Hannah noticed that her father had left to check on the cattle already. She hoped that he did not have too much to do this morning so that he could take a break from all the hard work that was ever present. "Is there anything that I can help with right now?" asked Hannah as she rose from the table with an empty plate.

"Not right now. There are some last minute preparations to do. Why don't you go ahead and get bathed and dressed while you have plenty of time?"

"Thanks, Mama. I won't be too long," Hannah said while thinking upon what she would wear.

Since it would be rather cool out despite the sun's warmth, she would choose her newest dress which was made of a heavier material. Anxiously Hannah bathed and dressed. Even though she knew that she must not put undue stock in appearances, she wanted to look especially nice for her birthday. Hating to admit, even more so for Isaac.

❦

"Hannah, I hope that you are about ready because it looks like Mandy has pulled up and is coming this way with bells on," laughed Sophie with a little excitement of her own.

"I'll be right there," spoke Hannah loud enough for her mother to hear. It was good to hear her mother laugh. It had been a long time since she heard the familiar sound. It gladdened her heart. It was the best birthday present she could have received.

Mandy didn't bother knocking on the door. She felt just as much at home here as she did in her own house. She and Hannah were like sisters. "Hannah! Happy birthday to you," Mandy loudly said as she searched the room for her dear first cousin. Just as Hannah entered the room, Mandy gave her a tight embrace and bright smile.

"Mandy I am so glad that you are here. It wouldn't have seemed like my birthday without you." Hannah couldn't keep a tear from slipping down her cheek as she stepped back to return a bright smile of her own. Grabbing Mandy's hand, Hannah led her into her bedroom and said, "So how have things been going for you? Are you still babysitting?"

"Yes, I really don't know how long that I will be there but those little children sure keep me on my toes. Makes me think twice about having any of my own," laughed Mandy. "Just kidding, you know how I love children."

"That I do. On a different note, you know that Josh is coming today don't you?" Hannah told Mandy with a knowing look.

Mandy took a deep breath while clasping her hands in her lap. "Yes, Mom told me. I know you can tell that I have feelings for him but I am so nervous when I am around him," Mandy pleaded with eyes that asked for some input about her dilemma.

"Just take things slow but don't be afraid to open your heart. You will know with time if Josh is right for you. Time has a way of bringing things to light," responded Hannah with what she hoped was good advice.

"Time is not something I can deal with very easily. You know how impatient that I can be."

"Love is something that can come quickly and unexpectedly or it can come slowly and gently and take root deeply within your heart."

The sound of Grandma Rose calling out to Hannah broke their thoughts.

They got up and went to the kitchen. There they found the rest of the women folk around the table. "Happy birthday, dear child, come and give me a hug," entreated her grandmother.

"I love you Grandma Rose. I am so happy that you are all here. How have you been?" Hannah asked her grandmother after she had given her Aunt Sarah a hug also.

"I am fit as a fiddle, for an old lady that is. I am living proof that a little hard work never killed anybody," chuckled Grandma Rose with that stubborn and determined look that dared anyone to say otherwise. Sarah raised her eyebrows as if she didn't fully agree that Grandma Rose was as well as she claimed.

Hannah sometimes wondered how a mother and daughter could be so different. Sarah was a very quiet woman while Mandy was exactly the opposite, a bundle of words and energy. Sophie and Sarah worked together to finish the dinner preparations. *"It is good to hear the chatter and laughter amongst them once more. Mama has been in a world of her own since Toby's death,"* thought Hannah as she watched them all enjoy each other's company.

Roman and Jacob had set up a table and chairs outside for the young people. Hannah walked over to the window to see where her father and Jacob were. They were by the barn throwing hay into the back of the wagon. Hannah wondered what they were doing that for. After a few moments, they began walking towards the house. They sat down into one of the chairs that they had placed under a shade tree, even though most of the shade was gone by this time of year.

Catching a movement out of the corner of her eye, Hannah looked and saw someone walking down the road towards their house. Hannah strained to see who it was. She could see that it was a lady and as she drew closer, she was surprised to see that it was Bella White.

Hannah turned to her mother. "I see Bella White coming down the road. Did you know that she was coming today?"

Sophie put down the large spoon that she was using to stir the corn. "No, I didn't. But this is a nice surprise though. Why don't you girls go out and welcome her?" Mandy jumped up quickly and pulled Hannah along as she walked swiftly out the door. Bella was already speaking to her father and Uncle Jacob. She turned and went to meet them when she heard them come out.

"Hello, Bella. Mandy and I are very pleased to see you," Hannah said. "Do come inside and say hello to the rest of the family."

"I hope that I didn't come at a bad time. It was a beautiful day for a walk and I thought that I would do some of that exploring that we talked about. It was also a good time to take you up on that invitation and come visit you and your family. Perhaps I am intruding by the looks of things," Bella said.

"You came at a perfect time. We are celebrating Hannah's birthday today," Mandy enthusiastically informed Bella.

"Yes. You must stay and have dinner with us. Isaac and his family will also be joining us any time now. I feel very blessed to have you all here today," Hannah expressed with genuine sincerity.

"If you are sure that I won't be imposing upon family time," Bella said with an undertone in her voice that sounded almost sarcastic. Hannah looked at Mandy to see if she had noticed but

Mandy had already turned to open the door. *"I must be reading too much into things,"* thought Hannah to herself.

℘

"Mama, Bella has been kind enough to stay and share the day with us," Hannah told her mother as she ushered Bella to the table to take a seat.

"What a pleasant surprise! Welcome to our home, Bella. I'm sure you have already met the rest of the family," Sophie said warmly, wishing to make Bella feel comfortable.

Bella could feel the love among the people inside the small home. Bella thought of how she had grown up in a large house with all the comforts. She was reminded today that love was what made a house a home. She knew that her mother had loved her in her own way but there was something missing in their relationship that Bella had always felt.

"Bella, Bella?" Grandma Rose spoke a second time to get Bella's attention.

"What, oh I am sorry. I was just admiring what a lovely and cozy home this is," said Bella.

"Yes, I agree. When a home is built with your own sweat and blood, it seems to take a piece of your heart and so everywhere you look there will always be a feeling of genuine thankfulness. A feeling that is impressed upon all those who enter," Grandma Rose said as she patted Bella's hands that lay folded upon the table before her. Unused to such tender gestures, Bella fought to hold her emotions in check.

Such a small display of the older lady's kindness must surely be taken for granted in a family where love was obviously in abundance. Bella again withdrew herself. She reverted back to the more familiar feeling of being sorry for herself. Hannah and Mandy had taken a seat at the table across from Bella. Bella took in their attire. She could tell that their dresses were homemade and probably one of their best. They were in no way comparable to Bella's specially ordered dress from St. Louis but they wore them with such pride, as if they were the best money could buy. There were many things about this family that were a mystery to her.

"Now that you have been amongst our small community, how do you like your visit so far?" Hannah questioned Bella. She could not help but admire Bella's beauty. She strikingly appeared to be without flaw.

"I find the people to be especially pleasant and the town much quieter than I am used to. It is a welcome change. In fact, I am thinking of extending my stay here. Cousin Katherine is in complete agreement and appreciates my company," Bella said taking in the reactions of those in the room.

"That's wonderful." Sarah spoke first. "You come visit us also when you get the chance."

"I think that I speak for us all when I say that we are very pleased about your decision to stay on for a while. We will have many opportunities to enjoy one another's company," Sophie bent to give Bella a hug to emphasize her words.

Mandy tapped her fingers impatiently upon the table. Leaning towards the window she said, "I wish everyone would hurry up and get here. I am absolutely starving. I didn't have any breakfast this morning, just so I could enjoy all of the delicious food here." Hannah thought to herself of how beautiful a young woman that her dear cousin had become. Her childlike exuberance often overshadowed her more serious and vulnerable side. Hannah also knew that food was not the reason she wanted the Daniels family to arrive soon. Hannah fingered the ruffled cuff on the sleeve of her dress. The antique lace also adorned the neckline and complimented her creamy complexion.

Hannah was unaware of just how rare her own beauty was. While her coloring was darkly vivid, her features were so delicate that they caused one to stare overly, much in appreciation. The clock on the mantle chimed the two o'clock hour. The conversation paused long enough for them to hear the rattling of the Daniels' wagon pulling up to the front of the barn next to Jacob's. Sophie and Sarah began putting the food into dishes while Hannah and Mandy finished setting the table. Plates and forks were set aside for the six young adults to eat outside. Hannah knew Katie would want to join them.

Roman entered the house first and collected everyone's coats as they all jubilantly greeted each other.

To gain everyone's attention, Grandma Rose tapped her spoon against her glass. Immediately, the room became silent and all looked to the eldest family member with respect. "Twenty years ago, the good Lord chose to bless us with our precious Hannah. God looks down upon all those who love and serve Him according to His purpose and with time reveals to us His will in our lives. I have watched my granddaughter grow not only in years but in faith as well," Grandma Rose said as she wiped tear filled eyes with her handkerchief that she always kept in her dress pocket. "I have no doubt that she will continue to press onward through the many hills and valleys that life presents her with and will always come out looking up," Grandma Rose concluded as Hannah rushed into her embrace.

Not a dry eye was found amongst them. Bella's expression held a mixture of both yearning and confusion at the same time. This was not lost on Grandma Rose. She knew that the girl had not been raised in the ways of the Lord and would take every opportunity to enlighten her.

Roman cleared his throat so that he might speak. "Before we all bow our heads to ask a blessing, I would just like to say that any birthday gift that we have for Hannah will pale in comparison to the beautiful and wise words of my dear mother. Thank you Mom."

§Ω

Hannah and Isaac filled their plates and went outside to eat. Everyone else followed shortly. Bella sat next to Isaac across from Josh, Mandy and Katie.

Mandy's curiosity began working full time when she started asking Bella about her life and where she grew up. "What were the people like where you grew up? Did you live in a big or small town?" Mandy asked.

"Well people were much the same there as anywhere, although there came to be more and more refined people from the east as time went on. The town of course has built up considerably." Bella informed them.

"I hope things never change here. Things have always been so peaceful in our small town," Mandy said.

They continued to talk of the differences between the more settled areas and the small remote settlements of the mid-west. Hannah and Isaac were content to listen. Isaac held Hannah's hand while they waited for the rest of them to finish eating. Sophie came outside and asked them to come in and have some cake while Hannah opened her gifts. Hannah hadn't even noticed the gifts setting on the table by the fireplace. Roman had placed one of the chairs beside it for Hannah to sit in. "Here Hannah, open ours first!" Mandy said as she reached a beautifully wrapped package to Hannah.

"Thank you," Hannah said as she tore the wrapping paper off. "I love it. Thank you all so much!" Hannah exclaimed as she ran her fingers over the brown and rose colored drawstring purse.

It was ornately decorated with rose colored jewel-like studs. The Daniels family gave her a set of gloves and scarf that had been lovingly knitted. She then opened her present from her parents. With special care of the ribbon, she opened the beautiful winter wrap. It was perfect.

She held it up to show how the dark brown color matched her hair and enhanced her creamy complexion. "It is absolutely lovely and I can't wait to wear it," Hannah thanked her wonderful parents with a heartfelt smile.

"You won't have to," Isaac said "We are going on a hay ride shortly. The evening air will be quite chilly."

"Here you have one more to open and it is from Isaac," said Josh as he handed the small gift to Hannah. Hannah pulled the ribbon from the box and opened its lid. Inside laid a set of the most unique hair combs that she had ever seen. They were adorned with flower shaped stones that were the color of Hannah's eyes. They changed colors with every movement, from green to gold and then to green again. With a choked voice Hannah said, "Thank you Isaac. They are so very special." Isaac only nodded his head in acknowledgement. He was glad that she was pleased with his gift.

"So are you all ready to go for that ride?" Mandy jumped up and went outside and Josh followed suit.

Bella walked up to Hannah and said, "I am sorry that I didn't bring a gift. But now I think that it is time that I should be getting back to Katherine."

"I am glad that you came. Why don't you stay and go for the hay ride with us? We will make sure that you get home safely," Hannah politely asked.

"Ok, I would love to. I told Cousin Katherine that I might be a little late."

"Then it's settled. Katie, are you coming with us?" Hannah asked the sweet girl.

"I don't think that I am feeling up to it, Hannah. I have a stomach ache. I probably ate too much cake."

"Of course, we will see you when we get back," Hannah smiled and patted Katie's shoulder in understanding.

Gathering their wraps, Hannah and Bella followed Isaac outside to where Josh and Mandy had already driven the wagon up to the front door. Isaac helped Bella up onto the hay that was stacked to provide seating for them. Hannah took Isaac's large warm hand and climbed up easily across from Bella and sat down.

Isaac hung two lanterns on the wagon, one up front by Josh and Mandy and the other one in the back for them. "We won't need the lanterns for a while but we will have them just in case," Isaac said as he swung himself up and sat down next to Hannah.

Isaac reached for Hannah's hand and held to it snuggly. When he had asked Roman to prepare the wagon for the ride, his intention was to be alone with Hannah. He had not anticipated on Bella being there.

"Have you ever been on a hay ride before Bella?" Hannah asked as she unconsciously scooted closer to Isaac.

"Actually, I haven't. I never did venture far from town and all of my friends were pretty much the same," answered Bella with a slightly proud look. "You tend to grow up fast in a town where there are saloons and many rough characters about." The wagon suddenly gave a jolt causing Bella to pitch forward into Isaac. Hannah observed that Bella was needlessly slow about getting up. She put both of her hands on Isaac's knees as she rose with Isaac's help.

"I am sorry about that. I wasn't prepared to be thrown at you like that," Bella said with a different story altogether showing in her eyes. Hannah tensed up and turned away as if taking in the scenery.

Isaac sensed the tension and sought to ease the mood. "That's ok. These roads are pretty bad in places. Hannah look at what a beautiful clear sky we have this evening. I bet the stars will shine like diamonds in a couple of hours," Isaac said and he felt the stiffness ebb from her body.

Hannah reached up to brush an errant curl that had escaped the ribbon holding part of her hair back. She heard Mandy let out a squeal of laughter and wondered what was so funny.

Turning to Isaac Hannah asked, "Where do you have Josh taking us?"

Isaac made a crooked smile and said, "It is a surprise. We will be there soon enough."

Josh had driven the wagon past the road that led to the Daniels farm. Not five minutes later, they pulled onto a barely noticeable untraveled, dirt road. It was very rough and the woodlands became denser and darker the further they went.

"Are you sure that we should be here? I hope we aren't trespassing on someone else's property," Bella inquired as she looked around.

"It's perfectly alright. This is still on my dad's land," Isaac answered.

There were large rocks on either side of them. They came close to the foot of the hill and again turned right. Winding around large rocks and tall trees, they came to what looked like a cave on their left. Josh drew the horses to a halt.

Josh jumped down and secured the horses to a tree limb. "This is where we get off." He motioned for Mandy to take his hand as she stepped off the wagon.

Hannah looked curiously around. "It looks like a cave but I can see daylight not that far in. It looks like a wide bridge made of rock or an entry way from one side of the hill to another," said Hannah.

Her pleased and excited expression was what Isaac wanted to see. They walked up the slight incline to enter the tunnel-like formation. As they went a little further inside, there appeared to be what looked like drawings or etchings on the walls to both their left and their right.

"Wow, I can't believe this! How did you find this place?" Mandy asked in awe.

Isaac said, "I wanted to see what the land looked like that bordered my father's place. I came across this place by chance."

"It is absolutely amazing! Look at the art work everyone. There are what looks like animals and symbols from no telling how long ago," Hannah said in childlike enthusiasm.

"Listen," Bella said inclining her ear.

"It sounds like water." Mandy said as she led the way to the other side. Isaac and Josh just smiled at each other and followed the girls.

As soon as they saw the small waterfall and the tranquil body of water that it spilled over into, they were met with breathless silence. There were wild ducks swimming leisurely and a female pronghorn deer that raised its head to stare at them when she detected their presence. Hannah thought that the little hidden oasis was a discovery that far outshined anything that the miners could find in these black hills. The only way down to the pool of water below was to climb down the rocks that hugged the side of the hill. The movement of a small red fox caught Hannah's attention as it walked over to the edge of the pool to quench his thirst. The deer and the ducks seemingly paid him no mind. Hannah had never seen a more serene display of wildlife. She looked around for the large more predatory animals, like the bear and wolf, but all seemed well. Even if they were close by, they wouldn't dare disturb the peace.

So intent upon the scenery, Hannah was caught unaware when a sudden blow from behind sent her plunging over the falls into the water below. The shocking cold took Hannah's breath away. She struggled to reach the surface, the weight of her clothes and shoes made her efforts slow and impeding if not impossible. When she finally broke the surface, she could hear Mandy screaming her name. After what seemed like an eternity, she felt strong hands grab her around the waist and pull her towards the bank.

Isaac held her as she caught her breath and calmed her racing heart. "Are you ok?" Isaac asked anxiously. There was a touch of anger in his voice that he tried to conceal.

"I think so. I am probably more scared and shocked than anything. What happened? It all happened so fast that I really don't know what caused me to fall." Hannah's shaky words were barely audible.

"We will find out for sure when I get you back up there with the others. I think that Bella tripped and fell into you," Isaac said with a puzzled look on his face.

Hannah lifted her eyes up to where the others stood looking down. Mandy was standing there with her hands still over her mouth in fright. Shifting her gaze towards Bella, the emotionless expression displayed there put Hannah's stomach into a knot. Surely there was some explanation for such lack of care. Isaac stood to help Hannah to her feet. With careful navigation, they made their way back to the others.

Mandy flew straight into Hannah's arms sobbing with relief. "What in the world caused you to fall? I was so busy telling Josh how beautiful this place is that it all happened before I knew it," exclaimed Mandy with eyes as big as saucers.

Bella stepped forward. "I am afraid that it was my fault. I wasn't looking where I was going. I tripped on the uneven surface and fell forward into Hannah. I am so sorry," said Bella apologetically. "I hope you were not injured."

"I'm fine, just a little shook up." Hannah managed the words with difficulty. "It was just an accident," added Hannah with little conviction.

Josh strode over to where Isaac still held Hannah close. "You were very lucky Hannah. There are a couple of protruding, jagged rocks that you came close to hitting on your way down."

"Yes, you could have been more than seriously harmed."

"I thank the Lord for watching over me and keeping me safe," Hannah said thankfully.

"I think it is time that we get you both home and into some dry clothes," said Josh as he began to lead the way back to the wagon.

"I am sorry that I spoiled the evening for everyone. If I hadn't been standing so close to the edge, this never would have happened," Hannah said.

"Nonsense, it was not your fault. I'm just thankful that you are alright," Isaac gave her hand a gentle squeeze. The ride home was very quiet.

❧

They dropped Bella off at the boarding house before continuing on home. The stars were shining like diamonds. Hannah and Isaac enjoyed the short ride back without Bella's presence.

"Isaac?" Hannah poked his shoulder to get his attention.

"What? I'm sorry. I guess I was lost in thought," Isaac turned his head to give her his full attention.

"What's on your mind? You have been silent for most of the trip home."

"I was just thinking about how close I came to losing you. I can't believe how Bella could have been so careless. I can't believe that she would do something like that on purpose," stated Isaac.

"I'm sure she feels terrible about what happened. It had to be an accident. It had to be."

"Your parents might not want to let you go anywhere with me when they find out what happened," sadly Isaac berated himself.

Hannah softly laughed. "They will do no such thing. They will understand when we explain what took place." Soon they were pulling up beside the barn. They could hear laughter coming from inside. Hannah couldn't wait to get inside to get warm. Even Isaac was having a hard time controlling his shivers. Mandy and Josh ushered them quickly inside.

℘

Everyone stared at them with their mouths gaped open.

Grandma Rose spoke first. "For land sakes child, what in the world happened to you?"

"Grandma it is ok. I just fell into a pool of water, that's all," explained Hannah.

Sophie had already gathered quilts from the bedroom. She handed one to Alice and they wrapped their children in them. They were then placed in front of the fire place.

"That's all! You won't believe what happened. She's lucky to be alive, that's what!" Mandy held her hands up in exasperation.

"Mandy is right. She is not exaggerating either," Josh seconded Mandy.

Roman stepped in front of Hannah and Isaac but he directed his question at Isaac. "Just exactly what went on out there?"

"Well, sir, I took Hannah and the others to see a special place that I had come up on while walking the far end of Dad's property line. It was a waterfall and pool hidden within the hills." Isaac stopped to clear his throat before continuing. "While Hannah was overlooking the pool of water down below, Bella somehow tripped and fell into her and knocked her over the edge," Isaac told Roman nervously.

"Hannah, were you in any way hurt?" Roman asked his daughter.

Hannah could see the tense movement in her father's jaw. She answered, "I am fine, thanks to Isaac. I don't know how he climbed down to rescue me as fast as he did. Being scared and wet are my only ailments."

Sophie put her arm around her daughter's shoulders and said, "Let's get you out of those wet clothes. Isaac, you do the same. Roman will get you whatever you need."

Sarah and Jacob put on a pot of coffee and some cookies on the table for everyone to enjoy. While waiting, they were all entertained with Mandy's account of their outing. Grandma Rose was unusually quiet.

"Are you feeling okay, Rose?" Sarah asked when she noticed the elderly lady's silence.

"I am doing very well, Sarah. Just a little tired I suppose."

Sarah set a cup of coffee in front of her saying, "We will be on our way shortly when Isaac and Hannah come back to join us."

Sarah could tell when Grandma Rose was not telling the whole truth. She would not look her in the eyes with her answer. Isaac entered the room with some of Roman's clothes on. They were close to the same height but the clothes were slightly loose because Isaac still had some filling out to do, at his young age. Isaac laid his own wet discarded clothes by the front door so that he would not forget them. Sophie and Hannah returned and Hannah sat close to the fire once again for some added warmth. The rest of the family stayed until their coffee was finished. Isaac was the last one out the door making sure Hannah was really ok. Roman and Sophie could tell that Hannah was exhausted and a good night's rest would do her good. They gave her a quick hug and insisted she go on up to bed.

Hannah could hear her parents cleaning up the kitchen. She climbed into her bed after adding an extra blanket. She immediately began going over the events of the evening in her mind. One minute she was entranced by her surroundings and the next she was falling hopelessly into the green, absorbing water below. She had never fought harder against the encompassing forces that worked against her. She remembered the strong hands grabbing her and taking away her fears with every move that brought her ever closer to the bank's safety. As Isaac had pulled her out of the water, she had caught a glimpse of piercing eyes at the edge of the woods. She remembered now that it had been Spirit. It was a comfort to know that he faithfully watched over her. They had a special connection. Hannah's eyes became heavy with sleep and the last thing she saw in her mind's eye was Bella's face and the mystery that seemed to surround her, a mystery that needed answers.

CHAPTER 11

Hannah awoke to a room filled with the morning's light. She yawned and stretched before pulling the covers back up beneath her chin. Her thoughts were trying to push through the cobwebs of sleep. Trying to remember what day it was, she realized it was Sunday and way past time to get up for church. *"I wonder why Mama didn't wake me up,"* thought Hannah as she rose and swung her feet over the side of the bed into her warm slippers. Grabbing her housecoat and making her way into the kitchen, she saw her parents sitting at the table with a cup of coffee in their hands.

"Good morning, sweetheart." Sophie rose to give her daughter a kiss on the cheek. "I hope we didn't awaken you."

"I had a restful night, thank you. Why didn't you wake me for church?" Hannah asked as she took her own seat at the table.

"Your mother and I thought that you could use a bit of extra sleep. We also wanted to make sure that you hadn't taken a chill from your plunge into the cold water," Roman stated with concern.

"Well to tell you the truth, I had a very exciting and overwhelming experience yesterday," said Hannah while accepting a glass of warm milk from her mother. Hannah noticed that her mother had dark circles under her eyes. She wished she wasn't the cause of her mother's worries but it couldn't be helped. A lot of reassurance would be in order to help her get past this incidence.

Sophie sat down across from Hannah. Her hands folded together tightly on the table in front of her. "The bacon and eggs will be ready shortly. I sort of got off to a late start this morning myself."

"I'm not that hungry anyway. I ate so much yesterday for dinner that it won't take much to fill me up for breakfast," Hannah assured her mother.

"Hey! Speak for yourself. I am more than ready for a plate of bacon and eggs," Roman declared with his laughing eyes and pouting mouth.

"Oh, Roman, you are always hungry. I don't know how you manage to stay so fit," Sophie lovingly replied back.

"It's called hard work. Speaking of which, I think that I will walk the fence down today to make sure everything is still in good shape. Would you girls like to come along and keep me company?" Roman invited.

Hannah shook her head back and forth. "Not this time. I need to prepare lessons for the children this week and clean up the beautiful wrap I received for my birthday if it wasn't damaged by all that water."

"It seemed to be in good shape except for a few spots of dirt here and there. If you don't mind, Hannah, I think that I will go with your father today. The exercise will do me good," Sophie said while rising to dish up the now done breakfast from the stove.

They quickly ate their breakfast. Sophie and Hannah tidied up the kitchen while Roman went to the barn to collect some fencing supplies in case there were some repairs needed. Sophie went to put something warm on beneath her skirts after instructing to Hannah that they would eat leftovers for supper.

After her parents left, Hannah sat down in one of the rocking chairs before the fire. She removed her feet from her slippers to feel the heat from the fireplace. Leaning her head against the back of the rocker, Hannah let the previous day's events unfold in her mind again. Things had started out so wonderfully. She couldn't believe how quickly things had made a turn for the worst. *"God must have surely been watching over me,"* Hannah thought. The jagged rocks that protruded from the waterfall went unnoticed until after her fall.

"Thank you Lord," Hannah said aloud once more.

A sudden knock at the door brought Hannah to her feet. "Who could that be?" mumbled Hannah as she slid her feet back into her slippers. Peeking through the window, she was surprised to see Isaac at the door.

Hannah quickly smoothed her hair back and tightened her housecoat before opening the door. "Hello, Isaac. I wasn't expecting you, at least not this early. I am glad you are here though," smiled Hannah, stepping back to allow Isaac room to enter.

"When I saw that you and your parents weren't at church this morning, I became worried about you. My parents also encouraged me to come and check on you," Isaac said while inspecting her closely for evidence of her well-being.

"I have to admit that I am a little shook up still but physically there was no harm done."

Isaac reached out and embraced Hannah, letting out a long sigh of relief. Hannah reveled in the comfort of his arms.

Isaac stepped back after noticing for the first time that Roman and Sophie were not there. "Where are your parents? Is everything ok? I didn't see them at church service either."

"Yes, they are just out checking the fence. I think they just wanted to leisurely walk and enjoy the day in each other's company," Hannah explained. "They also wanted to make sure that I was well so they allowed me to rest in to make sure I hadn't caught a chill from the cold water. You were completely soaked as well. How are you?"

"I am doing fine as well and I brought your father's clothes back." Isaac motioned to the table where he had laid the shirt and pants that he had borrowed. "Please tell them 'thank you' for me."

"Of course, let's go and sit by the fire. It still feels cool in here. Would you like something warm to drink?" offered Hannah.

"No I just wanted to check on you and apologize for ruining your birthday. I should have been watching over you more carefully," Isaac said in regret.

"Don't even think such a thing! I shouldn't have been standing so close to the edge," Hannah tried consoling Isaac with her words.

"We probably should go and check on Bella. I fear she may be blaming herself since the ride home was without conversation," suggested Isaac.

"I think you are right," Hannah agreed. She also felt a little guilty for not thinking of this herself. "I must wait on my parents to return and I also have some lessons to plan before we go."

"I will come back later this afternoon and pick you up." Isaac rose to his feet and waited for Hannah's acceptance.

"Great, I will see you later then." Hannah walked him to the door. He gave her a quick peck on the cheek and was off on his large black horse.

Leaning against the closed door, Hannah let out an uneasy breath. She knew the whole thing was an accident but her instincts kept telling her that something just wasn't right. She decided to walk down to her special place and pray for faith and wisdom to be a light to those that are walking in darkness.

℘

Roman slowed his pace to match Sophie's so she could keep up without tiring too easily. He adjusted his leather pouch that held the tools needed to mend any damaged fence. It was a beautiful clear and crisp fall day once again. Roman thought about how Sophie had just begun to laugh again after Toby's passing. Hannah's accident reminded her of how close she had again come to losing another child. He didn't know how to console her for he was rattled up himself.

"Let's rest for a spell Roman upon that large rock and let the sun's warmth relax us." Sophie's voice broke Roman from his thoughts.

Roman stepped up onto the flat surface and then reached out his hand to help his wife up. They leaned back and tilted their faces toward the cloudless, blue sky. The sun's rays seemed to be therapy for the mind as well as the body. Roman turned and leaned his weight upon his elbow to look at Sophie. She had her eyes closed and he saw that she had a more peaceful countenance upon her features than she did this morning in the kitchen. Their quiet reverie was interrupted by the call of a large hawk that floated aimlessly above them.

Sophie opened her eyes to see Roman's gaze fixed upon her. She could see the deep love in his eyes and thought of how the Lord had blessed her with such a caring husband.

"It really feels good to get out of the house. I had almost forgotten just how beautiful our little lay of land was. Thank you so much for bringing me along," Sophie said in an almost childlike voice.

Roman chuckled. "If it was up to me, I would have you always by my side, my dear Sophie."

"Let's continue on. I am anxious to see the new additions to the herd."

After helping Sophie down from the rock, Roman said, "Two of the cows are ready to calve any day now. With any luck, maybe we will have a surprise or two before we return home."

Roman and Sophie pressed on further around the side of the hill until they came to a small valley tucked between them and the next hill. There the cattle grazed contentedly on some late fall pasture. Soon they would start to hang close to the barn and nearby fields in order to feed on some hay.

The bleat of a newborn calf reached their ears before they saw it. Only a few hours old, the curious calf was still wobbly upon its legs, its anxious mother keeping a watchful eye on its whereabouts.

"How precious, I never get tired of such a miraculous sight," Sophie's appreciation evident on her face. Everything seemed to be in fair order. There were a couple of places where the fence had some broken strands of wire. The walk back to the house was done with their full attention drawn to nature's own form of entertainment.

❧

Roman and Sophie came home to the smell of hot coffee and warmed food on the stove. Roman took their coats while Sophie went to pour them a cup of coffee. Hannah's class preparations still lay on the table. Just as Sophie started to look for her daughter, she heard Hannah's bedroom door shut.

"I was beginning to think that you were not here. How was your morning?" Sophie inquired.

"I managed to get this week's lessons ready. Before I was able to get started, Isaac stopped by to check on me." Hannah hesitated before continuing. "He thought that we should go and see Bella to make sure that she was not blaming herself for the accident."

Roman immediately asked, "Why would she think that?"

"We were all very quiet on the trip back. You know how we all can sometimes get the wrong idea about things," Hannah answered without looking directly into her parent's eyes.

Sophie sensed that something was bothering her daughter. "Hannah, is there something on your mind?"

"I just have a gut feeling that something is not right. I'm sure I will work it out with a little time."

Roman had a feeling that Hannah was holding back but he trusted her to make good decisions. "If you are sure, you know your mother and I are here if you need us."

A knock at the door brought their conversation to an end. Hannah spoke as she went for the door. "That must be Isaac. I wasn't expecting him quite so soon," Hannah's eyes brightened as she mentioned his name. She smoothed her skirt before opening the door.

"Josh!" Hannah couldn't hide the surprise and confusion obvious in her tone and on her face.

"I know you were expecting Isaac but something has come up and he sent me over instead." Josh held his hat in his hands, looking seriously at Hannah.

"Please, come in Josh," Roman said.

"I'm sorry, do come in." Hannah stepped back to allow Josh to pass through.

"I can't stay." Josh fingered his hat nervously. "I came to let you know that Mom has taken sick. Isaac has gone for Doctor Hayes."

"Is there anything that we can do?" Sophie immediately offered.

"Thank you, but no. We will know more after the doctor sees her."

"Is it alright if I go back with you Josh?" asked Hannah.

"I was hoping that you would. Katie is very upset and you would be a great comfort to her," Josh responded gratefully.

Hannah rushed to grab her coat, scarf and gloves. She gave her parents a quick hug and kiss before going quickly out the door with Josh. She was glad that she had already eaten some dinner just before her parents had arrived.

Josh had ridden his horse because it was faster than bringing the wagon.

"Let me saddle up Goldie really quick. She has recently been watered and fed so she will be ready to go," Hannah said as she went to open the horse's stall door. Josh helped her saddle the horse and they were soon off at a fast gallop.

ᔆᓚ

Coming into the yard, Hannah saw that Isaac and Doctor Hayes were already there. She prayed that Alice was not seriously ill. She was not aware that Alice was having any health problems. Josh assisted Hannah off the horse and led the animals into the barn. Hannah went to the house ahead of Josh. She knocked before entering and was greeted by Isaac and Katie.

"I was hoping that you would come back with Josh." Isaac took Hannah's hands in his and kissed her cheek. He led her to the table and explained that his father and the doctor were with his mother right now. There was no news as of yet.

"Hello, Katie. Come and sit by me while we wait." Hannah patted the seat beside her. She turned to Isaac and asked, "What happened to your mother?"

"Mom seemed fine this morning, if you can go by that. We went to church and everything. Dad said that she suddenly became very weak and complained of her chest having pain shortly after they returned home. I got back just as Dad was carrying her to bed," Isaac said while he kept glancing toward his parent's bedroom.

"I pray that it is nothing serious. Whatever it may be, I am sure the doctor can help her."

"I hope so. Mom has never been seriously ill before. She has always been very strong."

Hannah looked at Katie and asked, "Have you had anything to eat yet?"

"No. I haven't gotten hungry. I have been too worried," Katie lowered her eyes to hide unshed tears.

Hannah hugged Katie and stood before saying, "Why don't I fix something simple for everyone and when you do get hungry it will be there."

"Thanks, that's very kind of you Hannah," accepted Isaac for them both. After putting on some coffee, Hannah rummaged through the kitchen until she found something to fix. There was a loaf of bread that was only a day old and some ham to be sliced and warmed up. She also quickly cut and fried some potatoes. Katie pointed out that there was also some molasses stack cake on the shelf still covered with a towel.

Josh had been waiting outside and entered the house just as Andrew and Doctor Hayes came from Alice's bedroom. Their faces were solemn as they both took a chair at the table with Isaac and Josh. Hannah sat a steaming cup of coffee before each of them.

Looking into his children's expectant faces, Andrew said, "Doctor Hayes feels that your mother has developed a weak heart. The best medicine for her right now is to have plenty of rest."

"Yes," spoke Doctor Hayes. "She must have complete bed rest for a while and then as time goes by and she starts to get stronger, she may begin to do light household chores. She must never overdo it and I will check on her regularly to monitor her progress."

After letting the information of their mother's condition sink in, Isaac said, "We will all pitch in and help so that Mom doesn't have to lift a finger."

"I can take care of the household chores," put in Katie.

"But what about school, you can't stay home from school for that long." Josh told her.

Andrew stood and looked at his children and said, "I know that you all want to do everything that you can for your mother. We will think on it and come up with a way that works best for everyone."

"I feel confident that Alice will be in very good care. I have to get going now and I will stop back by before noon tomorrow to check on her," the doctor said.

Josh jumped up to see the doctor out and to collect his buggy for him. The doctor reassured him again before signaling the horses into a trot. Josh's heart still had a heavy feeling of uncertainty. Hannah asked Andrew if she could get anything for Alice. He told her that Alice was resting and would probably be asleep for some time since she had been given something for the pain.

The family all sat down at the table and Hannah could tell that some of the tension had begun to leave their bodies. Hannah and Katie began to set the table for the small dinner that she had prepared earlier. While eating, they discussed how they could best see that Alice was taken care of. Hannah volunteered to come and stay with Alice but was quickly dismissed as an option because she was needed as the town's teacher. They decided that at least for a while someone would have to be available from morning until evening except for on Saturdays and Sundays. Andrew mentioned that maybe Mandy would be available but Josh explained how she was already caring for a neighbor and her children.

"We will just have to pray about it and trust that a solution will come our way," Andrew stated calmly. After a quiet meal, Hannah and Katie cleaned up the kitchen. The men went outside to do some necessary chores while Katie went and sat with her mother in case she awakened.

Hannah put on a roast and vegetables to cook for a late supper before deciding to return home. When Isaac entered and saw Hannah preparing to leave, he offered to escort her home but Hannah declined insisting he stay with his family. The trip home would be short since she had Goldie to ride.

"If you are sure and thank you for all your help." Isaac reached out and hugged Hannah closely. The embrace was comforting and helped to melt the tension away. Neither of them wanted to part each other's company but time and place demanded it.

With regret in Isaac's eyes, he said, "You should be going before it gets much later."

"I will stop by tomorrow after school and see how your mother is feeling. Tell Katie that it is ok if she chooses to stay home from school tomorrow. I will bring her schoolwork with me when I come," Hannah told Isaac as she gathered Goldie's reigns and put her foot into the stirrup. With Isaac's help, she was mounted and off.

Roman and Sophie were relieved when their daughter finally arrived home. They waited for Hannah to put her horse away and remove her outer garments before inquiring about Alice's condition.

"The doctor said that she has a weak heart. He feels that she will be ok but she will need plenty of rest and to do no work at all, at least for a while. She will have to be very careful after that and to not overdo it," Hannah explained with a rather exhausted look of her own.

"Thank God! We were so worried. It will no doubt be a challenge to refrain from doing all she is used to doing," said Sophie.

"Andrew is studying about how they are going to care for Alice while everyone is gone during the day," Hannah told them.

"The Lord will make a way," Roman said with conviction.

"Maybe I could go and help....," Sophie was interrupted by Roman. "No, it would be too much for you to care for two households."

"He's right Mama, especially since I am not home to help you around here," Hannah agreed with her father.

They spent the rest of the evening relaxing around the fire. Sophie and Hannah both occupied with many thoughts of the past couple of days and Roman absorbed with reading the scripture. The silence was broken from time to time by his quoting of verses that gave strength and lifted their hearts.

UNDER HEAVEN ❧ Karen McDavid

CHAPTER 12

Hannah tossed and turned all night and awoke well before daylight. What sleep that she did get was haunted by dreams of the cloaked figure that was always close behind her but never able to catch her. Having the same dream twice has put her on edge. Hannah decided that she may as well get out of bed and get ready for the day ahead.

The house seemed much cooler this morning for some reason. *"Maybe her parents weren't up yet and the fire had died down,"* Hannah thought as she rubbed the goose bumps on her arms. Leaving her room, she saw that they were at the kitchen table having a cup of steaming hot coffee. The fire was also blazing in the fireplace.

"Why does it feel so cold this morning?" Hannah asked with a shiver to support her question.

Sophie rose to pour Hannah a cup of hot apple cider. Reaching the heavy mug to her she said, "The temperature outside has dropped considerably from what we have been used to this morning. I'm afraid winter may be well on its way."

"I think we will still have a few more fair days ahead of us. It seems, this time of year, nature has a hard time making up its mind before cold weather is here to stay," Roman said.

"You will have to be sure and dress warm for your trip to the schoolhouse today," Sophie reminded her daughter. She knew that Hannah was old enough to know how to dress appropriately but the mother in her was not something that just goes away.

"I plan on it. Is there anything that you need from town today? I am out of some of the school supplies so I will be going to the store after school lets out," offered Hannah.

"Yes. I am out of thread and we could use some more coffee. But won't that be too much for you to carry?" said Sophie.

"No. I am going to ride Goldie today. I want to make a quick stop to see Alice on my way home, if that is ok with you?" Hannah said. "Dad, do you need anything?"

"I don't think so sweetheart. Your mother and I will make a trip to town in a few days."

ℰ

Roman saddled up Goldie and had her ready when Hannah stepped outside to leave. Hannah pulled her coat more closely around her. The trip to town would be much quicker on her horse and the extra time would be needed this afternoon after school. Hannah passed by the road that led to the Sullivan's farm. She should find some time to visit with Emma and her baby to see how they were fairing. Lately it seemed as if her well controlled and settled life had been taken away from her. Her time of peace had turned into an unwelcome warfare of life's uncertainties. The small town was very quiet for this time of morning. Luke was out sweeping the walk in front of his store. Three men were standing and chatting at the end of the boardwalk, one of whom she did not recognize. It was common for a stranger to pass through now and again due the talk of gold and the easier access by way of the railroad. Hannah took her horse to the stables and left her with some grain and water. The sun was starting to warm the air and lift her spirits as well.

Stepping inside the schoolhouse, Hannah was thankful that it was much warmer than she thought it would be. *"Luke must have come very early in order for the room to be so cozy,"* Hannah thought. After putting things to right, Hannah started writing math problems on the black chalkboard for each group of children. She had just finished adding some wood to the stove when the children began to arrive.

Later in the afternoon, Hannah had the students to silently read after they had finished their math problems. She noticed that one of the younger boys, Eli, had laid his head down on his desk. She walked back to check on him and found that he felt feverish to the touch.

"Eli, are you feeling unwell?" Hannah asked the small child.

Eli raised his flushed face and answered, "Yes, Miss Jamison. I have been feeling bad all day." Hannah looked to his older brother, Jeremy, and suggested that he take his little brother home early.

"Yes, Miss Jamison. Mom would appreciate that." Jeremy stood and gathered their things and helped his brother with his coat.

"We all hope that you get to feeling better soon, Eli." Hannah spoke for the whole class. Hannah went back to her desk and collected her spelling lists that she had made out for this week's tests. The children would have all week to study the words. She put them all to practice writing each one ten times. While the students did their work, Hannah sat at her desk and planned a special geography lesson that all the children could participate in.

Hannah turned to look out her window towards town. She saw Doctor Hayes come out of his office and quickly get in his buggy. He hurriedly left town, leaving a trail of dust behind him. Hannah prayed that no one was seriously ill or injured. Her thoughts went to Alice and wondered how she was doing. Glancing at her watch, she saw that it was almost time to dismiss for the day. After the children had left, Hannah went through her usual routine as she waited for the fire to die down. Hannah walked back to the front of the classroom to collect her belongings and the list of things that she needed from the store.

It looked as if most of the people that she saw milling about earlier had already gone home. It felt good to stretch her legs a bit after sitting in the classroom all day. The cold air was invigorating. She climbed the solid, wooden steps in front of Luke and Anna's general store. The small bell rang when she opened the screen door and entered.

Immediately Anna rushed to her and gave her a robust hug. "It is so good to see you dear! It seems like ages since I have seen you and your parents but it has only been a couple of weeks. How have you all been doing?" Anna said as she led Hannah further inside the store.

"We are doing very well, thank you. How are you and Luke getting along?"

"Oh you know us. We are tough as the bark on a tree." Anna laughed with her chubby, shaking shoulders going up and down. "I have heard tell of several people coming down with some kind of sickness."

Hannah shook her head up and down in agreement. "Yes, I had to send one of the children home early today. I just pray that it is nothing that a few days of rest won't cure."

"I certainly hope so. So what can I do for you?"

"Here is a list of some things that I will need." Hannah gave her the list.

Anna quickly started filling the order while Hannah admired the wide assortment of merchandise that lined the store shelves and walls. "Here you go. Be sure to tell Roman and Sophie hello for me." Anna handed her the sack of supplies and accepted the payment from Hannah with aged and somewhat arthritic hands.

"Have a lovely evening," Hannah smiled and waved through the screen door as she left. Hannah looked to her left and to her right before stepping out onto the street to cross over to where Goldie was stabled. To her surprise, she saw Josh leaving the boarding house and waving a goodbye to Bella White. Josh did not even look her way but hurriedly mounted up on his horse and left in the direction of his home. Hannah wondered what was going on. Hannah did not look to see if Bella was looking her way but could sense her eyes upon her. She hurried over to get Goldie packed and saddled for the trip to the Daniels' farm and then to home. Her mind was a whirlwind of thoughts. She was letting her imagination get away from her. *"I'm sure there is a very good reason for Josh talking with Bella,"* Hannah reasoned within herself.

Before she knew it the Daniels farm was in sight, so caught up was she in her surmising, she hardly noticed a thing on her way there. Tying Goldie up to the corral fence, Hannah smoothed her hair and straightened her skirts before walking to the front door and knocking.

Isaac opened the solid oak door and pulled Hannah inside. "I was getting worried Hannah. I thought you would be here by now," Isaac said as his piercing blue eyes questioned her.

"I'm sorry. I had to get a few things at the store before I left to come here," Hannah told him with a little defiance in her tone. Hannah didn't know that Andrew and Josh were silently watching them with a grin on their faces.

Josh cleared his throat before saying, "Come over and have a seat Hannah. My brother seems to have forgotten his manners." Josh pulled out a chair for emphasis.

"Thank you. How is Alice today?" Hannah asked. Andrew took a chair across from Hannah. He was a very tall man with hair the color of raven's wings and eyes almost as dark. Isaac must have taken after his mother's fairer coloring.

Andrew spoke as he settled more comfortably in his chair. "She seems much more rested. She has slept on and off all day long. She and Katie are both asleep at the moment."

"Good, I won't disturb them. Is there anything that I can do to help?" Hannah offered. She looked around to see if the house needed tidying up. Everything was in its place.

"Well actually, everything seems to be under control." Andrew said in a relaxed voice. "It appears that the dilemma about how to care for Alice during the daytime has been solved."

Josh quickly put in, "Preacher Carson stopped by today to see how Mom was doing. We were telling him about needing someone to stay with Mom and he came up with an idea that we hadn't thought of," Josh said while pausing to take a deep breath. "He suggested that we consider Bella White."

"Really, I thought that Katherine needed her at the boarding house," Hannah said with some surprise although her mind went back to when she saw Josh not long ago coming from there. Hannah felt a lump begin to form in her stomach.

"That's what we thought also but since we did not have any other options, we thought it wouldn't hurt to ask," Josh explained.

"So what did you find out for an answer?" Hannah asked. Hannah glanced in Isaac's direction and caught him studying her. She hoped her emotions weren't showing on her face.

"She was very happy that we asked her. She talked to Katherine and explained the situation. Katherine was more than willing to comply since business was very slow this time of year anyway. She told me that she would manage fine without Bella for a while." Josh informed her with a pleased expression.

"We hope Mom will regain some of her strength and the arrangement will only be temporary," added Isaac for Hannah's sake for he sensed her hesitancy of the arrangement.

"I hope so too," Hannah said. Hannah felt as though a cloud was hanging over her head preventing her from allowing her bright and cheerful self from shining through.

The door to Alice's bedroom came open and drew everyone's attention. Katie emerged rubbing her eyes after just waking up. Her face lit up when she saw Hannah sitting at the table with her father and brothers.

"I didn't know that you were here. I tried to stay awake so that I would know when you arrived," Katie said. Katie's wrinkled attire and uncombed hair showed that her entire day had been filled with caring for her mother and tending the house.

Hannah smiled at Katie and said, "I haven't been here long. I hear that you will be coming back to school much sooner than we thought."

"That's great! Did you all find someone to stay with Mom already?" Katie questioned while looking at her father and brothers.

Andrew spoke up first to answer his daughter. "Yes. We believe that we have. We have asked Bella White to tend to your mother for a while. She has agreed and will be here in the morning."

"That's very nice of her. I never even thought of her," Katie said in a rather grown up way.

"I would like for you to stay home again tomorrow and show Bella her way around the house. It would make things much easier for us all," Andrew told his daughter.

Katie turned to Hannah and asked, "Did you bring my schoolwork with you? I don't like to fall behind."

Hannah couldn't help but grin slightly at this more grown up Katie. "Yes. I brought you today's and tomorrow's lessons. You won't have to worry about falling behind, I promise." Hannah looked to Isaac and asked, "Has the doctor been back to see Alice today?"

"Yes, he said that she should stay in bed a few more days and he thinks with time that she will regain some of her strength back but will always have to avoid strenuous work." Andrew told all of them how hard it was going to be to keep his wife from doing too much. He also added with a chuckle how very stubborn that she could be. The Daniels children all completely agreed.

Hannah announced that she should be getting on home before it became too late. Isaac rose from his chair likewise and walked with Hannah outside to her horse. Hannah placed her arm in his as they strode over to the corral. The sun was becoming low in the western sky.

"It seems we never have time to be together for very long. I miss talking to you," Isaac's words were spoken with honesty as he looked into Hannah's eyes.

"We will just have to make time. I have no plans for the weekend," Hannah spoke a little too boldly than she thought she should. The last thing she wanted was to sound desperate, she chided herself. She lowered her eyes in embarrassment.

"I will see you then, sweet Hannah." He gently brushed a stray curl away from her forehead. Helping her mount the horse,

Hannah turned a blushing face towards him as she waved goodbye. Hannah was trying not to let her insecurities get the best of her where Bella was concerned. She would just have to try her best to trust that everything would work for the good. All the way home she prayed for God's help.

❧

That night at the supper table, Hannah told her parents about Bella being the one to help take care of Alice. They were as surprised as she was to hear the news. This meant that Bella White had definitely decided to stay on for a while longer.

Changing the subject, Hannah told them about the little boy that had taken ill at school and had to be sent home. Hannah also said, "When I was at the general store talking with Anna, she mentioned having also heard that something was going around. She didn't know what it was but it appeared to be contagious."

"Maybe it is just the change in the weather. Oftentimes, the colder temperatures bring along the sniffles with it," Suggested Sophie as she also looked somewhat puzzled as to the cause herself.

Roman took a large swallow of milk before saying, "You may have to close school for a few days if very many of the students start to show symptoms." Roman had seen his fair share of outbreaks of one kind or another over the years.

"I will pay close attention to them and try my best to keep it from spreading." Hannah covered her mouth while trying to hold back a yawn as she spoke. It had been a long day. She would go to bed tonight and on the morrow she would try to let her worries be sufficient unto the day.

Roman noticed how tired his daughter looked and said, "Why don't you go on up to bed. Your mother and I will clean up the kitchen."

"Thank you. I guess I am a little tired this evening."

Sophie hugged her daughter good-night and reassured her that it was no trouble cleaning what few dishes there were to do. Roman and Sophie exchanged worried looks as Hannah made her way to her room.

Sophie turned to Roman and in a low whisper said, "I just know something is bothering Hannah. She is just too stubborn to voice her concerns."

Roman agreed as he accepted another plate from his wife to dry. "She will confide in us when the time is right. In the meantime, we will pray that in God's time He will settle our dear girl's heart."

℘

The next couple of days went by quickly for Hannah. By Thursday afternoon, two more of the children were sent home early with what seemed like an influenza type of illness. Hannah had put Katie in charge while she had walked the two children over to Doctor Hayes' office. He said there had been several people in the township with the same sickness.

"It would probably be in the children's best interests if you would close the school for just a few days. We need to get an idea of what we are dealing with here," said the doctor.

"Yes, of course. I will go ahead and announce this to the students immediately."

"I am going in the same direction as these two children, so I may as well see them home. They are looking mighty peeked and could use the ride I suspect," offered the kind doctor. The town doctor was getting up in years but was as spry as ever. Although his hair was only slightly silvered, his age gave him away in his sun and time wrinkled face.

"Thank you. I am sure their parents will appreciate that very much," Hannah replied before turning and hurrying back to the schoolhouse to send the rest of the students on home.

❧

Hannah had walked to school this morning. The sun was still high and its rays made her shed some of her apparel that had been welcomed during the morning hours. Her mind kept going back to Isaac and his close contact with Bella now that they would see each other every day. Hannah did not like this newfound emotion that seemed to force its presence into her thoughts and feelings way to frequently now. Isaac had given her no reason to be jealous but Hannah was a novice when it came to affairs of the heart.

Roman and Sophie were standing just outside the barn when Hannah came into the yard. Their facial expressions were very serious and she knew something was wrong. When Hannah's footsteps drew their attention, they turned surprised faces towards her.

Hannah answered their question before they had to ask. "Doctor Hayes thought it best to turn school out due to the continuing spread of the illness that is plaguing our community."

Roman nodded his head in understanding before saying, "I'm afraid that we have some bad news. Paul Sullivan was just here and he has informed us that Jack Johnson has just passed away from the same thing that has everyone so sick."

Hannah's shoulders drooped as if in defeat. "Oh no, poor Ruth, she must be devastated. When should we go and see her?"

Sophie took some of her daughter's burden from her arms and they all walked to the house. "We thought it would be best to wait until tomorrow. Grandma Rose is going to be staying with her tonight. Paul was just over to Jacob's and he relayed the news to us."

That night, for supper, they all had cornbread and milk. No one had much of an appetite. It seemed that the dark cloud hanging over them had just gotten darker.

When they were finished, Hannah excused herself and went to grab her wrap hanging from a peg beside the door. "I will be right back. Do you want to prepare some food to take to Ruth's when I return?" Hannah spoke in her mother's direction.

Sophie shook her head no and said, "We will wait until the morning. We will have ample time then." Hannah grabbed a piece of leftover cornbread and walked to her rock to whisper a prayer for Ruth. She also wished that Spirit would be close by.

℘

She lingered upon the rock for several minutes just taking in the sounds of nature. Behind her she heard the crunch of dry leaves. Turning around, she saw Spirit lying still with his head resting on his front paws. Hannah took out the cornbread and laid it upon the rock at arm's length. Spirit licked his lips and looked from Hannah to the cornbread and back again. Hannah patted the hard surface in front of her. "Come. Don't be afraid. I've missed you boy," Hannah whispered softly. Spirit got up and cautiously walked towards her. He came just close enough to reach the food. Hannah did not move but allowed him to eat freely. When the peculiar dog had finished, he came close enough to lick the top of Hannah's hand. Hannah didn't move. She wanted him to know that he could trust her. The dog then placed his paw upon her hand as if trying to console her. Hannah's eyes filled with tears. He then turned and left. "Thank you, Spirit."

℘

That night, Hannah rested without the dream haunting her sleeping hours. The next morning, they cooked several dishes hoping to feed the many friends and family that would undoubtedly be at Ruth's home for the next couple of days. They loaded the wagon around noon and went the short journey to the Johnson farm. Hannah saw a team of horses come over the small knoll ahead of them. The closer they got, the more she was able to recognize Isaac as the driver. Hannah couldn't believe her eyes when she saw Bella sitting next to him on the buckboard seat. Hannah felt her stomach sicken. Roman slowed the wagon down as Isaac pulled his to a slow stop beside them. Hannah forced a smile and nodded a hello to the both. She couldn't have spoken if she had wanted to.

Isaac looked at Roman and said, "We are on our way back from paying our respects to Ruth. Josh is coming home a little later."

"Perhaps we will see you tomorrow then?" Sophie politely asked.

"Yes, we hope to see you both tomorrow," Hannah finally was able to manage a few words.

"Bella has offered to stay with Mom so we can all go to the funeral," Isaac informed them.

"We will see you then," Roman said as he signaled the horses to begin their steady trot again.

Isaac waved goodbye to Hannah but she had already turned her attention to the road in front of her. She never did talk to Bella about not blaming her for the accident that happened a few days ago. She was sure that Isaac had said enough for the both of them.

CHAPTER 13

Mrs. Johnson was sitting in her rocking chair with her eyes closed when Hannah and her parents entered the small farmhouse. Her hands were clasped around a delicately stitched handkerchief that was wrinkled with use. Her weathered features looked overcome by grief.

"Come children, you can put your food over here on the cabinet," Grandma Rose said in a low voice in an attempt to not awaken Ruth.

"Perhaps we should come back another time when Ruth has had time to rest," Sophie suggested. "Poor Ruth, she looks absolutely exhausted."

"No. She will be very upset if I let you leave. I am sure that she will awake very soon." Grandma Rose said as she took a seat at the kitchen table, moving about a bit more stiffly than usual.

They also took a seat at the table. Grandma Rose informed them that Josh was outside getting a start on digging the grave. Sophie told her that Roman had volunteered to help him. Jack was to be buried by the small child they had lost not long after being born.

Hannah had never been inside the Johnson house except for briefly for she never really had cause, but to relay news of some sort or another. She had never noticed the beautifully hand carved furniture that Jack had made himself. He must have been a very talented man were Hannah's thoughts.

"I had no idea that Jack had even been sick. Hannah told me that some of her students were coming down with something but I didn't think that it was anything serious," Sophie commented quietly.

Grandma Rose rubbed her lower back while saying, "I believe it all happened very fast. Ruth told me one minute that Jack was acting as if he had a common cold and the next thing she knew; Jack had taken to his bed."

"I am just so thankful that Jack was ready to meet his Maker. And as you have often told us in these sorrowful hours, our loss is Heaven's gain. This knowledge brings us great peace." Grandma Rose's eyes always held a twinkle in them at the mention of Heaven. She liked for it to be known that she was not getting older, only closer.

Turning her attention to Hannah she said, "Are you feeling unwell yourself Hannah? You look a little peeked to me."

Hannah laughed within herself. "I feel fine, Grandma. Just a little tired. I guess I still haven't got used to the teaching just yet. But what about you, how are you holding up?"

"I would say that I have led a blessed life. A little dab of arthritis is nothing to complain about. When I have done all that the good Lord would have me to do here upon this earth, then I will be a meeting my Maker same as old Jack has," Grandma Rose chuckled. It was obvious that she was looking forward to that day.

Sophie rose to get them all a cup of coffee and Hannah some warm cider. She asked Grandma Rose how long that she planned on staying with Ruth. Sophie knew that Jack and Ruth had a son that lived close to Denver, Colorado. She wondered if he would be bringing his family home with him.

Grandma Rose shifted in her chair before speaking, "Well as far as I know, Ruth received a telegram early this morning of her son's arrival in a few days. She didn't say if anyone was coming with him. I plan on staying until then."

"Sophie and Hannah, how good to see you both." Ruth re-pinned her hair and smoothed her skirts while coming in to greet them. She looked at them apologetically and said, "Rose you should have awoken me. I have slept half the day away."

"Nonsense, you need your rest. You have been up night and day and now it is time to let someone care for you in turn," Grandma Rose gently reprimanded her dear friend.

"Oh Rose, you old bird, I do love you." Accepting a cup of coffee from Sophie, Ruth blinked back the tears that threatened to spill once again. Hannah offered to get Ruth something to eat but she said that she would eat later.

Hannah busied herself with putting away all of the food that had been brought for safe keeping. She listened to Ruth tell about how Jack would try to console her while he knew that he was dying. She told of how peaceful his passing was. Sophie asked Ruth about her son and his family. It had been several years since Sophie could recall of having seen them. The last time Ruth's son was here, they were unable to come visit them.

Ruth's eyes lit up when she said, "Peter said he would be here within a week. I am so excited about seeing him but I wish it didn't have to be for this reason." Ruth pulled her wrinkled hanky from her pocket and blew her nose. Tears of sadness mingled with tears of happiness. "Guess what else he said in the message?" She paused for good measure. "My darling grandson, Seth, is coming also. I do so miss them. Peter regrets not bringing his wife, Lucinda, but she is duty bound to stay with her ailing mother."

"How old is that handsome grandson of yours now?" Grandma Rose asked.

"Well I believe that he is twenty-two years old now, Rose. And you got handsome right. That boy could charm the pants off a snake." Ruth laughed a heeling laugh.

Turning to Hannah she said, "I bet you and Seth would get on very well together. He's as honest as the day is long. Yes, I think that you could be very good friends."

"You know what Ruth? I could really use a good friend right now. I will look forward to his arrival. Do you think that he will stay for a long visit?" Hannah asked the elderly lady.

"I am not really sure. They did not mention anything about the duration of their stay."

Sophie stood as she looked around the room and asked, "Ruth do you have anything that Roman or I can do for you? Perhaps chop some firewood or care for your animals."

Ruth's tired eyes took in her house's appearance before saying, "I know my house is a mess right now. I have had to let it go in order to take care of Jack the past couple of weeks. I thank you so much for asking and for right now I think everything is taken care of. Josh has already seen to the firewood and animals with some help from Isaac earlier today. Please don't worry about me. Rose will see to it that anything needs done will be taken care of." Ruth's eyes were full of appreciation for the good friend she had in Rose.

Sophie glanced out the window towards where the men were digging the grave. "It seems the men are all finished outside so we will leave you to get some much needed rest. We will stop in and see you tomorrow Ruth. May God bless you and we will keep you in our prayers," Sophie tenderly embraced the dear lady.

Roman saw Sophie and Hannah come out of the house. He paid his respects quickly before they drove slowly and quietly home. They were each absorbed in their own thoughts.

By the time they had reached the house, the air had turned cooler and the clouds had begun to gather in the western sky. Roman told his wife and daughter to prepare for some north winds for the funeral tomorrow. He didn't expect it to snow, although it had been known to snow many times before this early, but a cold rain was more likely to chill a person to the bone with its dampness.

Hannah decided to ready some of those warmer clothes that her father was talking about while she had time to spare. She heated the iron to press the garments that would be appropriate for the graveside funeral. She walked into the kitchen to fetch a small pan of water and a cloth to better steam press the wrinkles out of the clothes. Her mother was standing in the kitchen window looking toward her son's grave. Hannah knew the recent death did much to revive the feelings of deep loss that always lay just below the surface.

"Mama," Hannah spoke softly being careful not to startle her. Sophie turned around slowly, as if coming from some faraway place where thoughts were like hands that kept dragging you back to memories that you would rather forget. Forcing a smile upon her face, Sophie said, "Yes, Hannah, what is it?"

Pretending not to notice the shine in her mother's eyes that was a result of unsuccessfully masking her feelings completely, Hannah cleared her throat and said, "I was wondering if you wanted to lie down for a while. There is not much to be done today and we cooked enough for supper, while making the food to take over to Ruth's this morning."

Sophie started to instantly decline the idea but after another moment's thought, she let out a deep breath and said, "Maybe you are right. I am a little tired. Don't let me rest too long."

"Don't worry, it is still quite early yet," Hannah encouraged her mother as she carried her water and cloth to the small room in the back of the house. Hannah watched the sky darken with the ever approaching clouds as she ironed in front of the window.

She saw a movement several yards away along the creek bank next to a large ponderosa pine. Straining to see what could be out there, she nearly burnt the hem of her dress. Hannah set the heavy iron down, out of harm's way. She was taken by surprise to see her father out there leaning on the tree when he was supposed to be mending some broken boards on the corral behind the barn. She saw him look to the sky as if seeking God's help. Tapping her nails against the window seal, she contemplated about what was bothering her father. The first drops of rain began hitting the window pane in front of her, bringing her out of her musing thoughts. Hannah finished ironing the necessary clothing for the funeral and went to check on her mother. Her mother still lay sleeping as far as she could tell so she put another log on the fire before going in search of her father.

Grabbing her everyday hooded cloak from its resting place, she opened the door and quietly stepped out into the rain soaked earth. The rain was coming down pretty steadily so she assumed her father must be in the barn somewhere. She made her way carefully from the house to the barn being sure to avoid the puddles of water that threatened the warmth of her feet inside her flat-heeled boots. Opening the large door, she peered inside to see where her father might be. She saw him working

213

on an old wagon wheel to the far right in the area where he kept all of his tools.

Roman sensed rather than heard Hannah's presence. He turned before she got halfway to him. "What brings you out in this rain Hannah?" Roman asked his daughter as he turned his attention back to his work.

"Nothing really, I finished up inside for the moment and Mama is still resting comfortably," said Hannah as she watched her father painstakingly chisel a wooden spoke to fit the wheel perfectly.

Pausing to raise his head and look at his daughter, Roman asked, "Is your mother feeling ok? She never mentioned anything to me earlier."

"Yes, I mean "yes" she is feeling well. But I can't help but wonder if there is something bothering her. Is everything ok?"

Roman returned to working on his project and said, "Everything is fine. If anything is troubling your mother, then she will share it with us if she feels that it is necessary. So don't worry your pretty little head needlessly, ok?" Hannah shook her head in agreement but she was far from being convinced that that was all there was to it.

Hannah knew it would be even more fruitless to ask her father if anything was troubling him. She stayed and helped her father, more like watched, until it was time to go back in and awaken her mother. She enjoyed spending time with him when she got the chance. She mentioned that Jack had made his own coffin quite some time ago. She said that if it was anything like the furniture he had made, it was bound to be beautiful.

"Yes, I saw it today after Josh and I got through digging the grave. Finer craftsmanship I have never seen," said Roman with an appreciative look in his eyes, as he thought of the unusual engravings that were so carefully embossed on the wood.

With eyebrows drawn together in consternation, Hannah asked her father, "Do you think Jack knew that he was going to die?"

"It's possible because with God all things are possible. Jack was certainly a God fearing man but only God knows what amount of knowledge a man can handle." Roman looked at his daughter curiously. He wondered what was going through her mind.

"Then it is also possible that if we look close enough and if it is God's purpose, then He may be showing and preparing us for future events if we are willing to see." Hannah said in what sounded like a whisper of hope in her voice.

"Yes but only if it is His will and in His own time," Roman stated firmly. He didn't want his daughter to start getting the wrong idea about things and start seeing things that simply were not there." Things must always be done through much prayer and with much patience." Hannah handed her father the last spoke to the wheel he had been repairing, before deciding that she had lingered far too long away from the house. Donning her cloak once more, she stepped outside the barn. The rain had nearly stopped and the earth smelled renewed.

ॐ

Hannah opened the door to find her mother at the kitchen table with the Bible opened before her.

Hannah removed her cloak and boots before saying, "I hope I am not disturbing your reading time."

"No, of course not," Sophie told her. "I just opened the pages knowing that I would find strength in the words wherever I turned to."

Hannah sighed as she lowered herself down into one of the chairs across from her mother. "I don't understand how people can go through life without God's help. How empty and lost they must feel. I think that if they would just start to honestly seek and get a small taste of heaven then they would become hungry and strive to be a fit subject for the kingdom."

"You are right. We must never cease praying for those less fortunate than us," Sophie insisted.

Before thinking Hannah said, "Even those that would do us harm?"

Curiously Sophie responded, "Especially those that would do us harm." Sophie's eyebrows drew together in concern at her daughter's question. "Hannah is someone out to do you harm?"

"No. I am really not sure. It is more of a feeling that I have than anything. I am sure that I am just imagining things with all of the bad things happening lately," Hannah said trying to convince her mother as well as herself.

"We must not let fear rule our lives. It will undermine our trust in God. And we must never lose faith," Sophie said with heartfelt conviction.

"Thank you Mama. I feel much better now." Hannah let out a little giggle as she thought out loud. "I bet Ruth's spirits have been uplifted since Grandma Rose has been staying with her. Grandma Rose can always pull the sun from behind a cloud in any circumstance."

Sophie joined in on the laughter, "You sure are right about that. There is no one else like her. Why don't you and I see what we need to finish up the baking for tomorrow and then we can spend the rest of the evening catching up on something more relaxing to do."

That evening Hannah forgot about her problems as she helped her mother bake and sing old hymns that carried out into the cool evening air, across the yard and into the barn to grace the ears of a man whose heart needed the words that rained peace upon his soul.

A drizzling mist stubbornly insisted on enveloping the land with its unwelcome presence, dampening the spirits even more for those already of such a sad countenance. Hannah studied the faces of the loved ones and friends gathered around the freshly dug grave. Preacher Carson wiped away tears as he spoke comforting words to those standing around. He and Jack had been very close friends for many years. Most of Jack's family lived close by including his two brothers and a sister. If only his son and grandson could have been here in time it would have been a great comfort to Ruth.

Hannah had to admit that her curiosity was peaked concerning her grandson, Seth. Ruth and Grandma Rose both were more than a little excited about his arrival. Hannah was looking forward to meeting him and his father. Hannah felt Isaac's hand rest in the small of her back. She knew the gesture was one intended for support but it only made her that much more aware of his presence standing there beside her. She had tried not to think about Bella staying at home with Isaac's mother but it always lay in her thoughts. *"Isaac doesn't even realize how much it bothers me that he is around Bella so much of the time. A little reassurance would do wonders."* Hannah thought to herself. *"Why does love have to be so conflicting? My heart does not question how it feels but my head keeps allowing uncertainty to enter in."* The words "Let us pray" broke Hannah's train of thought.

Just as the parting prayer ended and everyone raised their heads, the sun burst through a small opening in the clouds above and its rays reached down and touched the coffin and those gathered around it for a short space of time. Hannah heard Ruth say, "Thank you Lord."

A rather large group had turned out to pay their respects. It seemed practically the whole community. As they made their way down a couple of hundred yards or so to the house, Hannah noticed several people choosing to leave instead of staying to eat. She informed Isaac that she wished to help set the food out and would come find him later.

Isaac nodded his head before saying, "Sure and if it is alright with you, I would like to escort you home later. Dad is leaving now to make sure Mom is ok."

"I would like that, Isaac," Hannah smiled in return. Hannah had not expected to enjoy herself at the funeral. A little guilt was starting to set in. But with Mandy, Sarah, Grandma Rose and many other good friends and neighbors, they all sat around the kitchen and living room enjoying each other's company immensely. Dear Ruth had even broken loose with stories about Jack that no one had ever heard before. The afternoon went by so quickly that it was soon time to clean up and wake the small ones to go home.

The men had all gathered out in the barn and had brought their plates back some time ago. Mandy promised Hannah that she would come by soon and spend the whole day.

§

The mist had finally stopped when Hannah and Isaac were at last to themselves. Isaac had draped a heavy wool throw across her lap. There was a strong earthy smell coming from the damp forest on either side of them.

"I thought we could go somewhere and talk a while. We haven't had much time together lately," Isaac said looking at her expectantly.

"Where can we go that is not very far?"

"Just off the road up here there is a short trail that leads to the water's edge. We only have to walk a short distance if you are ok with that," Isaac explained.

"If we only take a few minutes, I don't want to worry my parents." Hannah felt nervous for some reason. Isaac seemed so serious today. She had noticed the twitching muscle in his jaw and it set her on edge. Isaac pulled the wagon to the side of the road next to a not so obvious foot trail through the trees. He walked around and encircled Hannah's waist with his large hands as he lifted her effortlessly down from the wagon seat. Within a couple of minutes, Hannah could see the water. They walked down the bank to where there lay an old log on which to sit.

"This is quite lovely Isaac; how did you know about this place?" Hannah asked.

"Actually, Josh is the one who found it and showed me a few days ago," Isaac said as he shifted himself more in her direction.

"I wanted to ask you if you were upset with me for some reason that I don't know about. Please feel free to talk to me about anything. I don't want anything coming between us." Isaac looked at her as if trying to discern her thoughts.

Hannah chose her words carefully before she spoke. "I am sorry if I gave you the impression that something is wrong between us. The truth is that with all that has occurred these last few months, I am afraid that I am letting everything get to me more than maybe I should."

"I understand." Isaac let out a breath of relief before he continued. "I know we haven't had much time together lately but don't worry and trust me that things will get better."

Hannah raised tear filled eyes to meet loving and determined ones. "Oh, Isaac, I am thankful for your reassurance. I desperately needed it." On the rest of their trip home, they were content to talk of things of a less serious nature and enjoy the carefree moment. Hannah knew things would not be as easy as Isaac expected them to be. Hannah was a novice at relationships and an easy target for firing darts.

UNDER HEAVEN ✷ Karen McDavid

CHAPTER 14

By Monday morning, news came that more people had contracted the illness, several of which had been at the funeral. Roman had gone into town to purchase a few supplies where he was informed by Luke of the unfortunate news.

"The doctor was in earlier and said that he was going to wire Doctor Lewis in Deadwood to see if he had come across any similar cases there. This sure has the Doc scratching his head. He has told everyone to stay home if they can until they can get a handle on what this here bug is."

Roman nodded his head, "Sounds like good advice to me. I will be sure to spread his instructions to as many people as I can."

When Luke saw Roman reach for the crate of supplies, he hurriedly spoke, "Be sure and tell Sophie and Hannah to take care and we hope to see them soon."

Roman walked through the screen door held open by Luke and said, "Tell Anna that I am sorry that I missed her." Roman carefully walked down the wooden steps in front of the store.

Besides a couple of men talking in front of the livery stables, there was no one milling about on this nice fall day. He sure hoped that everyone would try to stay home because he had seen how disease could rapidly spread and kill. What everyone thought might just be a common bug that was passed around every year, is turning out to be a very serious matter.

❧

"Sophie, Hannah!" Roman loudly voiced as he entered the house and saw no one in the living room area. Roman saw a piece of paper on the table held in place by a salt shaker. Hannah had written a note to let him know that she and her mother had gone to gather pinecones of different sizes and greenery to decorate with.

Roman gave a little chuckle to himself, *"That Hannah could always think of a way to get out of the house. No doubt it would be good for them both."* Roman went back outside to unpack and unsaddle his horse. The rattle of a horse and carriage caught his attention as he was leading his horse to the barn. When the carriage drew closer, he could see that it was Doctor Hayes and he acted like he was in a bit of a hurry.

"Good afternoon, Doc. What brings you out this way?" Roman said as he left his horse loosely tied to the corral fence in order to greet and shake hands with the doctor. Pulling a handkerchief from his jacket pocket, the doctor wiped the sweat from his forehead. Roman saw the fatigue in the doctor's face and asked him in for a few minutes to take a break.

Immediately the doctor began shaking his head no and said, "I wish that I could but I am trying to get around to as many folks as I can in order to see how many have taken sick."

"Just how bad are things, Doctor Hayes?"

"Well, I had heard back from the doctor in Deadwood today when I had stopped back by my office. It was as I suspected, it is diphtheria. A name has only been put to it very recently but the disease is one that has showed its ugly face many times."

"What kind of symptoms should I look for, Doc?" Roman rested his booted foot in one of the spokes of the wagon wheel and leaned his elbow upon his knee in a relaxing stance as the doctor explained.

"Well, the disease more commonly affects children but adults also. Look for a fever, sore throat, cough and difficulty with breathing. It can be mistaken for the influenza or even a bad cold. There are several children from neighboring farms that have come down with this," said the doctor as he picked up the horses' reigns preparing to leave.

"Is there anything that I can do to help?"

"Not at this time. Right now I am trying to keep it contained by keeping everyone at home if possible, a quarantine of sorts. If you will, help spread the word to those you might see, it would be a great help. I'll check back with you and your family in a couple of days."

Roman thanked the doctor as he rushed off to the next farm. Roman raised his face toward the heavens and whispered a prayer for those who were sick. He went to untie his horse so that he could put him in his stall to feed him.

Sophie and Hannah put their buckets at the back door and walked around the front of the house when they saw the carriage pulling away. Roman turned around when he heard the crunch of rocks under their feet as they approached. The look of love that passed between her parents gave Hannah hope that one day she and Isaac would share a love that would only grow stronger with time.

Roman's voice broke into Hannah's thoughts. "The doctor said that the illness that is plaguing the area is called diphtheria. It is a very serious disease as we are seeing its effects already."

"Did he say how many had taken sick with it? What should we look for?" Sophie said in a slightly panicked voice.

"He didn't give an exact number but several children and of course it is more than likely what took Jack down."

"Yes, I remember Ruth saying that Jack had a very hard time breathing. She thought that he had pneumonia," Sophie wiped at the tears that fell freely.

"We should watch for a sore throat, fever, cough and difficulty of breathing. There may be more symptoms but those are the ones that he passed on to me," Roman explained.

Hannah thought of her students and wondered who among them were ill. They had all become so precious to her in the short space of time that she had been teaching. Feeling restless and in need of a brisk walk, Hannah thought it would be a good idea to post a note on the school door.

"I think that I will go into town and post a note that school will be closed until further notice," Hannah said in a tone that stated more than asked for permission.

"That's a good idea. Would you like for your mother or me to go with you?" Roman asked his daughter.

"That's not necessary. I would like to stop by and check on Isaac and his family if you think it would be alright," Hannah asked.

"There is still much of today's beautiful sunshine left to enjoy," Sophie said as she lifted her face towards the sun's warmth. "We should take advantage of these clear fall days while they last. Please keep your distance from everyone until you know it is safe. Does that sound alright with you Roman?"

"Yes but don't be gone too long."

"Thanks and do you need anything while I am out?" Hannah asked. "Maybe I should check on Grandma Rose and the rest of the family."

"No, we will go and check on them together tomorrow. Your mother and I will see how Ruth is doing while you are gone." Roman said in a matter of fact tone.

✀

Hannah picked up her skirts and ran back to the house to freshen up. Excited at the chance to see Isaac, she quickly drew a brush through her shiny mane of hair and braided it so that it hung over her right shoulder. She donned a clean, pale blue blouse and grabbed her navy wrap on her way out the door.

Her mind was in a million different directions. She wondered how long she would have to keep the school closed. It would not be long before the holidays were upon them and it would be such a busy time. She would just have to post on the schoolhouse door a note that cancelled classes until further notice. It seemed that it was just one thing right after another lately.

Hannah's attention was drawn to a female elk that stood curiously observing her as she walked by. And then, as if deciding that she was of no concern, the animal continued sifting through the fallen foliage for non-confiscated nuts. Hannah wished her worries were so few but would trust that things would unfold more favorably for her in the not too distant future. Katie would be at home to take care of her mother now that school was out. That would mean that Bella would have to go home for a while and that was a guilty yet pleasing thought to Hannah. She could not push the strange feelings concerning Bella from her mind.

She had to continually force herself to concentrate upon more pleasant thoughts. Hannah had reached the road that led to Isaac's house and decided to stop by there before going on into town. The lay of the land really was magnificent surrounding the Daniels' farm. Hannah could see no one outside when she approached and found that to be very strange this time of day. Perhaps they were having a late lunch or had gone somewhere, were the thoughts that entered her mind.

Just as she reached up to knock on the front door, Josh opened it and almost knocked her down in his hurry to go out.

"Oh! For goodness sakes, Hannah," Josh said as he stepped back at the same time as he reached out to grab her arm to steady her.

"I'm sorry, Josh." Hannah's face was one big smile. She could not help but laugh at Josh's look of surprise when he opened the door and practically ran over her.

"It's okay. I wasn't expecting anyone to come and visit," Josh said while looking over his shoulder nervously.

"Is everything alright? Did I come at a bad time?" Hannah's brows drew together in worry. She stood on her tip toes to try and see if anyone else was in the room. It was difficult to see around Josh's broad shoulders.

"Yes." Josh finally got out before continuing on. "I mean, you shouldn't be here because Katie has become ill with the sickness that has been spreading," said Josh as he politely motioned for Hannah to turn back around and move away from the house. Walking a few yards away from Josh as he closed the front door behind him, Hannah waited for him to explain. She noticed that he hadn't mentioned anyone else being sick so she hoped no one else had been affected.

Josh stopped several feet from her and said, "As far as we know, no one else is sick. Isaac has gone into town after Doctor Hayes. Bella went with him to get some of her things. She will be needed to stay and help care for Katie also, now that she has been exposed."

Hannah's heart sunk. Now she wouldn't even get to see Isaac, even only for a short time. Forcing the depressing thoughts from her mind, she focused on what was important.

"Is there anything that I can do for Katie or Alice?"

"Thank you Hannah, but no. It's best if you don't hang around here too long just to be on the safe side." Josh told her before going on to ask her about Mandy.

"As far as we know, they are all well. We are going to go and check on them tomorrow. I am going in to town to post a note on the schoolhouse door to inform every one of the canceled classes until further notice. I'm sure they already guess that is the case but I need to just as a formality."

"Take care and let me know if anyone at Mandy's is sick, will you?" Josh made no bones about how he felt about Mandy.

"Sure but no news is good news." With a wave, Hannah turned and began her walk into town, her step not as springy as before.

§

The short walk went by quickly and before she knew it she was at the edge of town. The schoolhouse was one of the first buildings you came to and was situated off to its self so the children had room to play. She already missed the children and was surprised at how they had come to grow on her so easily. Hannah paused long enough on the first wooden step to look among the few gathered along the boardwalk and dirt street to try and catch a glimpse of Isaac. She didn't see him. Feeling disheartened, Hannah climbed the remaining steps and entered the classroom to see if all was in order.

Aside from leaves and pine needles that had blown from under the doors, everything was pretty much as she had left it. Hannah went to grab the broom in the corner where she kept all of the cleaning supplies. As she swept, she thought of how nice it would be to enjoy the holidays with the children. There were so many fun and special things that they could do to celebrate Thanksgiving and Christmas.

Walking past the windows to place the broom back in its place, Hannah saw Isaac and Bella come out of the boarding house door. Unable to move, Hannah watched Isaac help Bella up onto the wagon seat and walk around and climb up on the other side. Bella waved to her cousin, Katherine, and scooted closer to Isaac than was necessary. She wanted to run out and go to Isaac but her feet were glued to the floor. Many thoughts filed in line, one after another, like a trail of ants building together. *Why couldn't Josh usher Bella around some of the time? It seemed Isaac was always the willing servant. How much more could she stand? Was she just reading things into everything that she saw? Then again, how much is really just a case of naivety on her part?* With her lack of enthusiasm gone, Hannah wrote the note for the door and secured it with two small nails.

Hannah tried not to think at all on the walk home. She decided that she would put all of her time and energy into her family and friends. If she and Isaac were meant to be together then things would work in that direction. If not, she would have to find a way to accept it and move on. In the meantime, she would try her best not to make herself miserable with worry.

Roman and Sophie were standing at the corral fence watching the horses eat after their journey to Ruth Johnson's and back. Roman's arm was resting across his wife's shoulders and Sophie's right hand clasped his. Hannah would accept no less in a marriage than what she saw in her parents'. Maybe she was expecting too much but that is what she wanted, a true marriage.

At the sound of Hannah's footsteps behind them, Roman and Sophie turned around together. "You are back earlier than I expected. I hope all was well," Sophie said as she looked at her daughter questioningly. Hannah was having a hard time keeping her disappointment from showing but she was determined to make the best of things.

Hannah raised her chin a little and said, "When I reached Isaac's house, Josh was there and told me that Katie had contracted the diphtheria. I didn't get to see Isaac because he was gone with Bella so that she could gather some things to stay and help."

Roman took hold of Hannah's hand to calm her. He could tell that she was a little more than upset and was trying hard to hide it. "I am sure that Isaac and his family are doing what they feel is best right now. The doctor has given strict orders to try and keep this thing contained." Gently he squeezed her hand and continued, "I assume they did the right thing and kept you away from everyone."

"Yes, I know that you are right. I pray Katie will get well soon and no one else will catch it." Hannah perked up the tiniest of bits.

Sophie started leading them towards the house before saying, "Ruth is doing well and your Grandma Rose is going back home tomorrow. As a matter of fact, your father told her we would pick her up and take her with us when we go to see them all tomorrow."

Hannah's eyes brightened as she said, "I am so looking forward to seeing Mandy. What time will we leave?"

Roman scratched his chin, "Let me see here. Peter and Seth will be arriving around noon. So how does noon sound to you ladies?"

"Really, Seth will be there? I can't wait to meet him, and Peter of course. I almost forgot all about them coming," Hannah started pondering upon what Seth would be like as she helped her mother prepare supper for that evening.

CHAPTER 15

Hannah rose from her bed and looked out her window to see the ground adorned with shimmering diamonds. The window panes had all but frosted over except for a small space here and there. Donning her warm housecoat and slippers, she knelt beside the bed to say a quick prayer before beginning the day. She very much looked forward to seeing the rest of the family again.

Hannah's nose was tickled with the aroma of hot maple syrup and fried sausage. She went to wash up before entering the kitchen where she found her mother and father awaiting breakfast on her. Sophie rose to take the hot plates of food from the stove top and place them on the table. The flapjacks and sausage patties were ready to be smothered with hot maple syrup and butter. They each dug in after a silent prayer and they discussed what each of them had planned for the next several days.

Sophie looked at Hannah and said, "I thought that we could give the house a good cleaning before the holidays arrived. I would like to get that out of the way so we would have plenty of time to do any sewing or gift making that needed done."

"That sounds like a good idea to me, especially since any sewing or knitting done by my hand will take forever," Hannah said seriously because they all knew that sewing was not her cup of tea.

Sophie knew all too well that her daughter would rather do anything besides sewing or anything akin to it. The teaching job that she had was exactly what Hannah needed. It got her out of the house as well as gave her a challenge and a sense of fulfillment. Sophie also hoped that it would help soften the worried look on her daughter's face that she thought no one could detect.

Roman set his coffee cup down loudly getting his wife's attention. "Well I have no problem deciding on what I am going to do. I just have to decide what I want to do first," Roman said as he stood up and went to collect his hat and coat.

Pausing at the door he said, "I'll be back in time to change clothes and eat a bite before we leave." Roman quickly closed the door behind him before the cold morning air filled the room.

After the kitchen was put back in order, Sophie and Hannah discussed their concerns over the spreading epidemic that gripped their community as well as other surrounding communities. They had no way of knowing yet how many had been affected so far. They ventured a guess that it would be at least two weeks before school could resume. One thing was for sure, they would do a lot of praying between now and then.

Hannah and Sophie had put away the pinecones and greenery they had gathered out in the barn until they were ready for it. At least they wouldn't have to wade through deep snow in search of some if they waited until a later date to fetch it. All they would need is some red ribbon to set it off.

A growing sense of anticipation had been stirring within Hannah all morning. She had been able to push some of her troubles to the back of her mind whether they were concretely founded or not. It was not often that one got to make a new acquaintance around here. Finding a suitable dress, not too nice but not too shabby either, was not so simple a task. She knew Mandy loved to explore outside and what was her usual choice just did not seem up to standard for meeting someone for the first time. Hannah discarded several dresses before deciding on a moderately worn dark, brown skirt and a light green blouse that was far from being new but in very good condition.

"Hannah?" Sophie called to her daughter.

Hannah lay her hairbrush down and said, "I'm coming. Just one minute." Quickly straightening her clothes and grabbing her shoes, she went to eat a small meal with her parents before they boarded the wagon and were on their way.

The ride was invigorating. Although the sun shined brightly and was high in the sky, the air was yet crisp and the shaded areas still showed signs of this morning's frost. Hannah could honestly say that she loved every season. Each season had its own uniqueness and purpose, each no less important than the other. Spring is a time of awakening. The earth comes alive, within and without. Summer is a time of growth, a time for the earth to bring forth her fruit.

As Hannah looked around, she saw that they were in the very midst of fall, the great time of the earth's harvest, a time to reap of the bounty they are so wonderfully blessed with. And winter, glorious winter, the earth's time of slumber. The earth takes a long healing sleep from its labor.

"Did you hear me Hannah?" Roman's voice cut into Hannah's thoughts.

"No, I'm sorry. My mind was wondering as usual." Hannah smiled apologetically at her parents.

"Your mother and I thought it would be nice if you asked Mandy to come and stay a couple of days with us. What do you think?" Roman asked, all the while knowing the answer he would get. The pleased expression on his daughter's face was a dead give-a-way too.

Hannah clapped her hands together like a little girl. "Oh, it would be like old times. We have both been so busy lately," Hannah paused for a moment with her eyebrows drawn together. She then asked, "Do you know if Mandy is still babysitting?"

"Grandma Rose told us that Mandy is staying home now. As far as she knows, her job is finished as long as the mother continues to recover," Sophie explained.

"That's very good news. She has been sick for too long. I will be so relieved when all of this recent sickness is past and we can get back to our normal lives." Hannah let out a giggle and said, "I never thought that I would wish for an everyday routine but that is exactly what sounds good to me right now."

"It sounds good to me also, sweetheart," laughed Sophie.

Roman joined in, "The doctor said that he would swing by tomorrow. Maybe he will have some encouraging news for us all."

"I hope so," Sophie and Hannah responded in unison. Hannah could see the smoke from Ruth's fireplace curling up in the distance. Although the air had seemed to warm slightly, due to the sun's rays, since they had left the house, the lazy, rising smoke was an inviting welcome to her cold fingers. Hannah's mind again went to wondering what Ruth's son and grandson would be like. It was exciting to meet someone from so far away. Then she remembered Bella and the thought made her a little wary. Hannah scolded herself for almost sabotaging what promised to be a happy day.

The strange buggy that was pulled up to the front of the house was sure to be Peter and Seth's. Roman pulled up along beside it and swung down to help his wife and daughter to the ground. Before they could reach the solid oak door, it opened wide to reveal a tall, dark-haired man.

Reaching out his right hand, Peter said, "Hello, you must be Roman. It's such a pleasure to meet you."

Roman took a liking to Peter at once. He took the offered hand firmly and said, "I'm very glad to meet you also, Peter."

Peter stepped aside to allow them entrance into the house. After shutting the door, he turned and motioned to a younger version of himself. Nodding his head towards his son, he said, "This is my son, Seth. Seth I would like you to meet Roman."

Roman shook Seth's hand and then turned to introduce his wife and daughter. "Peter and Seth, I'd like for you to meet my wife, Sophie and my daughter, Hannah."

After pleasantries were exchanged between them, they took a seat at the table with Ruth and Grandma Rose. Hannah felt uncomfortable for she could feel Seth's eyes upon her. She tried to maintain what she hoped was a calm demeanor.

Grandma Rose spoke as soon as she received her hug from Hannah. "I was just discussing with Peter about all the beautiful pieces of furniture that his father so enjoyed making. As it turns out, Seth has taken after his grandfather in that respect," Rose informed them before turning to Ruth. "Isn't that so Ruth?"

With an abundance of love in Ruth's eyes and voice, she easily replied, "Yes, I just knew that Jack's love of woodworking was as much a part of him as his brown eyes or crooked grin. It doesn't surprise me one bit that Seth has found that same talent ingrained in his very being."

Hannah glanced towards Seth as they spoke and found him already looking in her direction. He awarded her with one of the most devilish crooked and handsome grins that she ever saw. Hannah just knew her face turned beet-red because she could feel the heat from it. She quickly looked away and stomped her foot under the table before she could stop herself. She hoped no one noticed but realized differently when she heard a satisfied laugh at the end of the table.

"I hate to bring up more unfortunate circumstances going on around here but Mom has been telling me about the disease that has been spreading amongst you. Do you know how bad it is yet?" Peter asked Roman.

"Not for sure. Everyone is being careful not to come in contact with anyone infected or that may appear to be. The doctor is fairly certain that it is diphtheria," Roman told him.

"Yes, we had a run in with that same thing in our area a couple of winters back only we didn't know what it was called then. It mostly hits children but it can take adults as we saw with Dad." Peter sadly looked at his mother and took her feeble and small hands in his for comfort.

"I trust that all of this will be over quickly if we all stay on guard. Even I am going to get cabin fever if we don't soon get to go back to church," Grandma Rose spoke in mock firmness with that familiar sparkle in her eyes.

Seth spoke up with a little sparkle in his own eyes. "I wonder if a fellow would be allowed to have two grandmothers," Seth said as he comically watched the two elderly ladies let what he said sink in. "You know, sort of like grandma one and grandma two."

Ruth was the first to speak up. "Hold on just one spanking minute now. I expect to be number one, of course. Don't you agree Rose?"

Hannah could not believe her eyes and ears. He was riling them up on purpose! Looking at everyone else's reaction to Seth's antics, it seemed they thought it was all in fun. *"Surely it was, wasn't it?"* Hannah almost spoke the last thought aloud.

"Well I suppose, but you mustn't hog him all of the time," Grandma Rose retuned in a possessive tone.

"Now Grandmothers, I will make sure that each of you get your fair share of me. Besides, I'm sure there are a few young ladies around here that I will have to save a little charming companionship for also," Seth said with convincing sincerity.

Hannah spoke up in a rather smug voice, "I hate to be the bearer of bad news but there are very few ladies around here that you will be able to cast your charming spell upon."

Seth winked at Hannah undeterred. "Well Hannah that is just more of me to go around for each lucky lady."

Peter reached over and gave his son a playful shove on the shoulder. "Now Seth, you must stop the teasing. Hannah is going to think that I raised a regular rascal." Peter couldn't help but laugh at his son's playful banter.

Sophie watched the interaction between father and son. It brought back memories of Toby. She wondered what he would have been like as a man. There was no doubt that he would have been a loving husband and father. His affectionate nature played a role in every part of his life. *"Oh, God,"* Sophie thought. *"Why must I be haunted by all of these things that were never meant to be? Will I ever be able to come to terms with this life changing tragedy."*

"Isn't that right, Sophie? Sophie?" Grandma Rose leaned in closer to gain her daughter-in-law's attention.

"Yes? What? I'm sorry, my mind was elsewhere," Sophie turned a little in her chair so that she could look more directly at her mother-in-law.

"I was just telling Hannah that it sometimes done a body good to be more light-hearted and less serious sometimes," Grandma Rose said as she looked at both Sophie and Hannah before she continued.

"There has been ample enough time to weep and to contemplate upon serious matters. Now maybe it's time to laugh and let our hearts be lifted. I think Ruth would even agree with me. She has seen her fair share of sorrow in her lifetime and dwelling upon what could have been only takes away from what is."

Hannah knew that she was being politely reprimanded by her grandmother and if she was not mistaken, so was her mother. There was no one like Grandma Rose to keep them all marching on. She would do her best to take her advice.

Sophie smiled and said, "You always know what to say at the right time." "Thank you, Grandma Rose,"

Hannah added. "How does apple pie sound to everyone?"

Ruth said before everyone could get up. "Rose and I baked them fresh this morning."

"Are you kidding? I thought that you would never ask," Seth said as he started rolling up his sleeves as he got ready to dig in. "I have been sitting here smelling that wonderful aroma the whole time. I was just about to get up and help myself."

Hannah and Sophie served up the pie. Hannah was sure to give Seth his piece first. She couldn't help but laugh at the outrageous way his eyes got as big around as saucers and he licked his lips for good measure. Hannah thought that there was never going to be a dull moment while Seth Johnson was around.

Roman and Peter talked of their farms. As it turned out, Peter also owned a rather large farm outside of Denver a few miles. Peter explained the business of breeding horses to Roman. Roman asked him if that was all he used his land for. Peter was self-sufficient because he grew his own corn and oats and cut his own hay.

"How about you, what gets you out of bed every morning," asked Peter?

"I like to fool with cattle. Although I don't own a great deal of land, there's good pasture and water supply. If there is ample corn for the herd, then I sell the rest. Over the years I have obtained some buyers who come to me."

Peter placed his laced fingered hands in front of him upon the table and leaned in closer to Roman. With a look of intrigue in his dark eyes, he said, "I've heard talk that there is going to be a lot of money in pure bred cattle. While Hereford cattle are very popular still, there is some convincing talk coming out about the Angus breed of cattle."

Roman's interest was piqued. He looked at his wife to see if she was listening to the conversation. "Sophie and I would be interested in learning more about this cattle breeding," Roman said and glanced his wife's way again and Sophie smiled her agreement.

While the men continued to talk business, the ladies talked of the very soon upcoming holidays to be preparing for. Grandma Rose was the driving force behind the family getting together. She was almost like a child when it came to getting her way or maybe she would be better described as a general. Either way things got done.

"Ruth, you will, of course, come to our homes for the celebrations," Grandma Rose said and continued on before Ruth could turn her down. "There is always so much to do that an extra pair of hands will be appreciated not to mention the company."

Sophie and Hannah exchanged looks and the mutual thought that passed between them was easily interpreted. Grandma Rose was not about to allow her dear friend Ruth to spend the holiday season alone without Jack who was so soon gone from her life.

Sophie asked Ruth the question that Hannah was interested in knowing herself. "How long are Peter and Seth planning on visiting?"

Ruth's countenance changed with her reply, "Peter says that he will be staying for a week and to my surprise, Seth has announced that he would like to extend his visit for several weeks," said Ruth with pleasure evident in her voice. The men were so caught up in their discussion that they didn't even hear their names mentioned.

Ruth continued, "Peter would like to bring Lucinda back with him when he returns for Seth if her mother is on the mend."

Sophie smiled and said, "That's wonderful news! You will bring him along for our gatherings, the more the merrier."

Ruth nodded her acceptance before saying, "I have a feeling he will keep me on my toes. I probably won't see a moment's peace with that boy around." Ruth's eyes told a totally different story. She was so excited that she was beside herself.

Grandma Rose said, "Well he is not a boy anymore and you are right, you won't see a moment's peace." Ruth and Grandma Rose both started their cackling laugh that sounded funnier than anything they had said. Sophie and Hannah joined in on the fun. This finally got the men's attention and Seth got up and walked over to the elderly women.

Putting his hands on each of their shoulders, Seth said, "Now what has got my two grandmas laughing so hard?"

"Nothing, Seth, we are just so glad that you are going to stay with us for a while," Ruth replied.

"Yes, Seth, we are just happy," Grandma Rose added.

"Well isn't that nice. I just hope I can make the rest of the ladies in these parts happy that easily," Seth said with a kiss to each of their cheeks. Seth looked up in time to catch Hannah rolling her eyes. He just grinned and patted her on top of the head in passing. This only aggravated her more.

Roman stood and asked Grandma Rose if she was ready to go. Hannah went to gather their things while they said their farewells for the time being. Ruth's tearful embrace was all the thanks that Grandma Rose needed.

Roman shook Peter's hand once more and said, "It was very nice meeting you Peter and Seth. You both must come over to our place soon for supper. We can continue our discussion then."

"Yes, we would like that. It was a pleasure meeting you and your family also."

Almost out the door, Hannah heard Seth say, "See you soon Hannah."

Hannah smiled and nodded before she closed the door behind her. She just knew he was standing with that smile on his face right now. Letting out a deep breath that she did not realize she had been holding, Hannah climbed up and sat beside her mother in the second seat in the wagon. Hannah did not know quite what to make of Seth. She had never met anyone like him before.

"I have to admit that it feels good to be going home. I like sleeping in my own bed and sitting in my rocking chair. That's just the way you get when you get old," Grandma Rose said.

"Well I must be getting old Mom because I am already just about that way myself now." Roman lovingly told his mother.

"Oh my, you are going to be as set in your ways as your father was." Rose turned to Sophie and said, "I feel sorry for you Sophie for Roman's father was a stubborn man indeed." Sophie only smiled in return because she could see the love in her mother-in-law's eyes every time she mentioned Roman's father.

Sophie prayed that Hannah found a love that endured all things. Sophie knew she had so much to be thankful for and knew also that she like many others may never have the answers to the burdens that weighed one's heart, at least not in this life.

A jolt of the wagon from hitting a rock brought Sophie's thoughts closer in. She noticed that Hannah was also being awfully quiet. It would do her daughter good to spend a couple of carefree days with Mandy. As a matter of fact, Mandy's cheerful ways would do everyone some good. The cleaning could wait a little longer. The thoughts brought a smile to Sophie's face.

<p>

Roman saw his mother sit up a little straighter when the home place came into view. Jacob was out front standing next to a pile of wood ready to be chopped. By the looks of things, he hadn't been at it very long.

Grandma Rose chuckled as Jacob swung the axe over and over at the knotty pine piece of wood. "I see Jacob has finally met his match. That piece of wood looks to be just as stubborn as he is, maybe more so," she said continuing to laugh even more.

Jacob pulled out a handkerchief and wiped his forehead when he saw his family driving up. "Well it's about time you decided to come home." Jacob reached up strong arms to help his mother down.

After helping his wife and daughter down, Roman gave his brother a firm handshake and asked, "I trust you all are well?"

"Yes. We have been worried about you all too. We have been sticking close to home just like the doctor ordered." Jacob laid his axe down and led them into the house.

A loud squeal sounded as soon as they entered. There was no room for doubt that Mandy was happy to see them. Hannah barely had time to remove her wrap before Mandy's embrace almost knocked her down in its exuberance.

Mandy calmed down enough to say, "I didn't know if Uncle Roman would bring you along considering the sickness and all. I'm so glad he did."

"Me, too," Sarah joined in. "Welcome home Rose. It's good to have you back."

Grandma Rose sat down at the table with a loud sigh and said, "It is good to be back."

"It was a beautiful day for a ride," Sophie said as she smoothed back a stray portion of dark, silky hair, with a hint of silver, from her forehead.

Before Hannah had even taken a seat, Mandy asked, "So, did you get to meet Seth Johnson? And Peter, too, of course," she quickly added.

Hannah took a seat and slowly straightened her skirts in mock calmness just to tempt Mandy's impatient nature before saying, "Yes, they were already there when we got there. Peter was a very nice man. Wouldn't you agree, Mama?"

"Yes, so much like Jack."

"And Seth," Hannah paused as if trying to find the words to describe him. "I have never seen anybody as full of himself as he is."

"Now just a minute there, Hannah," Grandma Rose interrupted before Hannah could say more. "Seth was just teasing you, my dear. You just made it easy for him to know which buttons to push. He's really very smart."

"But is he good looking? Not that it matters, but it seems to me that he is already stirring things up a bit," laughed Mandy.

Hannah sighed and said, "Yes, unfortunately, he is very good looking." This got them all to laughing. Sarah told them that they should all stay for supper. The conversation stayed light-hearted while they all pitched in and helped. The afternoon passed swiftly.

Roman helped Jacob split the wood, so there would be enough daylight left to travel home by. It just about bested them both. It was time to eat when they were done.

When they had finished eating, Hannah invited Mandy home with them. "I would love to!" Mandy was up and out of her chair before thinking to ask for permission. She caught herself and said, "If that is alright with you that is."

Sarah said to her daughter, "I suppose we can get along without you for a couple of days. Why don't you and Hannah go and pack up your things before it gets much later."

Sophie rose to start cleaning up but Sarah said, "Please leave it. I have plenty of time to do that after you have left. With it getting dark so much earlier now, the evenings seem so long if there is nothing to keep you busy."

"I agree with you completely. I hope to make some plans for some Christmas gifts and start spending my evenings working on them."

"I'm afraid that I will need more than just a few hours in the evening to work. These old hands don't want to sew and knit like they used to." Grandma Rose displayed her arthritic hands as she talked.

Sophie could hear Roman telling Jacob about the discussion that he had with Peter earlier this afternoon. Roman seemed more than interested about what Peter had to say about cattle breeding. She was pleased to see her husband have the look of excitement that she had not seen for far too long now. Mandy and Hannah reentered the room with a clothes bag each. Roman and Sophie stood to their feet because they knew the girls were ready to be on their way. Soon they were back on the road after a long day out.

CHAPTER 16

The air had turned considerably colder as the sun began setting. The wind had picked up slightly bringing along with it some cloud cover. Hannah reached down and picked up a wool blanket and threw it across their laps. The wind decided to strengthen and began to howl and to whip any loose debris all about them. Roman urged the horses into a faster pace while everyone held their hats and scarves to their heads.

Sophie could hear the girls chattering behind her above the rattling of the wagon and whipping of the wind. She almost envied the girls' carefree time in their lives, a time that she herself was robbed of. Sophie would always remind herself that all things worked together for the good for those who loved God. The comforting words were a lifeline to her. Off in the distance, a loud crack of lighting brought Sophie's thoughts back to the present.

The mountainous view was fast becoming obscured by the approaching cold rain. The first large drops fell just as they pulled up in front of the house. Sophie looked up and smiled her thanks to God for watching out for even the little things.

$$\wp$$

Hannah and Mandy talked until way into the night. The rain turned to snow overnight as the temperature dropped. A dusting of snow covered the ground announcing that winter was here. It would be a lovely day to explore and enjoy the landscape.

The aroma of bacon frying sifted its way into Hannah's room and enticed the girls from their warm bed. They made plans to go and check on Katie in hopes that she was doing better and that no one else had contracted the disease, especially Alice in her weakened condition. Of course the opportunity to see Isaac and Josh was an added benefit.

The cold floors sent them scurrying to find their house slippers when they climbed out of bed. The door to their room had been partially shut to allow them some privacy but at the same time, much of the heat from the fireplace sought much easier accesses. Entering the kitchen was a great comfort to their chilled bones. Sophie placed hot plates of food on the table, while the girls snuggled close to the cook stove's warmth. Sophie guessed that she would always look at them as little girls more often than the young women that they had become.

Sophie smiled and asked, "Did you girls have a good night's rest?"

Mandy spoke up first. "Yes, at least what few hours we slept after talking until after midnight."

"I hope we didn't disturb you and Dad. We tried to be quiet," Hannah said as she snatched a piece of bacon crumble from the plate.

"No. As a matter of fact, I slept like a baby," Sophie replied as she began to put some eggs and biscuits on a plate for Hannah and Mandy. "So what do you girls have planned for today?" Sophie asked after the girls raised their heads from prayer.

Mandy swallowed the bacon that she had already taken a bite of and said, "Since I haven't been able to visit anyone for the longest while, I asked Hannah if it would be alright to go and check on Katie, Alice too. We would keep our distance, of course," Mandy was quick to add.

"Isn't the doctor supposed to stop by soon with some news on the gravity of the situation?" Hannah inquired.

"That is what he told your Father. He should be back by here anytime now," Sophie told them. "Mandy do you know of any recent cases since you have been home?"

"No, but we really haven't been in touch with many people either. Doctor Hayes told Mom and Dad that the disease was a very serious one. In many cases, it caused a thin membrane to coat your throat which made it very difficult to breathe. I couldn't believe such a thing as that could happen. It's very scary," Mandy said as she emphasized her words with a shivering of her whole body.

"That's sounds horrible. I am so concerned for my students. I wish that there was some way of knowing if they are alright," Hannah said.

Sophie rose from her chair as she said, "We will just keep praying that God's will be done. Please be careful while you are out today. How long will you be gone?"

Hannah wished she could give her worried mother an exact time but she could not. "I am not sure. I would like to get some things from the schoolhouse so that I will be prepared when the classes do resume. It will probably be later this afternoon so don't wait lunch on us."

Sophie nodded her head and said, "I will pack you a light lunch then."

Hannah and Mandy finished their breakfast and then went to get washed up and dressed. They each chose a warm skirt with blouse and matching jacket. Hannah's was a deep green and Mandy's was a complimenting navy blue. Although they had worn them many times before, the material was still in excellent shape.

Hannah finished her long braid and asked, "Mandy, do you want to ride or walk today?"

"Walk, if it's alright with you. I need the exercise."

Hannah laughed, "Oh Mandy. You are as skinny as ever. In fact, you could stand to gain a couple of pounds." Donning their coats and all of their other outerwear that is needful on such days as this, they headed out to brave the clear but cold day. It didn't look as if the snow was going to melt today.

Roman was standing inside the barn doorway when they walked by. He raised his hand in a gesture of goodbye. They both waved with an enthusiasm that told Roman that they were very glad to be on their way. Hannah had a hard time keeping up with Mandy's fast pace. Hannah would swear that Mandy would skip instead of walk if she thought she could get by with it. Oh, how she sometimes envied Mandy's spunk.

"So tell me more about this Seth character. He sounds interesting," Mandy said as much with her hands as with her mouth.

"He's a character, alright. I think his interests lie far too much in himself. Mom says that I shouldn't be too quick to judge a person after such a short encounter though."

"That's true you know. People often think that I am not a serious person until they get to know me better. Let's just keep an open mind and see what transpires," Mandy wisely suggested.

Hannah said, "It's a deal." Mandy never failed to be good medicine when duly needed.

The sound of a buggy and horses reached their ears before it came into sight up ahead. It was Doctor Hayes going at a slower trot than his usual ample pace. That had to be good news. As he came closer, his blonde head stood out against the black inside of his buggy. Hannah and Mandy stepped to the side of the road and slowed to a stop.

"Hello girls. What brings you out on such a cold morning?"

As usual, Mandy spoke up and said, "We were on our way to see Katie Daniels or rather just to inquire as to her condition."

"And we have all been wondering how bad things are," Hannah added.

"Things are not as bad as I feared they would be." The doctor paused to push up his glasses. "We separated everyone before it could spread to every household. Although several children in as many families have contracted the disease, we have been fortunate enough to where most seem like they are going to for sure pull through. There are three children and an infant that I am worried about but the rest seem to be on the mend." The doctor rubbed his tired eyes before continuing, "We are still not out of the woods. You will need to continue to be very cautious."

"Yes, Dr. Hayes, thank you." Hannah said wanting to ask him who the children were that had not recovered. Doctor Hayes stopped the buggy after just a few feet and said, "I forgot to tell you that Katie is doing well but wait a few more days before seeing her."

Hannah and Mandy waved and smiled as he rode off.

Even though it had only been a few days since the illness had presented itself, it seemed much longer. Hannah found that she missed teaching more than she expected she would after such a short time. Mandy turned to see if Hannah was close behind and adjusted her pace a little.

"Hannah, I noticed that while I went on and on about Josh last night, you barely mentioned Isaac to me. Is everything ok with you two?" Mandy asked out of concern.

"I know this seems crazy but when we are together it seems like everything is perfectly fine and then when we are apart, all of that changes. It is like something always happens to make me doubt his feelings for me," Hannah's worried look left no doubt as to her troubled thoughts.

Mandy thought for a moment before saying. "Maybe you should try talking to Isaac about how you feel. He is the only one that can lay your fears to rest."

Hannah turned her head in the direction of Isaac's home. "I can't, at least not yet. I need to sort out if these feelings I am having are meant to show me something or if I am just being insecure."

"Well, if you want my opinion, I think that you and Isaac were made for each other. So just hang in there and let time do the telling," Mandy said very bluntly, as usual.

Hannah turned grateful eyes on her dear cousin but most of all, friend. "Oh Mandy, what would I ever do without you?"

"You would sit around and mope all day and get lost in your worries," Mandy told Hannah with a teasing twinkle in her eyes. Hannah laughed and picked up her pace to match Mandy's exuberant one. The crisp air seemed to clear one's mind while the bright sun lent some cheerfulness to the heart. Today she would lay aside worries and fears to enjoy all the things that she had to be thankful for. She would rejoice and be glad in it.

"Mandy, how about we sing a song as we journey along?"

"What a wonderful idea! What would you like to sing?"

"How about, What a Friend We Have in Jesus," Hannah said as tears were already beginning to roll with a blessing from above.

"That's perfect," Mandy responded with watering eyes of her own.

℘

They turned down the road leading to the Daniels' farm. Their voices reached a pair of inclined ears long before they could be seen rounding the last bend in the road. Bella paused in the middle of hanging some laundry on the clothesline outback in hopes of it somehow drying. Thinking the singing was coming from Katie and Alice from inside the house, she continued to pin the clothes on the line. *"For some reason,"* Bella thought to herself. *"The genuine love of God that shown forth brightly by the people she was now surrounded by made her uncomfortable. It was as if she had always been in a dark room that suddenly allowed a flicker of light to enter."* The musical voices became louder causing Bella to grab her now empty basket and walk around to the front of the house.

Surprised to see Hannah and Mandy, she looked around to see if anyone else had noticed their arrival. The men had all left directly after breakfast to cut firewood. Thinking about those that she considered friends back home, they wouldn't be caught dead finding enjoyment singing church songs. Mandy waved enthusiastically as she drew closer to Bella. Bella walked slowly to meet them. Hannah looked around the premises to try to catch a glimpse of Isaac but it seemed that Bella was the only one around.

Hannah stopped a few feet away from Bella to allow a safe distance. "Hello Bella. How are you?" Hannah asked.

"I am doing well, thank you. How have your families been concerning this ugly disease?" Bella asked them both.

Hannah and Mandy both replied at the same time. "We are fine." Mandy laughed.

"We were concerned with how Katie and the rest of the family were doing. You look as beautiful and healthy as ever Bella."

"Thank you, Mandy. Katie is doing much better but the doctor advises her to stay in for a few more days just to be safe. The rest of us are still disease free," Bella filled them in.

"That's great news. Where is everyone, by the way?" Hannah said scanning her surroundings still hoping to see Isaac.

"The men went to cut firewood and I assume that they will be gone for quite some time," Bella said a little smugly. A strange look of pleasure was in those startling green eyes of hers. Hannah looked at Mandy to see if she had noticed Bella's attitude. Mandy however, was too busy looking and waving at Katie through the kitchen window. Hannah waved and smiled at her also.

Hannah tugged on Mandy's coattail to get her attention. "I suppose that we should be getting on. We just wanted to stop by and see if everyone was well."

Mandy said, "Be sure and tell Josh that I stopped by."

"Sure, no problem, they will be sad that they missed you," Bella said as she started toward the house. "Have a good day." With one last scan of the area, Hannah turned and started walking quickly back the way they came. This time Mandy had a hard time keeping up with Hannah's steps that were induced by frustration. Hannah never managed to come away from a visit with Bella in a good mood.

"Slow down Hannah. What's wrong?" Mandy asked a bit breathlessly. Hannah slowed her pace before saying, "Just disappointed that I didn't get to see Isaac." Hannah chose not to share the whole reason for her troubled mood. "He will just have to make time to come and see me."

"That's right. We don't need them to have a good time!" Mandy said a little too positively. They talked of old times back in their early childhood days, precious memories of innocent pranks and shared moments, both happy and sad. Mandy and Hannah were sisters to each other in every way except blood.

℘

They were so absorbed in their reminiscing they didn't notice the people up ahead that had stopped to talk. Upon closer inspection, Hannah could see that it was Paul and Emma Sullivan and surprisingly Seth Johnson.

Mandy squinted her eyes while saying, "I can't tell who that is talking with Paul and Emma. Do you know Hannah?"

With a slight sigh, Hannah said, "Yes, it is Seth Johnson. It looks like you will get to meet him sooner than you thought." Mandy let out a small squeal of glee as she sprang forth excitedly. She picked up her pace almost leaving Hannah behind.

Mandy spoke over her shoulder without slowing down, "It looks like Emma has her baby with her. I can't wait to see her!"

As if in defeat, Hannah shrugged her shoulders and practically ran to catch up with Mandy.

Hannah could see that Emma did indeed have her baby with her. Emma smiled and waved when she saw them coming. Hannah hoped they had all been well. It had been a while since she had seen them.

"Well, well, if it isn't Miss Hannah Jamison." Seth greeted them with an exaggerated bow of his head as he placed his large black hat on his chest.

"Hello, Seth, it's nice to see you again so soon," Hannah politely replied. She could sense Mandy's eagerness to be introduced to Seth.

"Seth, I would like for you to meet my dear friend and cousin, Mandy Jamison."

Seth offered his hand and said, "Hannah I thought that you said there were very few young ladies in these parts, let alone one this lovely. It's wonderful to meet you Mandy." Mandy was obviously flattered and intrigued by Seth. It was the first time Hannah had ever seen Mandy speechless. He was stunningly good looking but once you got past all of that, he was rather exasperating were Hannah's thoughts as she observed their interactions. She then remembered that she had promised to keep an open mind and give Seth a chance.

Mandy found her voice and said, "It is so nice to finally meet you. I've been hearing a lot about you."

"Well good then, I can concentrate on getting to know more about you," Seth smiled and winked at Mandy before he turned his attention back to the Paul and Emma. "It looks as though I am going to enjoy getting to know a lot of wonderful people while I am here."

Hannah had stepped around the wagon to take a look at Emma's baby. "Oh Emma, she is absolutely beautiful," Hannah said as she stepped upon the wagon's wooden sidestep to better see the small child. "She has grown so much and she looks just like you."

Emma just laughed. "Thank you for saying so. Paul won't have it though. He swears that she is his spitting image."

"Let me see and I will decide who she looks like." Mandy demanded behind Hannah while yanking on her coat to get her to climb down. Mandy climbed up and looked from the baby to Emma to Paul and then back to the baby. "She definitely looks like both of you," Mandy snickered as though she had pulled a prank on them all.

Paul laughed along with her and said, "I guess I can live with that if you can Mama."

Emma playfully rolled her eyes before saying, "Whatever you say Papa."

Paul grabbed the reigns in preparation to leave as he said, "It was real nice meeting you, Seth. I hope to meet your father before he heads back south."

"It was a pleasure meeting you and Emma and the little one. If you get time, come on over to Grandma's house. I know Dad would be delighted to meet you also."

"I might just do that."

Emma waved to Hannah and Mandy as they pulled away. For a moment there seemed to be an awkward silence amongst them. But as Hannah looked around, she saw that Seth was standing there with a big grin on his face and Mandy was grinning right back.

Hannah felt like stomping her foot. "Just what are you two grinning about? Did I miss something?"

Mandy motioned with her finger for Hannah to look down in front of her. To Hannah's mortification, the front of her skirt was folded upon itself, exposing her stocking clad legs. Red-faced, Hannah quickly pushed her skirts down to once again properly cover her legs. When Hannah looked back up, she couldn't help but to burst out laughing at the comical expression on their faces. They had been holding their laughter in for her sake.

"Oh, for goodness sakes, go ahead and laugh. I don't know which is the funniest: my dress all hiked up or you two, standing there looking so goofy," Hannah said as the tears rolled freely from joy.

They all stood there and laughed with each other and at each other for what seemed like several minutes. And so a bond was made that time would prove to be unbreakable and steadfast. It was the most carefree Hannah had felt in what felt like months.

Mandy placed her hand on her chest as she made an effort to calm down enough to speak. "This has turned out to be a grand day." Turning to Hannah she said, "You see, I told you we could have a good time without Isaac and Josh."

"You are absolutely right. I should have known better than to have doubted you," Hannah agreed.

"I'm not even going to ask who Isaac and Josh are, at least not yet. I don't want to spoil our good time," Seth said a little sheepishly. "Where were you two headed before you ran into us?"

"We were going into town or rather to the schoolhouse to check on things and gather some essentials needed to prepare assignments with," Hannah answered politely.

"Don't tell me that you are the town teacher," Seth said in mock surprise.

"You sound shocked to learn this bit of news," Hannah played along.

"Well, you don't wear eye spectacles and your hair is not in a tight bun," Seth prodded.

Hannah could hear Mandy chuckling under her breath. "Like I told you before, there are not very many unmarried ladies to select from around here."

"That's too bad for both of you then. It looks like you both will be seeing a lot of me because I definitely enjoy spending time with ladies," Seth gave them an over exaggerated wink.

Mandy clapped her hands quickly together in her usual excited manner before saying, "Well I don't think that it will be such a bad thing. As a matter of fact, an unexpected friendship is a wonderful blessing. Don't you agree Hannah?"

Hannah looked into Seth's eyes and said, "Absolutely." Seth could see the vulnerability that involuntarily surfaced within Hannah's carefully controlled expression. Seth didn't think he would ever be able to stand it if she were to ever wear her heart on her sleeve. He also knew that if he was to ever be a true friend to Hannah and Mandy, he would have to reveal unto them his more serious side.

"In that case, would it be too much of an imposition if I tagged along with you both today? Maybe you could show me around and introduce me to a few people in town," Seth implored.

"Sure, we would love to," Mandy answered for them both as she so often did. Seth looked at Hannah for confirmation. She nodded her agreement, pleased that he wanted her approval as well.

For the remainder of the walk into town, they pointed out to Seth where everyone lived and a little about each family as they passed by. The area was still largely unsettled but was quickly becoming popular for cattle barons. The Indians were no longer as much of a threat but Hannah often wondered how the earlier settlers managed. She herself couldn't help but feel that the Indians were sorely mistreated. Perhaps that is why the grasshoppers came and destroyed everything in their path in the year of 1874. Hannah believed there was a time and purpose for all things.

The small assortment of buildings came into view and it looked as though Seth wouldn't be meeting many new folks today. It seems the sickness is still keeping everyone at home. Hannah wondered how the larger towns such as Deadwood and Spearfish were fairing.

"It almost looks like a ghost town instead of a quaint small and friendly town," Hannah observed aloud. "I am afraid that there will be little acquaintance making in store for you today Seth." Hannah said, this time in Seth's direction.

"What about Luke and Anna?" Mandy suggested. "I'm sure they are in."

"Who are Luke and Anna?" Seth questioned.

"Luke and Anna Calder, they own the town's general store. They are two of the nicest people you'll ever meet," Hannah told him.

"Let's go then." Seth motioned with his arms for them to lead the way. The store appeared to be vacant at first. The door was unlatched so they walked in.

Mandy yelled out their names to alert them of their presence. A few seconds later, Luke and Anna came in from the storeroom in the back.

"What a pleasant surprise! We weren't expecting anyone in today. Everything has been very quiet around here," Anna said with her naturally friendly demeanor. Her curiosity kept drawing her gaze back to Seth.

Hannah said a quick hello before stepping next to Seth and saying, "Luke and Anna, I would like for you to meet Seth Johnson. He is Ruth's grandson."

Luke quickly grabbed Seth's hand in an enthusiastic handshake. "It's an honor to meet the grandson of two of my dearest friends. If you don't mind my saying so, you remind me a great deal of your grandfather. God rest his soul."

Seth smiled, showing even white teeth. "Thank you, I count it a blessing. It's very nice to meet you both. My grandparents have told me a lot about the two of you," Seth also extended his hand towards Anna.

While Anna had Seth's attention she asked, "How is Ruth getting along dear?"

"She is doing well. My father is there with her now. It has been good for her to have him there."

"I'm glad. As soon as Luke and I are able to get away, we are going to pay her a visit," Anna said.

"I will be sure and let her know," Seth said before being drawn away by Luke to check out some new tools that had arrived a few days ago.

Hannah saw some lovely material that must have arrived recently. She supposed Luke and Anna were ordering extra stock in preparation for Christmas. The snow on the ground outside was just what the doctor ordered to put one in the holiday spirit. Mandy had wandered off in the direction of the ready-made clothes. Hannah spied the school supplies and noticed some paints that would come in handy for decoration making when the time came. She would have to wait and purchase them when she had enough money with her. The town people donated a good amount of money for school supplies at the beginning of the year. Hannah knew they would not mind a small portion going towards something that would cause such enjoyment for the children. Hannah made a mental list of the artistry supplies that she would pick up the next time she was in town.

"Hey Hannah, would you look at this dress! Isn't it just lovely?" Mandy exclaimed while holding up a long burgundy dress that was trimmed with wide, delicate, antique lace.

"It is quite stunning," Hannah smiled. "It would complement your beauty perfectly."

"You would say that no matter what I wore. In any case, it is much too expensive. I could purchase two dresses for the price of this one," said Mandy holding up the price tag for Hannah to see.

"My goodness, you are right," Hannah said. "Maybe we will have time to sew something similar before Christmas."

"Maybe but I am not holding my breath. I will be busy enough making gifts between now and then." Mandy hung the dress back up in its place with one last longing look. Hannah shook her head up and down in agreement, "I am afraid you are right."

Walking back up to the front of the store, they inquired as to where Seth was. Anna told them that Luke had taken him out back to look at the larger inventory. They said their goodbyes and went to rescue Seth before leaving.

Seth repositioned his hat on his head. "That Luke sure is a talker. I bet a stranger he's never met."

"They have no children so I guess they especially enjoy their customers company. I would say probably even more than their purchases." Hannah said as much to herself as to them.

$$\wp$$

They walked up the steps to the schoolhouse door. Hannah slowly opened the door as if afraid of what she might find on the other side. She let out a breath of relief. Everything was as she had left it.

"Wow, this is much nicer than I expected!" Seth commented as he looked around, admiring the craftsmanship of the student's desks and also that of the large teacher's desk up front.

Mandy saw Seth run his hand over the smooth wooden surface of the desk beside him. "You know, Seth, your grandfather was the one that made these beautiful pieces of furniture for the school. I was very small but I can still remember how happy everyone was when they placed them in here."

Hannah overheard their conversation and joined in as she went around gathering the necessary books needed for the assignments that she wanted to plan. "I can recall how everyone came to school that day to admire Jack's handy work. Since all of the adults kept interrupting, the children didn't have to do any work," Hannah laughed at the recollection.

"Grandpa must have really loved woodworking. He was very talented," Seth said with pride evident in his eyes.

Mandy swept out the debris that had blown in the front and side door. Seth brought in some firewood from outside so that it would be good and dry when classes took up again. Hannah divided her load up between the three of them and they left to make their way back home.

As they walked, Seth talked of his life back in Denver. He told Hannah and Mandy about his friends and about his mother's family that live close by. Mandy asked Seth if there was anyone special in his life back home. Seth informed her that there used to be but it didn't work out. He knew that it was for the best and they were just friends now.

"So this is my stop. I really enjoyed today. Next time it is my turn to be nosy," Seth grinned when the girls looked at each other uncomfortably.

Mandy was soon excited about their next get together and said, "Fair is fair. Isn't that right Hannah?"

"I suppose. There is not much to tell though," Hannah agreed although reluctantly.

"I'll still be at Hannah's tomorrow so if you want to come by we can continue our visit. What do you think Hannah?" Mandy's eyes were pleading.

"That sounds great. Come by anytime," Hannah invited.

"I just might do that, little ladies." Seth handed Hannah her books and turned as he whistled.

CHAPTER 17

Hannah could hear someone calling her name over and over again. Hannah. Hannah! No matter how hard she tried, she couldn't answer them. All around her was this thick, white fog making it impossible to see what was in front of her.

"Hannah? Hannah?" Mandy said while trying to shake Hannah awake. Slowly reality began to clear its way into Hannah's thoughts. She could feel the unfamiliar warmth beside her. The shaking became more desperate and Hannah began to open her eyes. For a moment she wondered why Mandy was there with her but the cobwebs faded and she saw the puzzled look on her cousin's face.

"I'm sorry, Mandy. I must have been sleeping pretty soundly," Hannah said while scooting up into a sitting position.

"I'll say, you must have been having some dream," Mandy said while pulling the covers closer about her.

"How long have you been awake?"

"Just a few minutes, the cold air awoke me. I thought that I heard the wind howling last night." Mandy couldn't control the shiver that traveled the length of her frame.

"As did I. Let's go and warm ourselves by the fire," Hannah said as she hopped quickly out of bed and wasted no time leaving the room.

"Good morning girls. How did you sleep?" Sophie asked when she heard them come scampering into the room.

"Great! At least until it started getting much cooler," Mandy explained.

"It sounded like we had a storm last night," Hannah said wishing to avoid her mother's question. The dream she had left her feeling very unsettled for some reason.

"It was more wind and freezing rain than snow but a good coating none the less."

"Where's Dad gone off to in such cold weather?" Hannah's eyes had searched the room for her father.

"He went to make sure the animals had plenty to eat. It seems to take more feed when the weather turns colder," Sophie replied as she poured pancake batter into the hot skillet set before her.

Hannah noticed the dark circles under her mother's eyes. "Mama, aren't you feeling well? You look rather tired this morning."

Without looking up, Sophie said, "I am fine. The storm kept me up also." Hannah didn't believe her. Her mother never would look her in the eye when she was keeping something from her. Hannah also knew when not to push for more information.

Hannah walked over to the kitchen window to look outside. The landscape took her breath away. "Mandy, come and look at what God has graced our eyes to view this morning!"

A little unwilling to leave the warmth of the fireplace until she saw the pleasure sparkle in Hannah's eyes, Mandy walked over and looked out the partially frosted glass. "Oh my goodness! Everything has a coating of ice and snow. It's a winter wonderland!" Mandy exclaimed.

"I wonder if there is enough snow to go sleigh riding." The trees were all bowed down with the weight of the ice that clung like rivers of glass over every inch. Her father's tracks out to the barn were the only disturbance to the pure, white cleanness that cloaked the earth. Winter has definitely announced its arrival.

"Come on, Hannah, let's eat. We need to decide what to do today." Mandy impatiently motioned her over to the table where a plate of hot pancakes sat waiting for her.

"I'm not surprised that you girls want to go out. The wind is still quite biting at times," Sophie warned them.

"We promise to dress warmly and Seth said that he might come by also," Mandy looked at Hannah pleadingly.

"Yes, we will dress warmly and not venture too far if that is alright," Hannah said as she sought permission with her eyes.

Sophie knew that she probably always worried too much. "Please, just take care and don't stay gone too long before coming home to warm up."

"Thank you, Mama. We will be fine. You should just rest today. I will help you with anything that needs doing tomorrow."

They ate their hearty breakfast before dressing and heading outside.

§

The ground was a hard layer of yesterday's snow with last night's ice and snow on top of that. They decided that getting the sleds out of the barn was not such a bad idea after all. Hannah went to the back of the storage section of the barn where they kept such things and saw the sled that lay next to hers. Memories came flooding in as Hannah knelt beside Toby's sled. The rope she had always used to pull him around with was still attached. Blinking back the tears that threatened to spill, Hannah reached for both of the sleds.

Thinking Mandy was coming to help her, Hannah waited before deciding to go and see what was keeping her. Hannah picked the sleds up and out of the corner and placed them beside the doorway. Looking at the many things that reminded her of Toby, Hannah felt all over again, the empty space that he had left behind in their lives. Just as Hannah turned to leave, a small wooden chest caught her eye. It was in the bottom corner under a shelf, almost invisible. She couldn't remember ever having seen it before. Hannah stretched out her arm and reached far enough to nudge it forward and grab a hold of.

"Umm, I wonder where this came from," Hannah whispered to herself. Wiping a thick layer of dust off the top of the small chest with her hand, she unlatched the lid and raised it. The inside was lined with red velvet and in the bottom laid an infant's gown along with yellow knitted booties. She raised them up to see if there was anything else underneath and found a lock of black hair with a white ribbon tied around it.

Puzzled, Hannah shut the lid and placed the small chest back where she had found it. Hannah thought that it was probably something that belonged to a relative. Mama kept hers and Toby's baby things in her bedroom along with other treasured things that she held dear.

"Guess what?" Mandy said right behind her.

"Oh! You startled me, Mandy. I didn't hear you come in," Hannah said as she regained her balance after almost falling forward onto her bent knees. Brushing the dust from the front of her skirt, Hannah replied, "What is it?"

"Seth is outside. He is talking with Uncle Roman right now. Isn't that great?"

"Yes, I didn't really expect him to come. It is a nice surprise." Hannah motioned for Mandy to grab one of the sleds while she grabbed the other and they went outside.

Seth looked over and smiled a hello as he talked. Hannah wished Isaac could meet Seth. She thought they would become fast friends. Although Hannah was feeling a little guilty for liking Seth as a friend and found herself enjoying spending time with him, on the other hand she knew Isaac spent much more time with Bella than she would care to think about.

Hannah and Mandy, well Hannah, stood patiently while Roman and Seth conversed. The sky had darkened and the clouds had brought with them a fresh burst of snow. The flakes were large and the girls held out their gloved hands to catch a glimpse of their unique formations before they melted away. Something many people missed because they never took the time to see.

Seth shook Roman's hand and headed over to where Hannah and Mandy stood waiting. "So I see what you two have planned for today," Seth observed as he looked at the sleds on the ground in front of him.

"I am kind of surprised that you were brave enough to venture out in all of this ice," Hannah bluntly said.

"Well I couldn't stand the thought of sitting in the house all day. I also knew that you two would be up to something so I decided to come on over and see what it was." Seth spread his arms wide as if to say, here I am.

"Let's go," Mandy said as she picked up the rope to one of the sleds and began to pull it after her. Seth picked up the other rope before Hannah could and said, "Where to ladies?"

"It's a ways behind the house into the woods until you come to a clearing. There is a very suitable hill that you can ride down with plenty of stopping room," Hannah explained as she pointed him in the right direction.

They walked in silence for several minutes. The scenery spoke for itself. The snow stopped but not before it had put another quick coating on the ground. They were almost to the clearing up ahead when they heard someone calling from behind. Hannah turned too quickly at the sound of Isaac's voice and she would have fallen if Seth hadn't grabbed her to steady her.

Gathering her senses, Hannah thanked Seth for his rescue. Hannah's heart picked up its tempo as it always did when Isaac was near. She waited nervously as his long legs soon closed the distance between them. As he drew near, Hannah saw an unfamiliar emotion in Isaac's eyes that she had never seen before.

Hannah walked towards Isaac with a smile and said, "Hello Isaac. I must say that I am certainly surprised to see you here."

"I gathered as much. Katie told me that you came by yesterday. I am sorry that I missed you," Isaac said with his eyes on Seth curiously.

"Isaac, this is Ruth Johnson's grandson, Seth. He and his father, Peter, are here from Denver. I'm sure you have heard her speak of them before," Hannah said.

Seth offered Isaac his right hand and said, "It is nice to meet you Isaac."

"The pleasure is mine," Isaac replied back in return. The muscle in his jaw was twitching beneath a day's growth of beard. "Hannah has told me a lot about you and your family," Seth said. He then added with a chuckle, "Also, with Mandy's help, they have filled me in on just about everyone they know around here."

"Hey there, Isaac," Mandy yelled as she retraced her steps to join them. "Where is Josh? Why didn't he come with you?" Mandy said a little breathlessly as she came to stand next to Seth.

Isaac focused his attention on Mandy. "He stayed home. He is helping Dad with the animals."

"That's too bad. We were just about to have a lot of fun," Mandy explained by pointing to the sled lying on the ground next to Seth.

"I am sure that he would have managed to come along if he knew that you were going to be here." Isaac's consoling voice did not seem to pacify Mandy.

"Maybe," Mandy said. "So where is Bella? She is usually with you." Hannah felt like telling Mandy to be quiet but knew Mandy had only spoken what she herself had already thought.

Hannah stole a quick glance at Isaac's face. She could tell that Mandy's question had irritated him a little. "She is at home with

Mom, of course. Mom was having an especially bad day and needed to be closely watched," Isaac informed them.

Hannah spoke with an apologetic tone. "I am sorry to hear that. I would like to come and see Alice as soon as Katie is cleared by the doctor."

"The doctor is supposed to stop by tomorrow. I am sure that he will find her to be completely recovered," Isaac told them. Then with a more sorrowful note he said, "I am afraid for a couple of families that the outcome was not a happy one. There were three very small children that did not make it."

Hannah's voice was choked up when she said, "We must keep the families in our prayers. Not only them but those of our neighboring communities as well who have been stricken with this awful disease."

Mandy said, "I feel so bad. Here I am having so much fun while so many have lost loved ones." Mandy turned to Seth and said, "You know that you and your family haven't been forgotten. You are still in all our prayers."

"Thanks Mandy. I appreciate that."

"So Seth, how long was you planning on staying for?" Isaac asked to lighten the mood.

"I'm not sure. My father suggested that I stay on for a while. You know, to help keep Grandma busy during these first very lonesome weeks. I am still thinking on how long that I wish to stay away from home and my responsibilities there."

"Oh please say you will stay for a long visit!" Mandy practically jumped as she spoke to emphasize her approval.

"Well that is an invitation that is hard to turn down," Seth laughed. "What are we all standing here for? Let's go have some of that fun that Mandy has been itching to have."

Hannah turned to Isaac and asked, "Can you stay for a while?"

Isaac's gaze was intense when he replied, "If you are sure you want me to." His answer made her uncomfortable.

Hannah took his hand and said, "Of course I do. Don't joke around like that." It felt good to have Isaac by her side again. He seemed a little distracted as they made their way up the hill behind Seth and Mandy. Hannah's mind had been so cluttered with worry and doubt that she had almost forgotten how Isaac's mere presence affected her.

"Hurry up! The snow is going to melt before you two get up here," Mandy exaggerated in fun.

"Just hold on to your horses. We will have a race to the bottom of the hill," Isaac suggested with a little enthusiasm of his own.

Hannah saw Mandy jump up and down and clap her hands together. She was already instructing Seth on where she wanted him to sit on the sled. Seth just threw his hands up and did as he was told.

Soon they were off down the hill on their sleds, the girls in front with the guys on the back. Isaac and Seth lost their hats on the way down the hill. The race was close but Mandy and Seth won by just a few feet. Hannah wouldn't have had it any other way. She knew that Mandy had a competitive side that did not like to lose. While Mandy was exclaiming about the close race, she was suddenly hit square in the chest with a snowball. That did it. She fired back at Isaac and soon they were each participating in an all-out snowball war.

Hannah knew that this would be a memory long remembered. She couldn't recall when she had felt so carefree. After everyone had yelled uncle, they grabbed their sleds and took a couple of more rides down the hill. Hannah hated to see the excitement come to an end but they were cold and wet from their snowball fight. They walked back to the house. Hannah and Mandy walked ahead of Isaac and Seth. Hannah was pleased that Isaac was getting to know Seth.

℘

When they reached the house, Hannah invited the guys in to warm themselves.

Sophie turned around from stirring a simmering pot of beef stew to greet Isaac and Seth. "Hello, you are just in time for some hot stew. I hope you both can stay."

"You can count me in Mrs. Jamison. My mouth is already watering," Seth responded eagerly.

"Sophie, you know I am always open to one of your delicious meals. Beef stew sounds perfect, thank you." Isaac and Seth got more acquainted while they ate their meal together.

Hannah noticed that Mandy seemed to be somewhat withdrawn which was not like her at all. If anything was wrong, Hannah knew that Mandy would put a voice to her worries soon enough.

"Mama, where is Dad?" Hannah asked.

"He came in and ate his dinner a little while ago. He said that he had to go and check on one of his first time mothers to make sure she was still doing well," Sophie said as she drank a cup of coffee while the rest of them ate their dinner.

"So, Isaac, why haven't we seen much of you and Josh lately?" Mandy asked.

Isaac looked at Hannah before speaking. "Dad has been trying to get caught up around the place so that he can spend more time with Mom. We didn't realize that there was so much to do until we started checking everything out. I'm sorry if we have been neglectful."

Mandy's eyebrows were raised in indignation. She said, "A word or two would have been nice. Isn't that right Hannah?"

Startled at being brought into the exchange, Hannah said, "Yes, a word would have been appreciated."

Isaac smiled slowly and charmingly and replied, "We will surely try and do better from now on." A loud pounding on the door broke up the conversation between them. Sophie swiftly rose and went to answer the door to see who was being so persistent.

As soon as she swung open the door, an out of breath Bella ran straight to Isaac. "Isaac, you have to come home immediately. It's your mother. She has taken a turn for the worse," Bella laid her hand upon Isaac's shoulder as she spoke excitedly.

Isaac took Bella by the shoulders. "Calm down and tell me exactly what has happened."

Bella raised beautiful eyes to Isaac and said, "She had just eaten her dinner and was resting as if to take her afternoon nap. She then all of a sudden opened her eyes and clutched at her chest with her hands. I immediately sent Katie after your father and brother."

"When they got there, how was she doing then?" Isaac questioned.

Bella dabbed at her eyes with an expensively crocheted handkerchief before saying, "She had lost consciousness. Your father sent Josh after Doctor Hayes and me after you."

Isaac turned to Hannah and said, "I'm sorry. I must go."

"Yes, of course you do. Shall I come with you?" Hannah suggested.

"No, I must hurry home. I will take Bella's horse and she can fetch mine out of the barn and bring it back after me."

Sophie said as they went out the door, "Our prayers are with you."

Hannah stood up and walked over to the window and looked out. Bella was quickly out of the barn and following close behind Isaac. Hannah wished that she could be there for Isaac. She should be the one caring for Alice and helping the family. Hannah chided herself for her thoughts. The important thing was that Alice would soon get well. Everything else would take care of itself.

"So that was Bella White. Wow!" Seth said with that sheepish look of his.

Mandy and Hannah both turned "don't you dare say another word" eyes on him.

"Oh, don't go and get your dander up. She doesn't hold a candle to you two." Seth crossed his arms over his chest and stared right back at them.

"Since we will probably have to wait until tomorrow for any news of Alice, why don't we all just enjoy one another's company for the rest of the afternoon?" Sophie placed a plate of oatmeal cookies on the table that she had made earlier that morning.

Sophie hated to see the troubled look return to her daughter's face when only moments ago she was more like her old self. She and Roman had been praying fervently for a healing of their little community. To see a time of the rebuilding of the hope that will lift their spirits again.

CHAPTER 18

The rest of the week seemed to go by slowly. Mandy had left early the next day when Uncle Jacob had come by to accompany her home. Roman had ridden over to the Daniels' farm to check on Alice's condition. Doctor Hayes was there when he arrived so he waited outside until he came out. The doctor and Isaac came out and informed Roman of her condition when they were finished. The attack had set her back into an especially weakened state and she would not be allowed visitors for a while.

Hannah and her mother spent the next couple of days going through their sewing supplies. They had much of what they needed to start making their Christmas gifts. Hannah had already gotten a very productive start on a beautiful silvery-gray shawl for Grandma Rose. Sophie chose some flannel material to make a warm quilt for Jacob and Sarah. With

Thanksgiving coming in just a few days, it was time to get busy. Hannah was determined to let the joy of the season to work its magic, to allow her heart to be light and her thoughts to be pure.

$$\wp$$

It was Saturday morning when they finally received word that their time of confinement was over. Doctor Hayes had stopped by after seeing Alice to inform them that everyone should go about their normal routines beginning Monday morning. Hannah asked the doctor how Alice was fairing. He told them that there was a slight improvement but she had a long road to recovery ahead of her. He said that he would allow only limited visitation for the time being.

Hannah helped her mother catch up on the household chores and then spent the rest of the weekend preparing class work and other more enjoyable projects for her students. She needed to get back to her teaching, more probably for herself than for her students. She needed to keep busy so that her mind would stop dwelling on the unknown. Thanksgiving was this upcoming week so they would have a short week for their first few days back to school.

⌇

Sunday night Hannah was having trouble getting to sleep. The wind kept howling making it impossible for her to ignore the screeching of the tree limbs against her bedroom window. She climbed from her bed and made her way towards the kitchen for a warm glass of milk. She felt a cold draft and tightened the belt on her housecoat. She immediately noticed the front door was slightly ajar. *"Why was the door opened?"* thought Hannah to herself. Thinking to shut the door, she walked over and reached for the knob but halted when she caught sight of a flicker of light out in the distance. Hannah turned to go and get her father but was startled to find him standing directly behind her.

"What is going on? Did you see the light outside?" Hannah questioned him nervously.

"Come Hannah and close the door. There is no cause for you to worry," Roman told his daughter in a calm voice. Roman ushered his daughter into the kitchen and began to prepare her the warm glass of milk that she had forgotten to do, when she became alarmed by the light outside. Hannah waited for her father to explain what was happening. She looked around for her mother but assumed that she was either in bed or outside.

"Why would Mama be outside at this time of night?" thought Hannah as she watched her father pour them both a full glass of warm milk.

"Hannah I am sorry that you were startled a few moments ago and are probably wondering what is going on." Roman tried to explain without worrying his daughter, at least no more than she already was.

"Is that Mama out there by Toby's grave?" Hannah asked.

"Yes. She has many sleepless nights and for some reason she feels the need to go out there no matter what hour of the night it may be. She goes less often than she did at first but she has never completely stopped," Roman said without being successful at hiding his own worry completely.

"Isn't there something that we can do to help? How could I have not known how hard she has been grieving?" Hannah asked with desperation in her voice.

"We will just have to wait until she is ready to talk. She knows we are here for her," Roman patted his daughter's hand. Finish your milk and go on back to bed before she comes back in. She will only worry the more if she thinks that you are upset."

"You are right. I will." Hannah drank her milk quickly and gave her father a hasty hug before going back to her room.

Hannah lay awake until long after she heard the front door open and close again. When she did finally fall asleep, she dreamed once again of the cloaked figure that was continually close behind her. She awoke from her sleep and dream sitting straight up in the bed. Hannah untangled her gown and covers from about her and lay back down in hopes of a couple more hours of sleep before she had to rise again.

The aroma of coffee reached Hannah's senses causing her to stir and to stretch in wakefulness. She had hoped to be much more rested as she headed out to school this day. She was actually tempted to have a cup of that coffee which to her smelled significantly better than it tasted. Hannah reluctantly climbed out of bed and quickly washed and dressed before going and having some breakfast. Sophie looked up at the sound of

Hannah's entrance into the kitchen. Sophie's bright smile did much to lift her daughter's spirits.

Hannah could not help but wonder if the smile was a true indicator of her mother's feelings or if it was just a camouflage for her sake. "Are you ready to get back to teaching?" Sophie asked.

Hannah finished swallowing a bite of bacon before saying, "Yes. What will you be doing today?"

"Your father and I are going into town to pick up some special items for Thanksgiving dinner. Can I get you anything while I am there?" Sophie offered.

"No, I don't think so but if I think of anything I can pick it up since I am close by anyway." Hannah was relieved that her mother was getting out for a while today. It would surely do her good.

Sophie laughed softly and said, "I have a feeling there will be several people in town today after the mandatory shut in that we have all endured over the past number of days."

"I would say that you are probably right," Hannah snickered a little. Hannah ate the last of her biscuit and jelly and went to put on her coat and warm accessories. Grabbing her books and kissing her mother's cheek, she went out and braved the cold trip to the schoolhouse.

℘

The morning air did much to revive her body of its sleepless night. Several of the children were already outside playing when she walked into the schoolyard. It was soul-cheering to hear the laughter ring out once again. Hannah looked on down the road that took you further into the main town and saw that there were indeed several people already milling about. Laughing to herself, Hannah thought of what her mother had said earlier.

Hannah was greeted by a nice warm room upon her entrance. She was thankful to be surrounded by such thoughtful people like Luke and Anna. She arranged her books and papers on her desk before going to call on the children. She was pleased to see that she had perfect attendance for their first day back.

The day seemed to pass swiftly by. They had worked in each one of their subjects with much attentiveness after having been away and coming back more rested and alert. They even had time to work on their special Thanksgiving projects at the end of the day. Hannah's heart went out to one of her students who had lost a baby brother to the dreadful disease that had plagued their community.

After dismissing the students, Hannah made a list of things needed to complete her plans for the holiday season. As soon as the fire had died down enough to leave, she swept her eyes over the room to make sure all was in order for the next day.

Hannah donned her coat, scarf and gloves and stepped out the door. She noticed that it was beginning to look later as it was the time of year that the days grew shorter. She would not have time to dawdle if she wanted to get home well before dark. Hannah greeted several people on her way to the general store.

ॐ

She almost ran right into Katherine Barkley when she stepped out her door onto the boardwalk right in front of her. It had been quite a spell since Hannah had last spoken with Katherine. She knew that she must stop long enough so as to inquire of her welfare.

"Hannah, dear, it is so good to run in to you," Katherine spoke first. Katherine leaned upon the door frame as if too tired to stand alone. Hannah thought Katherine seemed to be somewhat agitated.

She calmly replied, "It is so nice to see you, Katherine. How have you been fairing these past worrisome days?"

Letting her shoulders sag as if very weary she said, "I am doing well, I suppose, but I was wondering if you have spoken with Bella lately."

"Why yes. It hasn't been long since I last spoke with her. Is something wrong?" Hannah asked.

"I am not sure. She hasn't been by to see me in ever so long. She must know that I am worried about her. At the very least, she might have checked on my welfare." Katherine was almost in tears as she voiced her troubled thoughts to Hannah.

Hannah tried to reassure her. "I can tell you that Bella is doing fine and that she is still staying with and caring for Alice Daniels. I do not know the reason for her neglect in checking on you and your wellbeing."

Hannah laid a comforting hand on Katherine's shoulder before saying, "If you like I can find a way to get word to her of your concern if I see anyone who will be going that way."

"Thank you dear. I would be ever so grateful. I hope you and your family are well and please give them my best," Katherine said in a stronger voice than before.

"I must be going now. It was good to see you," Hannah patted her shoulder once more before walking away. Katherine turned and walked back inside as if somewhat appeased.

Greeting several acquaintances as she continued on her way to her intended destination, Hannah was not surprised to see a number of familiar people coming and going from the general store. She wanted to get ingredients for a special dish to take to Isaac and his family for Thanksgiving. At the rate at which people were shopping, she would likely start to find many of the store shelves beginning to empty.

Hannah was soon stepping back outside onto the boardwalk in thankful relief with her purchases tucked away in her arms. The sun was low in the sky. She would have to soon start thinking about riding her horse to school for she didn't want to be caught out after dark without her.

There were some new faces that she didn't recognize in town today. She knew that there were cattle drives being made through the area before winter. The land was fast becoming a cattle baron's paradise. Progress always seemed to steal the simplicity from life.

℘

Hannah's restless night began to catch up with her on her way home. She was unable to take in the sounds around her as she usually liked to do. She simply could not keep from yawning. Her mind was only half aware of her surroundings when the snapping of a twig startled her into alertness. Hannah quickly scanned the woods to her right where the sound had come from. It sounded like a large branch or stick that had snapped. A small animal was definitely not in question here was Hannah's first conclusion. It was hard to see through the dense trees with dusk already beginning to fall upon the forest, the black barked pine trees only aiding the obscurity.

Hannah felt a shiver run through her. She could feel eyes upon her. Man or beast, she did not know. Hannah did not know why but for some reason her dream came before her mind's eye. She knew something was wrong and she knew the answer was close. Hannah turned and began to walk briskly towards home, trying to resist the urge to look back. Who or what was back there had definitely succeeded in spooking her, if that was the intention. She had never felt threatened or unsafe before, that she could remember anyway.

By the time that she had reached her front yard, she had convinced herself that she had probably just blown everything out of proportion. She knew of no one that would want any harm to come to her.

❧

Hannah entered the house to find her father at the table and her mother at the stove. Hannah's sigh of relief did not go unnoticed by her parents when she came in and sat down at the table across from her father. Slowly taking a sip of his coffee, Roman gave his daughter time to talk about what was on her mind.

After a moment, Roman set his cup down and asked, "How was your day, Hannah? Did everything go well?"

Hannah's eyes brightened a little at the thought of seeing the children again. She answered, "Oh, yes, things went splendidly well. It even seemed as if the children were happy to return to school if you can believe that."

Hannah's beautiful features then just as quickly began to tense up again with unwanted thoughts.

Sophie joined them as she sat a glass of warm milk in front of her daughter on the table. "You look a little flushed. Are you sure that you feel well?" Sophie asked with concern etched in her own face.

Hannah nervously ran her fingertip along the rim of her glass as she spoke. "I guess I just got a little spooked on my way home this evening. I heard a loud noise to my right in the forest but I couldn't see what had caused it."

"What kind of noise?" Her mother asked.

Hannah had been keeping her head down in fear of appearing foolish to her parents. Raising her eyes Hannah said, "It was like a large stick snapping in two. My first thought was that it was a rather large animal but I never saw one. Then I came to the conclusion that someone was out there watching me. This thought bothered me even more than the first."

"You more than likely would have seen the animal. They either would have run away or stood and stared at you," Roman concluded. "Although the bears are preparing for hibernation, there are still a number of large animals such as the elk, mountain lion or bison that are in the area."

"Maybe it was too dark for you to see what was out there," Sophie suggested hopefully.

Hannah shook her head up and down in agreement with her mother. "It was beginning to darken along the edge of the trees. But it wasn't just the noise that bothered me so much," Hannah paused before continuing because she didn't want to sound unreasonable.

"It was the feeling that seemed to saturate my being, a feeling as dark as the forest was fast becoming."

"Oh Hannah, surely you were just scared. I can't believe anyone around here would have reason to do such a thing. I can't bear the thought of any harm coming to you," Sophie said as she frantically cradled her head upon her hands in weak defeat.

Hannah quickly realized that she had made a mistake in confiding to her parents, especially her mother. She looked to her father for guidance. He would know how to calm her mother's fears.

Roman quickly added, "I am sure that you are right, Sophie. I can think of no one that would have aught against our Hannah."

He then turned his gaze upon his daughter and spoke in a tone that tolerated no argument. "Just to be on the safe side, I will escort Hannah to and from school for the next several days." Hannah opened her mouth to speak but knew her father would not let her go against his wishes.

"I really wish that I had not brought this matter to their attention," thought Hannah regretfully.

"Furthermore I think that it is time to start taking the horses since the days are becoming much shorter and the weather is becoming more unpredictable," her father stated.

"That sounds like a fine idea Roman. I will feel much better if you are with her." Sophie's relieved words were what Roman wanted to hear.

"I hate to be so much trouble. Just being on horseback would be a great comfort." Hannah gave one last stab for her independence.

"Nonsense, it will only be for a few days. Maybe your mother will venture out and ride along with us part of the time. The fresh air will do her good." Roman looked at his wife hopefully.

Sophie smiled back, making no promises. The matter settled, Sophie rose to place supper on the table. Hannah did not have much of an appetite. She just didn't understand why things couldn't go smoothly for a change. *"What was she doing wrong?"* She wondered. *"Was everything really just her imagination? After all, what proof did she actually have that any of her concerns were warranted?"*

$$\wp$$

After pushing her food around on her plate, Hannah excused herself and went to her room to change into her everyday clothes. She helped her mother clean up the supper dishes while they discussed the holiday menu. Hannah also described the projects that she had planned for the students over the next couple of days. There were some items that she needed to collect outside such as turkey feathers and some of the colorful field corn that was out in the barn drying out.

Sophie retired to the rocking chair to finish up one of the gifts that she had been working on.

❧

Hannah slid her boots and coat on to venture out into the now starlit sky and glowing moonlit night. She grabbed the lantern from its hook where they kept it within easy reach. Between the cloudless sky and the soft light of the lantern, Hannah could see quite well. The call of the wolves in the distance gave an eerie feel to her already taunt nerves. Every sound seemed to be magnified to her ears. She had asked her father where everything was before she came out.

When she reached the barn door, she could hear the horses acting a bit restless. Hannah hung the lantern on an iron hook just inside the door as she entered. After calming the horses, Hannah got busy searching for her wanted items. She found everything except for the turkey feathers which were kept up in the loft. Hannah decided to light another lantern for extra brightness. She took her time going through the feathers in order to choose the most colorful ones.

She heard the horses moving in their stalls again. Rising from her knees, Hannah picked up her choice feathers carefully. A strange smell reached her senses. The smell of smoke was her first thought but she dismissed it quickly. She continued placing feathers in a neat pile before returning the unwanted ones back to their place. The smell became stronger. Hannah walked over to the loft's edge and was terrified to see the straw on fire in front of the barn door. She flew down the ladder, almost getting tangled up in her long skirt, and grabbed one of the large horse blankets hanging over the stall rail.

With great determination, Hannah managed to choke out the flames with the blanket and a bucket of water that was always full for the horses when they needed a refill.

Hannah stood completely stunned and horrified at the still smoldering floor and barn door. The flames had even begun licking their way up the first post of the horse's stall. Hannah looked to the hook where the lantern had been hanging securely. It now lay in burnt ruins directly below its appointed place of occupancy for years.

Hannah tried to think back to when she had first entered the barn. She couldn't remember for sure if she had closed the door behind her or not. Her next thought was that she did not recall hearing the lantern fall from its hook. She would have heard it as it crashed to the ground. She also remembered the horses acting agitated when she first came in and then again just before the fire started.

"Something was very amiss here," Hannah said aloud to herself. She had never been so careless before. No. The only explanation was that someone else had been there. She could think of no other plausible explanation. An explanation that she knew she must keep to herself for the time being.

"One thing was for sure," Hannah told herself. "If I wasn't spooked from my walk home earlier, I definitely am now." Hannah knew that this was not some harmless prank. Things were becoming very serious. After sweeping and cleaning up the mess the best that she could, she took a deep breath and headed out the door to explain the situation to her parents.

Hannah cautiously left the barn. Her senses tuned to every sound about her, every shadow catching her eye. The trip from the barn to the house seemed like a mile. When Hannah entered the door, she did not have to say a word. Her carefully planned explanation went unheeded as soon as her mother saw her. She didn't realize her face was smudged with soot and her clothes were even blacker.

"Hannah, whatever happened to you?!!" Sophie burst out as she ran to her daughter's side.

Roman rose from his chair in front of the fireplace almost as quickly. Leading them over to the kitchen table he said, "Come, we will take a seat while we let Hannah tell us what happened out there."

Hannah spoke as calmly as she could for her parent's sake. "I guess that I accidently caught the barn on fire."

"Caught the barn on fire?!" Roman barked as he ran to the door and opened it up to see out to the barn.

Hannah spoke loudly to gain her father's attention. "No, I mean I did catch it on fire but it is ok now. I am so sorry!"

"Thank the good Lord that you are alright. But how did it happen?" Sophie asked much calmer than before.

Taking a deep breath Hannah said, "I am not really sure myself exactly how it happened. The lantern must have fallen from its hook. I had no idea that it had until I smelled the smoke. The lantern lay amongst the burnt remains." Hannah's eyes were watering. She knew it was because of the ordeal but her parents would probably assume it was from the smoke.

"Don't worry daughter. Sometimes these things happen. We must be thankful things were no worse than what they were. You could have been seriously hurt."

Sophie hugged her daughter closely. "Your father is right. Let us go and get you cleaned up and then we will have some hot cocoa."

Roman stood and grabbed his coat from beside the door before turning and saying, "I will check to make sure things are well with the animals."

What Roman didn't say was the same thing that he knew his daughter had chosen to allow remain unspoken. It was not like Hannah to be so careless. Things just did not seem right, were his thoughts concerning the events happening to Hannah this evening.

Hannah went off to bed as soon as she finished her warm drink. She had put on a face for as long as she could for her mother. Her troubled mind prayed often throughout the night. She knew that in time, that which was hidden would be brought to light.

CHAPTER 19

The next morning Roman did exactly as he said that he would. He was ready and waiting outside with Hannah's horse saddled beside his own. Hannah also noticed that her father had hung a sack of Indian corn and carefully wrapped feathers from her saddle.

It was all Hannah could do to keep from letting the tears course down her cheeks. "Thank you, Dad. I had completely forgotten why I had gone into the barn in the first place," Hannah said with a shaky voice full of emotion.

"Everything is fine in the barn. It's a beautiful day for a ride. I thought that I would even go and see Grandma and Jacob while I am out. I would like to make sure they will all be over for Thanksgiving dinner on Thursday," Roman said trying to steer his daughter's thoughts away from yesterday's events.

"I can't wait. I am thinking about letting school out a little early tomorrow. Do you think that would be ok with all of the student's parents?"

Roman scratched his unshaven chin as if to think it over. He then turned and said with a smile, "I don't see why not. It would probably be a good idea to send a note home with the children today informing the parents though."

"That is just what I will do then. I also thought it would allow me more time to help Mama get started on the cooking."

"Then it's all settled." Hannah knew how very blessed she was to have two God fearing parents. They had taught her of God's ways from her youth up. She knew now after having been amongst children not as fortunate, the difference that it made in a child's life. She hoped that by prayer and example that she could, with God's help, be an influence to those in need.

Hannah pulled her coat more closely about her as they road in silence. The wind had decided to get an early start this morning. Even though the sun was bright and the sky was cloudless, Hannah felt gloomy inside. Her thoughts were that she wished that she had someone she could confide in, really confide in. She believed that even Isaac would think that she was overreacting. No, she would not burden him with her problems anyway. He had enough worries of his own over his poor, sick mother.

They were soon pulling up to the front steps of the schoolhouse. The smoke was curling from the chimney sending a warm invitation to enter. Roman opened the door for Hannah before leaving to take her horse to the stables to board until school let out.

Hannah quickly got started on the student's projects for which they will be spending a good part of the next two days working on. Soon the entire day passed so fast, it was soon time to lay their work to the side and go home for the day. The children had accomplished much and Hannah was very proud of them. Hannah's mind was exhausted for no matter how hard she tried to keep busy, the events of the day before kept haunting her.

Her father was there waiting when all the students had left. He too seemed to be preoccupied with distant thoughts as they road back and forth the next day also. Hannah felt miserable being the cause of the tense expression that graced her father's usually carefree one. Hannah kept telling herself that surely things would brighten up over the holidays.

ᦓ

That evening Hannah and her mother busied themselves with desserts for the dinner. They made pumpkin pies, which were a special treat this year only because Luke had saved them one that had come in with his orders. They also made a pound cake and molasses cake to boot. By the time Grandma Rose and Aunt Sarah brought food and dessert, there would be enough food to feed the whole town.

Hannah had thought to take some food over to the Daniels family but decided against it. She knew it was just pride talking but why must she be the one always trying to find ways to see Isaac, not that she didn't think so very much of his family but she would not chase him. Hannah then told herself that it was more a sense of principle than pride.

That night as Hannah looked into her dressing mirror, she had the same drawn look upon her face as the one that she had seen on her father's. She picked up her Bible and took it to bed with her. She awoke the next morning with the Bible still opened and feeling much more rested.

§

The house was filled with the smell of spices and she couldn't wait for the rest of the family to get there. By the noon hour, they had managed all of the cooking and had a beautifully set table in anticipation of the gathering loved ones. Hannah took advantage of the spare time to ready herself for the day ahead. The bedroom was even cozily warmed because of all of the cooking and baking they had done that morning. They would probably have to let the fire die down in the kitchen stove to keep the temperature down from the extra bodies in the house.

Hannah chose to wear her hair up to feel more comfortable which only accented her delicate features and somewhat too full lips that were overly red from her biting them in nervousness the last couple of days. She wore a simple gray blouse with an unencumbered navy skirt. Hannah was just leaving her room when she heard the commotion in the front room.

The family had arrived and with bells on it would appear. "Hannah, where are you?" Mandy's voice was already cheering up her day. "Look who we brought with us," Mandy said as Hannah entered the now quite crowded room.

Hannah's eyes traveled the room until she set her eyes upon Seth and his grandmother, Ruth. "What a lovely surprise. No one mentioned that you and your grandmother for sure would be joining us," Hannah said as she walked closer to where Mandy and Seth were standing.

"Grandma Rose was adamant that Ruth spend the holidays with us this year. I guess we will just have to put up with Seth as well," Mandy rolled her eyes in mock dislike.

Hannah hugged Mandy and said, "Oh you silly goose. It is a good thing that Seth has you and I all figured out or he might become offended at our playful banter."

"I don't think I will ever have you women all figured out. I'll just have to stay on my toes when I am around you two lovelies," Seth rejoined right back as usual while receiving a friendly hug from Hannah as well.

"I am sorry that your father had to return home so soon. It would have been nice to have enjoyed his company as well," Hannah told Seth.

"He had to get back to Mom. It is difficult for her to care for Grandmother as well as the ranch on her own," Seth replied.

"Of course, we understand completely," Hannah returned. Hannah excused herself and went to help her mother and Aunt Sarah get ready for the dinner.

Soon they had all gathered around the table and bowed their heads. Roman gave a very heartfelt thanks for their many blessings and the faith to see them through their trials. Grandma Rose and Ruth began to reminisce about childhood Thanksgivings of long ago. Grandma Rose told them all about how they as children would never have had such a bountiful table of food like the one set before them now. Some years, they were fortunate if they had a turkey and a few potatoes to eat.

Grandma Rose had a faraway look in her eyes as she spoke, "But you know we were always a close family and most especially close to God."

Ruth chose that moment to join in to say, "We were very much the same. Through my childhood and in to adulthood, I saw God answer many, many prayers for us. My trust and faith grew. I saw too many miracles take place for anything to make me waiver."

Grandma Rose wiped her eyes with a table napkin before saying, "Yes, to those looking on it would appear unto them that we were always wanting. Little did they know that we were being blessed beyond measure." The small exchange between the two elderly women left everyone else at the table rethinking their worries.

They all continued their meal with more stories of times past, feeling a little more light-hearted and a great deal humbler.

The men had stepped outside to talk while there was still some daylight left. The women cleaned the kitchen in the pleasure of each other's company. Mandy never stopped talking as she washed one dish after another. Hannah paused to look around. She wanted to remember this Thanksgiving. She wanted to start treasuring every special family gathering instead of taking them for granted. Sophie went and called the men folk back inside once the kitchen had been cleared. The aroma of a fresh pot of coffee brewing rode on the air in the small house. The crackling of the flames that strove to finger their way up the chimney put a feeling of relaxing comfort to their overworked minds.

Jacob went to the small table beside Roman's chair and picked up a song book and reached it to his mother.

Grandma Rose willingly accepted the love worn songbook and said, "What is it you would like to hear, son?" Jacob's voice was a little raspy as he requested, "I'd like to hear "Amazing Grace" and then whatever else you have a mind to."

Everyone found a seat and began to sing along as Grandma Rose led them. As the evening went on, they all seemed to have a particular song that they wanted to hear. Hannah made sure that Seth had a songbook in case he was unfamiliar with some of the hymns. She took notice of the curious look upon his face that he unknowingly displayed. Hannah assumed that Seth's family was not in the habit of singing together with such enjoyment.

It was fast becoming dark and Jacob thought it was time that they must be leaving. Although everyone was hesitant to get moving, they were a little appeased when he reminded them that Christmas was soon around the corner and they would all gather again. While the women wrapped themselves warmly, Jacob and Seth stepped outside to ready the horses and to light the lanterns they had hung on their wagons to help guide their way.

§

The next morning, Roman informed Hannah that he and Seth had come to an agreement concerning her safety to and from town. Roman saw the defiant look enter Hannah's eyes quickly.

Before she could protest, Roman immediately said, "I know that you probably didn't want me to mention anything about our concerns but I thought it wouldn't hurt to have an extra set of eyes looking out for you. It will only be for a couple of weeks."

"What kind of agreement are you talking about?" Hannah asked as she fought hard to control the irritation in her voice. She knew better than to show any disrespect to her father.

"I will continue to ride along with you in the mornings while Seth has kindly offered to escort you home in the evenings," Roman said. He also added when Hannah opened her mouth to speak, "Now I realize how independent you are by nature, but under the circumstances, it will not hurt to be on the cautious side just for a short time."

"Yes, Father, if you think that it is absolutely necessary."

"Good." Roman was glad to have gotten that out of the way. He could see his daughter wanting to buck at the arrangement but was pleased that she was able to control her stubborn nature.

✀

The rest of the weekend was spent making presents and new decorations for the tree. They would always go as a family and hunt for a tree a few days before Christmas. Hannah even talked her mother into going out and collecting pinecones to paint.

✀

Come Sunday morning, the entire church house was full. Everyone was so happy to see one another after the long absence. The church service and singing was thankfully taken in by hungry hearts. It seemed that everyone had something to contribute to the meeting, even if it was to sit and let the tears flow.

Hannah had noticed that Isaac was not at church. She knew that he must have stayed home with his mother. She had high hopes of him being there today. Katie had informed her at school that her mother was only slowly improving.

When church had let out, Hannah made her way over to where the rest of the Daniels family stood outside the church house.

Hannah smiled and said, "It is so wonderful to see you all. I trust you all had a happy Thanksgiving."

Andrew gave Hannah a warm embrace. "It is good to see you also, Hannah. I trust you and your family had a good holiday as well. Alice was able to sit with us at the table for a short spell. We are very thankful indeed."

"I am so pleased for you," Hannah said in return. "I presume Isaac stayed home with his mother this day," Hannah inquired and stated at the same time.

"Yes. We urged Bella to spend some time with her Cousin Katherine today since she insisted on staying and cooking for us on the holiday. I don't know what we would do without her," Andrew replied.

"I'm sure," Hannah could think of no other words.

Hannah excused herself as others came to inquire of Alice's health. She saw Josh and Mandy laughing and talking off by themselves. She was just about to climb up onto the wagon when someone called out her name from behind. "Miss Jamison. Hannah Jamison?" A very tall and middle-aged man said.

"Yes, I am Hannah Jamison. How can I help you?"

The man initiated a handshake before saying, "My name is Jake Chesterfield. This is my son, Carl."

Hannah accepted his handshake and reached out to Carl as well before she replied, "It's nice to meet you both." Hannah waited to see what the man wanted to talk to her about.

"I hear that you are the town's teacher." Hannah nodded her head yes to his question and he continued on.

"I was wondering if it would be alright for you to accept Carl as one of your students." Hannah was a little surprised by the request. It must have showed on her face.

Mr. Chesterfield quickly added, "I know Carl looks kind of old to be going to school but he is only sixteen and his schooling is lacking to say the least."

"Yes. Please send him to school in the morning. He is very welcome." Hannah said to Mr. Chesterfield while looking at Carl also.

"Yes, Miss Jamison. Thank you!"

Hannah stared as they turned and walked to their horses. She had not noticed them in church. "*How could she have missed them,*" she thought to herself. She had many questions going through her mind. On the way, her parents confirmed that the Chesterfields were not in the church house that morning. Roman's only guess was that they were waiting outside for church to be over in order to speak with Hannah. It was a bit of a mystery to them because no one had mentioned having seen or heard of them being in town or moving nearby.

Roman worried about a student that was a stranger and much older and larger than he felt comfortable with Hannah being in charge of. He was uneasy.

CHAPTER 20

Hannah awoke the next morning a bit anxious about her new student. She hoped that he would get along well with the rest of the children and not disrupt the comradery among them. Hannah chided herself for judging the young man before she even got to know him. It was not like her to be so unfair.

Roman left his daughter at a warm schoolhouse and went to visit with Luke for a spell after he dropped Hannah's horse off at the stables. His true intention was to remain in town for a while, until he saw how things were going with Hannah and the new student. He also thought Luke might have some information on the newcomers. Roman politely greeted several men who were standing about on his way to the store. Luke caught sight of Roman immediately.

The storekeeper rushed to greet him with enthusiasm. "Roman so good to have you stop in. Did Sophie come along with you?" The unkempt store owner stretched forth his hand.

Although his appearance might not be as tidy as some would expect, there was not a more honest or friendlier person to be found.

Roman shook his extended hand and said, "No. She is resting up over the busy weekend. How is Anna? I don't see her anywhere."

"Fine, fine, she is still in the back. Can I get you anything? We have gotten stocked up on just about everything for the Christmas season," Luke offered.

"Well, actually, I am here looking for some information," Roman paused to better gain Luke's attention. "Do you know anything about the new neighbors we have by the name of Chesterfield?"

Luke scratched his chin in thought before saying, "Yes, Paul Sullivan was in one-day last week and he mentioned having some new neighbors move in next to his property. He said that they had been there a few weeks before he even knew it. He said that they pretty much like keeping to themselves."

"I was only curious because the boy is starting school today. I hope he is well behaved and there are no problems," Roman's concern was evident on his face.

"If it would make you feel better, I can go over and check on the wood supply and make sure all is well later on today," Luke kindly offered.

"Yes, that would make me feel a lot better. I appreciate that very much, Luke."

"Think nothing of it. I am glad to do it."

Feeling somewhat relieved Roman rode slowly by the schoolhouse on his way home. The children were starting to gather in and after scanning the area, he saw Carl walking slowly behind the rest of the children up the steps and into the building. The young man looked familiar to Roman. He didn't get a close look at his father yesterday after the church service. He would have to try and remember where it was that he had seen him before. All of this stuff with Hannah was beginning to make him suspicious or "spooked" as his daughter would put it.

Hannah called roll and got everyone started on their reading assignments so that she could spend time analyzing what stage Carl was at in all of the subjects. So far, it appeared that Carl was a well-mannered and well behaved student. Hannah had been very nervous initially but was beginning to become more relaxed and confident as the morning went on.

Just before the noon hour, a light knock was heard at the door. Hannah allowed one of the students to open it and grant Luke entrance. He announced that he was just checking on the wood supply, as well as, add an armload to the wood box by the back door.

"Thank you Luke. Please send Anna my greetings," Hannah smiled with a nod of reassurance as Luke smiled back and waved in his departure. Hannah knew that he was just checking in on her. More than likely her father has been talking to him.

It seemed her father had several people watching out for her. First it was Seth and now Luke has been recruited. Hannah checked Carl's math and spelling abilities while the students were having their lunch recess. It seemed that judging by the written skills tests on these subjects that he was somewhat behind but not as far as she had feared. She would be able to get him started as soon as they returned from lunch.

Checking the watch that she kept in her dress pocket, Hannah saw that there was still some time to go outside and grab a quick bite of her own lunch before resuming class.

Locking the back door so none of the children could come in without her knowledge, Hannah stepped out and sat down on the front steps to eat and watch the children play. She saw that the children were already fighting over which team got to choose Carl for their side.

The town was bustling for such a small place. Hannah would like to think that she had made the acquaintance of everyone living around these parts. Lately it seemed that she had been noticing a new face from time to time amongst the townspeople. Evidently their little community was beginning to grow.

❦

The rest of the day went smoothly and Hannah was able to let out a sigh of relief. She had forgotten that Seth would be there to collect her until he poked his head inside the door with that silly grin of his.

Hannah smiled and said, "Come in. I just have to get my things together and I will be ready to leave."

"There is no hurry. Can I help with anything?" Seth asked as he walked around observing the room.

"No, you are already doing enough. I really wish my father had not asked this of you Seth. I really don't feel that it is at all necessary." Hannah's voice held an apology in its tone.

"To tell you the truth your father did not say much about his reason for you needing some company for a while. He only said that you had reason to feel threatened and that he felt precautions needed to be taken. Do you want to talk about it?"

"No, not yet at least. I am still not sure if I am not just crazy. Time will tell, of this I have no doubt." Hannah checked the stove before they locked up and stepped outside.

Seth held Goldie's reigns while Hannah climbed onto her back. Seth handed Hannah back the reigns before he mounted his own beautiful horse with great ease. They were riding towards the road that led out of town when they heard Hannah's name being called out. Hannah turned in her saddle to see Isaac and Bella with Katie in the wagon behind them. Hannah was surprised to see Isaac but not that Bella was with him. That seemed to be the only thing that she could be sure of these days.

"Hello Isaac. It is nice to run into you. And you also Bella," Hannah managed to get the words from between lips that were shaking. She had to bite them in order to appear calm.

"So what are the two of you up to this afternoon?" Isaac asked with a smile that did not reach his eyes.

Hannah hurriedly spoke first. "Seth has kindly showed up to keep me company home." Hannah continued on quickly before Isaac had time to respond and begin asking questions that she did not care to answer, "What brings you and Bella out this afternoon?"

"We just needed some supplies at home. We managed to grab Katie just as she was on her way home also," Isaac told her.

"How is your mother doing? I hope she is improving."

Bella leaned forward a little as she spoke to gain their attention. "Yes Hannah. Alice has shown some improvement over the last couple of days. She has even been getting out of bed and joining the family at breakfast and supper time. We are becoming very close friends," Bella said as she turned a beautiful smile towards Isaac whose attention was still on Hannah and Seth.

"I am very happy to hear that. As soon as I get a chance, I will bring mother over for a short visit." Hannah shifted in her saddle to look at Seth who seemed to be in a world of his own.

Hannah continued, "Seth and I won't keep you. Maybe I will see you soon." Hannah looked at Isaac for a reply.

"Yes soon. It was good to see you again Seth," Isaac said.

Seth only nodded his head and said, "Goodbye." With that short exchange, Hannah and Seth nudged their horses and they went slowly on their way without looking back.

Hannah had never seen Seth so quiet before. She wondered what could be wrong. "Seth, are you alright? Are you feeling ill or something?" Hannah questioned worriedly.

Seth turned her way and said, "Oh no. I was just thinking about Bella."

"What a surprise!" Hannah said sarcastically.

"Now, hold your horses there Hannah. Don't go jumping to conclusions. I am not thinking about her in the way that you may think." Seth explained but not without that twinkle in his eyes that he always had when he sees her temper begin to surface.

With confusion written all over her face, Hannah said, "I don't understand."

"I am not sure that I really understand myself. There is something about her that I can't quite put my finger on. It's like she is two different people. I know it sounds crazy."

"No, it doesn't sound crazy to me at all. I have been trying to put my finger on something that has bothered me about Bella ever since her arrival. You just described it better than I ever could." Hannah felt such a rush of relief that she wanted to cry. Finally, someone saw what she saw or was at least beginning to.

"I hate to say this but I think that she likes Isaac more than just for a friend. He's such a noble guy that he doesn't even see it," Seth gently told her.

Hannah went on to express some of her thoughts that she had kept bottled up for some time. "I am almost positive that she has a great dislike for me. I am assuming that it is because Isaac has feelings for me and not for her." Then with downcast eyes Hannah said in almost a whisper, "Lately, I am beginning to wonder who Isaac really has feelings for."

"If it is any consolation, I think you just gave him a dose of his own medicine back there." Hannah looked at Seth with a puzzled expression. Seth continued, "He could have burnt a hole right through me with that fiery stare of his if I had stuck around for much longer. He definitely was not pleased to see us together," Seth surmised sheepishly.

"Well there isn't much that I can do to remedy the situation. As long as Bella is staying with Alice there is not a thing I can do to change what is happening between Isaac and me."

"Would you like me to have a word with him?" Seth sincerely offered.

"No, I absolutely do not. As a matter of fact, I do not want this to go any further than between us. You are the only one I have confided in," Hannah admitted.

"As you wish," Seth stated with finality.

"Thanks." They rode the rest of the way talking of more mellow topics.

Seth told her that while he was in town, he stopped and talked with Luke and some of the other men sitting and talking outside of the store. They had all been seeing a lot of new faces because of the opportunities pouring out of the surrounding areas. Many were just passing through. "You know that since the

Indians were forced onto the reservations, more and more changes will occur in the name of progress," Seth told her.

"I guess I am a fool in thinking that things will always stay the same for future generations that come along."

"We should be thankful that we don't live in the eastern part of the country. It is really booming out there."

Soon they had arrived at the Jamison farm. Hannah invited Seth in but he declined. Seth waved and said that he would see her tomorrow.

ℰ

That night after Hannah went to bed, she kept replaying the scene that transpired between her and Isaac that afternoon. He did seem to be disturbed but she couldn't understand why he never came to see her. Surely he was not that busy.

Then she thought about Josh. He was almost as absent as Isaac was. Mandy was sure to say something to him.

Hannah told her parents at dinner that evening about Carl Chesterfield. She eased their fears by telling them that he had been well mannered and eager enough, for a boy, to learn. She did not think that there was anything for them to worry about.

Roman added, "I hope that's true. We should still keep our guards up. There seems to be many passersby going through our area."

"Did you ever remember why the boy looked familiar to you?" Sophie asked her husband.

Roman had forgotten that he had mentioned to his wife that he thought he had seen them before. "Yes. Several months back, I believe it was in the springtime, a couple of men and a boy came up to me in town asking about where they could purchase some cattle. I told them that I had none for sale and they went on their way. They didn't appear to look too happy about that as I recall."

"I am sure that they were just having a bad day. We must try and remember to not be too quick to judge," Sophie reminded them both.

That night after everyone had retired, the wind howled fiercely. Hannah snuggled deeper into her covers. Every time it stormed, Hannah was reminded of how thankful she was to have shelter. The fiercer the storm the more content she felt.

CHAPTER 21

Hannah had to admit that even though she appreciated the company going back and forth to school, she preferred to be alone. The past couple of weeks had gone by faster than she had expected them to. She was running out of things to converse about with Seth. Seth informed her that he would be making a trip to Deadwood to see about arranging the purchase of some purebred horses for his father. He said that he expected to only be gone for a few days. Since he would be home before the end of the week, Hannah had dismissed his trip from her mind.

Sunday afternoon Hannah suggested to her mother about paying a visit to Alice. Hannah noticed that Isaac was absent from church again that morning. The only ones there were Andrew, Josh and Katie. Hannah's only conclusion was that Isaac had no desire to see her. Somehow she must muster up the courage to face what she felt was a failing relationship.

As soon as Hannah and Sophie had eaten their dinner, they again dressed warmly for the trip to see Alice. It had been a good while since Alice was well enough to receive visitors. They would not be able to tarry long because they would need to get home before dark.

The wind hit them square in the face as they drove at a moderate pace. Grandma Rose told them after church that it would not surprise her one bit if they had some bad weather coming in. Hannah had taken notice that her Grandma Rose was oftentimes right about these things.

❧

Finally, they pulled up in front of the long porch that stretched the length of the house. Hannah was so nervous that her hands shook as she helped her mother down from the wagon seat. She knocked on the solid oak door that boasted a beautiful small, stain-glassed window in its center.

Several seconds passed before a smiling Katie answered the door. "Miss Jamison!" A surprised Katie exclaimed. "Mrs. Jamison, please come in," Katie said as she stepped back and swung the door wider to allow them entrance.

Hannah smiled at Katie and greeted her as she took in her surroundings. "Hello, Katie. We were hoping to visit with your mother for a short spell if she is up to it."

Hannah wondered where everyone was on a Sunday afternoon. She knew that Josh went to see Mandy after church. *"But where was Isaac?"* She kept repeating in her mind.

"Katie, who is that you are talking to," Alice asked from her bedroom?

Katie smiled and said, "Please have a seat while I go and get Mama." They took a chair at the kitchen table. Soon Katie was pushing her mother into the room on a wheelchair. It was the first time Hannah had seen a chair like it, a convenience to be sure.

"Alice dear, what a pleasure to see you looking so well," Sophie said while rising to give Alice a gentle embrace. Hannah did the same and sat back down.

Hannah had to say that she expected to see a much frailer woman. It was a pleasant surprise to see her with a relatively healthy appearance.

Alice clasped her hands in her lap. "It is wonderful to see you both. I have had so little company and I am growing weary of my own."

"I am sure you needed your rest. You have been in all of our prayers," Sophie said.

"Thank you Sophie. I hope it won't be long until we can all get together again."

Hannah couldn't refrain from asking, "Where is Isaac? I didn't see him when we rode in."

"Oh, I am sorry dear. He drove Bella into town to visit with her Cousin Katherine. The poor sweet thing needed a break from always looking after me."

Hannah could feel her face burn. She hoped no one could see how upset she was. It seemed Isaac was the only one capable of escorting Bella around. She was sick to her stomach.

Katie set a mug of hot cocoa in front of them and they talked for a while longer. Sophie and Alice had a great deal to catch up on. Alice couldn't help but feel better because of the good conversation shared between them.

Alice felt an uncontrollable shiver run over her. "It must be getting colder outside. I can feel it in here. Katie?" Alice looked at her youngest.

"Yes Mama."

"Would you go into Bella's room and retrieve the blanket that she mended for me? She had just finished it, I think."

Hannah stood and said, "Katie you go ahead and finish putting on the coffee and I will fetch the blanket for your mother." Hannah could tell that Katie was getting a little frustrated with one request coming after another.

"Okay."

Alice informed her that Bella was staying in Isaac's room and that Isaac had moved in with Josh for the time being. This only served to aggravate Hannah's mood further. Hannah had just about had it.

Hannah stepped inside the room expecting to find the quilt lying on the bed. Her eyes scanned the half-dark room looking elsewhere for it. The only quilt in the room was draped across a chair in the corner of the room.

Walking over to the chair and picking up the quilt, something fell out of the chair and on to the floor. Hannah bent over and picked up what appeared to be a book. Hannah almost dropped the book back down upon the chair from which it had fallen when she noticed that it looked like a journal or diary. It was leather bound and held together by a red ribbon tied into a bow. Hannah's curiosity got the best of her and she strained her eyes to better see what was written on the front cover. It was a name. Hannah fell into the chair beside her. She was shocked by the name on the cover. The name was "Sophie". Was it her mother's or someone else's by that very same name? Hannah's frantic thoughts were confused. It had to be her mother's diary but what was Bella doing with it?

She knew that she had to find the answers. She had no choice. She must take the diary with her. Hannah slipped the small book down inside her dress pocket. It was completely hidden. Her heart was about to beat out of her chest. She must regain her composure or everyone would know that something was wrong. Hannah took a deep breath for courage and reentered the kitchen with a bright smile and a warm blanket.

"Here you go Alice. This should make you much more comfortable," Hannah said while placing the quilt across the sickly woman's lap.

"Thank you, Hannah. You are a dear."

"You are very welcome." Hannah paused only a second before continuing, "When do you expect Isaac and Bella to return?"

"I am not sure, probably not for a while yet. It is too bad that they missed you," Alice replied.

Sophie sat her cup down and said, "We should really be going. We don't want to tire you out Alice. I hope that you quickly regain your strength."

"I feel that I am finally on my way to recovery. It sure has been a long difficult few weeks," Alice said with a tiredness to her voice. Sophie and Hannah donned their outerwear and with one last farewell they were on their way back home.

§ℭ

The wind was to their backs which made the ride more bearable. There was not a cloud in the sky which made her wonder why her Grandmother thought that bad weather was in the offing. Hannah ran her hand along her thigh to feel the book resting inside her dress pocket. She would have a hard time waiting until bedtime to get some answers. She only hoped that she didn't regret what she had done. She didn't think that it was by mere chance that she found the diary or journal. She felt better thinking that it was meant for her to find it. How long would it take for Bella to realize that the diary was missing? That she was the one who had taken it. These questions and many others kept forcing themselves through her thoughts.

Hannah wanted so much to be able to confide in her mother. Maybe she could put this whole matter to rest. Hannah also knew that she couldn't risk upsetting her already fragile mother unnecessarily either. Hopefully this book with her mother's name on it was just a big coincidence. Hannah glanced her mother's way. She appeared to be lost in thought, in a world of her own. Losing a child was the one thing that a mother could never get over. Hannah knew that without God in one's life a person would be most miserable. The time to heal would surely come soon in their lives.

The ride home seemed to take forever. The temperature had dropped considerably; dusk was approaching by the time they reached home. Roman came out as soon as they drove up and grabbed the reigns to lead the horses and wagon to the barn.

℘

Sophie and Hannah were thankful to get inside where it was warm and cozy. The fire was blazing in the hearth. Roman had left his Bible open on the table beside his chair. Hannah wondered if he was searching for answers as she was. Hannah quickly made a direct path to her room and removed the small book from her dress pocket and shoved it under her pillow for the time being. Roman had told them, over a supper of left-over beef stew, that he would be mending fences the next day and maybe longer. The winds that they had the other night were pretty stout.

Sophie said, "That's no problem. I have plenty of gift-making still left to do. What about you Hannah? Christmas is fast approaching."

Hannah sighed, "I know. I really need to get busy. With school and all, I am feeling a bit overwhelmed."

"Don't worry. I will help you. We will finish gifts and then we will make decorations for our tree," Sophie said with a little bit of that old light back in her eyes.

After the kitchen was clean, Hannah excused herself in order to plan for school projects the rest of the week. Her mother had already settled into her rocking chair with knitting needle in hand.

Finally, Hannah shut her bedroom door, lit her lamp and picked up the mysterious diary. Running her finger across the written name on the front made a shiver run down Hannah's body. She was almost afraid to open it. Such things had the power to change one's life forever, or what they had thought was their life, their truth.

Taking a deep breath, Hannah opened the diary to the first page. There it was. Her mother's whole, given name on the inside cover. The pages were yellowed with age. Her hands shook as she began to read and turn the pages that were written by a very young girl. Hannah was getting to know her mother as never before. She couldn't believe her mother could be so witty and carefree. Hannah read about half of the diary before she went in and told her parents goodnight. They were getting ready to retire also. She told them that she still had some material to go over before she turned out the light. She hated only telling them a half truth and keeping the diary a secret but she didn't want to cause her mother to worry for no reason.

Hannah immediately snuggled under a blanket and picked up where she left off. Her eyes were starting to get heavy when she noticed a sizable gap in the next date entry. Perking up, she began to read words that made her jaw drop and her heart stop with shocking revelation. Hannah wanted to put the diary down and stop reading. Pretend that she had never laid eyes on it. *"What good could come of this?"* Hannah thought. *"But she had been praying for answers and maybe this was God's way of providing them."* Gathering her inner strength, Hannah continued to read. The pages were sprinkled with tears. Finally closing the diary, Hannah looked up and softly whispered, "Oh God, grant me wisdom."

CHAPTER 22

Hannah had tossed and turned all night long. She had finally fallen asleep about an hour before she had to rise and get ready for school. Her mind was still having a difficult time absorbing what she had read. Question after question came upon the heels of one another. Hannah knew that she had to be very careful about how she handled this information. There were too many unknowns for her to just go straight to her parents with this.

It felt good to make the trip to school this morning alone. It was perhaps one of the hardest things that she had ever done in her life, when she entered the kitchen this morning and pretended everything was normal. Hannah hated herself for thinking the thought that came next as she guided Goldie along the dirt road. She had wished that Seth was back from his trip. She needed someone to talk to and he was the only one that she could trust with this.

The schoolhouse came into view before she knew it, so entranced was she, with her racing thoughts. The smoke was curling from the chimney only to be blown down to the ground with the already gusting wind. Grandma Rose would say that we were in for some bad weather because the smoke blowing to the ground was a sign of it.

§

Hannah hurried to put Goldie in her stall and quickly made her way into the warmth of the schoolhouse. One of the projects this afternoon for the children was to make a Christmas wreath for Luke and Anna, a thank-you gift for their kind thoughtfulness. Each student would cut out an ornament made of paper with their name on it and tie it to a pine wreath with a big red bow on it. Hannah just hoped that she could keep her mind on the day at hand.

Just as Hannah had finished writing an assortment of arithmetic problems for each grade level, the children had all gathered in and taken their seats. Hannah was glad to have perfect attendance.

The morning passed productively so they could use their creative side when they returned from their lunch break. Hannah walked over to the edge of the schoolyard next to a large ponderosa pine. The pinecones were large and plentiful and would make lovely decorations. She had the students help gather them on their way back in from lunch.

"Miss Jamison?" Hannah turned at the childish voice behind her.

"Yes, Katie, what is it?"

Fingering one of her braids in habit, Katie said, "I would like to take home a special ornament for Mama if you don't mind. I think she could use some cheering up."

"Of course you may, whatever you would like."

Hannah suddenly had an idea come to mind. She must get answers. The only way to get them would be to talk to Bella. Hannah did not know if Bella had found the diary by chance or if she had acquired it some other way. Whatever the reason, she had to find out.

Hannah went to her desk and took out a pen and paper. She wrote a brief note to Bella requesting to meet her after school tomorrow. Bella probably noticed the diary was missing already and would know the reason behind her desire to meet with her. They would meet at the old abandoned shed just a way off the road a little distance from town. They had passed by it when they had all went out for her birthday, a night that she would never forget.

As the children were cleaning up and preparing to go home, Hannah called Katie to her desk. Poor Katie, Hannah thought the young girl looked very tired.

Hannah smiled, "Katie, I would like for you to do me a favor. I need you to give Bella this note for me. It is very important that she gets it. Ok?" Hannah stressed the word important for she knew how forgetful children can be.

"Sure, I can do that." Hannah watched as Katie shoved the note into her dress pocket. Katie had already turned to leave before Hannah could say thank-you.

After the students had left, she swept around the stove really good and tidied up the rest of the room. She wanted to be able to leave immediately after school tomorrow. Oh, how she prayed that she wasn't making a big mistake by meeting with Bella.

❧

Hannah's mind was so absorbed in thought that she was riding into their yard before she knew it. Her father was still out mending fences and would not be home until after dark. She and her mother waited upon his return to set supper.

They talked of happy times. Roman shared some stories of his childhood. Sophie's laughter felt like a balm upon rough skin, so soothing and comforting was its sound to her loved ones. Hannah had always cherished these moments when they were so cautiously shared. Only now, did Hannah understand the many times that she would see the dark place that her mother would retreat to, a place where no one else was allowed to offer comfort or understanding, a place where her mother felt that only she must walk alone.

Hannah wondered if her father even knew. Hannah kissed both of her parents' goodnight, as soon as the dishes were put away. She was exhausted and ready for bed.

Hopefully sleep would not avoid her this night. She would need all of her wits about her tomorrow afternoon when she confronted Bella White. It must be getting colder outside because she could swear that she could see her breath right here in her bedroom. She threw an extra blanket on her bed before climbing in. Finally, she warmed up enough to fall into a fitful sleep.

℘

Morning introduced itself much the same as any other. The fire could be heard popping its warmth out into the room and the smell of coffee floated ever so subtly into her nostrils. Hannah made quick work of getting dressed and taming her hair into a thick braid down her back. The hot oatmeal she ate for breakfast hit the spot. By the time she got her things together and dressed appropriately, her father had Goldie waiting outside for her. He, as well, looked ready to start work and to begin mending the fence again.

℘

As Hannah rode at a generous trot, she saw the clouds start to darken the distant horizon. Overhead an eagle flew gracefully, without care or need. Her shoulders slumped in defeat. Hannah knew that life was no bed of roses but she sure could use a little of what that eagle had. Just before Hannah reached the edge of town, she felt the wind develop a sharp bite. She looked at the sky again and there was no change. She tried to be responsible enough to make sure the children did not have to walk home in a storm. The weather was unpredictable at times, especially this time of year.

Hannah called roll and noticed that several of the younger children were absent. She hoped that they had not come down with something. Today the children were going to do their mid-term testing. Hannah decided to get it over with so the students could enjoy their last few days before Christmas break. The day seemed to drag by and the stove was having a difficult time keeping the schoolhouse warm. The wind was making its way through every crack there was.

Hannah thought that she was going to run out of wood. She had used all that there was inside so she went out the back door to fetch some more. There were a few snow flurries and a light dusting on the ground. After she put a couple of logs into the stove, she went to check the time on her watch, which lay on her desk. It was a few minutes early but she would let the children leave in case it started to snow more.

Hannah used the extra time to get a head start on grading the test papers. She didn't know how long she would spend with Bella. If she could get any answers out of her, that is. Hannah almost let the time get away from her. She quickly put her papers in her satchel and tidied up the room. She also checked the stove and shut the draft. The fire would soon burn out.

After tying her wool scarf around her head, she went out the door. Goldie was eating some grain when she entered the stables. The temperature had dropped considerably in the last couple of hours and the sky had darkened ominously in the distance. It was as if the weather had slowly worsened all day. Hannah judged the worse of it to continue to hold off for a while assuming today's forecast was anything to go by.

Hannah headed out of town with her head bent down. The wind was stinging her face with bits of snow. Grateful that she had sent the children home already, she kept an eye towards the sky. The tree tops were bending in the now snow-filled air.

Having seen no sight of Bella, Hannah thought that maybe she was already at the old shed. She could still see a slight path as she traveled through the woods in the direction of their meeting place. There were no horse footprints but Bella may have come in another way. The shed came into view and Hannah saw that Bella was nowhere in sight. Hannah climbed down off from her horse and went inside to shelter herself from the wind until Bella arrived. There were no windows to look out of. Her mind was so distracted with worried thoughts that she had not noticed the increase in the storm's intensity around her. She had her own storm raging inside which seemed of a much greater ferocity.

Checking her watch, she decided that she had a few minutes to wait. "Surely," she thought out loud. "It was as much in Bella's best interest to resolve this matter as it was in hers." Maybe Bella had no link to the diary whatsoever. What if she had just found it and had not had a chance to return it yet.

"No, there was much more going on than that," Hannah said in a low voice. The large cracks in the walls of the tiny shed did almost nothing to stop the now howling wind from blowing through. Hannah paced back and forth across the length of the floor, out of nervousness and for the added warmth of movement. Continuing to analyze the situation while she paced, she lost track of time.

A whinny from Goldie brought Hannah out of her focused state. Opening the door, she was blasted with snow and wind. It was a blizzard. Hannah could barely see Goldie who was only a few feet from her. Visibility was almost zero. Hannah untied the blanket from Goldie. After she mounted, she wrapped the blanket around her in an effort to shield herself as much as possible. She scolded herself for not keeping alert on the storm's progress. *"So much for meeting Bella,"* Hannah thought to herself.

The storm began to bear down even harder. Hannah had no way of knowing if she was going in the right direction. She had given Goldie the lead. A loud crack sounded above. Without time to react, a large limb broke free from above Hannah's head and fell. The limb knocked her off her horse and rendered her unconscious. Goldie bolted and ran away in fear.

Hannah's body had rolled against a very large rock. The snow and temperature both continued to fall. Hannah had no awareness but watchful eyes were close by. Appearing out of nowhere, Spirit looked upon Hannah with soulful eyes. A mysterious connection between man and beast, ordained of

God. Spirit licked the snow from Hannah's face and laid his large, thickly furred body along the length of hers.

CHAPTER 23

When the time came and went that Hannah was due to be home, Sophie became increasingly worried. Roman had come in from the hills hours ago. Sophie stood staring through the kitchen window at the total whiteness.

"She should have been home by now Roman." Sophie was working herself into a frenzied state.

"You are right. I am going to go and search for her," Roman said calmly for his wife's sake.

Sophie started for her outer garments. "I am coming with you."

"No. I need you to stay here and have some warm water ready. Just in case," Roman added softly.

"She is probably just moving really slow or decided to stay in town."

"I'm scared Roman."

"I know Sophie. Have faith." Roman kissed Sophie on the forehead. He was scared too. "If I am not back then I had to stay in town."

❦

Soon Roman was out the door and on his way. He tied an extra blanket and lantern on his horse. It would be dark before long. The only reason he knew that he was on the road was because trees lined both sides of it almost the entire way to town.

The going was slow and with every minute that went by with no sign of his daughter, Roman prayed that much harder. With the Lord's help, he made it to the edge of town. He could barely make out any lights from this distance. Once in a while the wind would carry with it the smell of smoke leading him onward.

Roman was very disappointed that he had seen no sign of his daughter, thus far. There was still a chance that she might be here with someone waiting out the storm. The snow was piling up. The boardwalks were hidden with only the posts marking their whereabouts. He strained his eyes to see which place had the lights shining from the windows.

It looked like the general store and the boarding house were still lit up. He would check with Katherine first. The heavy snow was beginning to take its toll on his horse also. They both needed to recharge if they were going to be able to search further. He left his horse in the stables across the street. He almost fell into the steps as he blindly made his way to the door. He entered the boarding house as a frozen, white figure.

Katherine jumped at the sound of the doorbell. She stood there staring for a moment trying to recognize him.

"Mr. Jamison, what in heaven's name are you doing out in this storm?" Katherine spouted as she rushed towards him to help him to a seat.

Roman was too cold to speak right away. Katherine ran to get a blanket. She removed Roman's hat, coat and gloves and wrapped him in the heavy blanket that was draped across the fireside chair.

"I have some coffee on. I will be right back," She said as she took his things and laid them on the hearth.

Katherine brought the coffee and Roman said, "Thank you. I didn't realize how cold that I really was."

"Is something wrong? No one is out on an evening like this without a very good reason," Katherine's concern was evident in her drawn eyebrows.

Roman's voice shook as he spoke, "Hannah never came home after school. I was hoping that she was here."

"Oh my, no! No one is even staying in the establishment at present. I had a few guests for an early dinner but they left hours ago."

"Maybe she is at Luke and Anna's. That is the only other place that I can think of that she would go to except for Isaac's," Roman hopefully said.

Katherine seemed a little troubled when she said, "From what Bella tells me, and that's not much lately, Hannah and Isaac have been somewhat distant lately. I am not sure what she meant by that. Bella rarely comes to see me and she acts rather peculiar whenever Hannah is mentioned."

Roman sat his empty coffee cup down and said, "You are probably right about her not being at Isaac's, whatever the case may be. It is too far out of the way to travel on such a night and Hannah would know better."

Roman thanked Katherine again before leaving. His only hope now rested with Luke down the way.

§

The short walk to the general store only dampened his spirits all the more. He had to knock twice to raise Luke from inside. Luke opened the door with a shocked look on his face. This told Roman that Hannah was not there. His heart sank.

"Roman, what in the world brings you here? Come in, come in. You'll catch your death out there." Luke ushered him in to where a chair sat beside a potbellied stove.

Roman removed his already snow covered garments again before saying, "I suppose that you haven't seen Hannah, have you?"

"Why no, she left the schoolhouse the same time as always. I know because I went over there right after school let out to be sure everything was shut up nice and tight," Luke told him. A worried look crossed over Luke's weathered and time worn face. "She's missing ain't she?"

"I am afraid so Luke. You were my last hope." Roman's shoulders slumped as he bent his face to the floor.

"Anna! Bring Roman a glass of warm milk," Luke yelled to his wife who was still in their living quarters.

"Roman?" Anna loudly called back. "What's he doing here?"

"Just bring the milk, dear." In quick order, Anna entered with milk. Luke explained the situation to his puzzled wife. They all sat there in silence and in earnest prayer. Roman did not know what to do next.

"Roman, I know that you do not want to hear this but I think it would be best if you would wait until daylight to continue your search," Luke wisely advised his longtime friend.

"Yes dear, it is absolutely pitch black out there and the storm is still raging," Anna said as she let the curtain fall back down on the sill of the window that she was trying to look out of.

Roman felt defeated by the storm. He hated the thought of leaving Sophie at home by herself. He knew that she was not handling things well. There was no choice but to wait it out. In the morning he would solicit some help and find his daughter. His only hope was that she had found shelter with one of the neighbors.

℘

While Roman lay in the spare bedroom, praying without ceasing almost all night long, Sophie paced the floors at home imagining the worst. She could not lose another child. She kept asking, "Oh Lord, do not take her away from me please!"

Roman had fallen asleep for a short time. When he awoke it was still dark outside. He looked at his pocket watch. It was five o'clock in the morning. He could hear his dear friends stirring about. He walked to the window and parted the curtains. It was still snowing but from what he could tell, it had slacked down on its intensity some. Daylight would answer his unspoken question of just how much.

Anna had fixed a big breakfast. "You both will need your strength for the day ahead," Anna said before Roman could refuse.

Roman slightly bowed his head humbly and said, "Thank you Anna. Thank you both for everything." By the time they ate it was very close to dawn.

He didn't expect to see anyone in town this early or really at all. They would have to stop at their houses as they searched and request their help. He would go to Isaac's first thing. Maybe his daughter somehow had made it there.

Just out of town, Roman and Luke parted ways. The sun was just starting to brighten the eastern sky through the thick mass of clouds that still showered a goodly amount of snow upon the land. He knew that he would have to push his horse hard if he were to cover any ground. The snow was deeper in places where the wind had driven it into piles. He was thankful the wind was not nearly so fierce this morning.

Luke had ridden in the direction of Paul Sullivan's to ask for his aid in the search. Roman's eyes took in both sides of the road and as far into the woods as he could see. *"Where could Hannah have gone that would have been so important to her as to put herself in such peril?"* Questions came and went without answers.

Finally, Roman came to the short lane that led to the Daniels' farm. He could see someone outside trying to clear some of the snow away. As he drew nearer, Josh saw him and raised his hand in greeting.

"Roman what brings you out in this?" Josh asked in his usual cheerful manner. Roman's heart sank again. Hannah was not there or Josh clearly would have known his reason for showing up on such a day.

"Hannah's missing. She didn't come home after school yesterday. Does anyone have any idea where she might have gone?" Roman's wearied voice started to sound hopeless.

"Climb down from your horse and come on in. We will see if anyone inside can be of some help."

"Thanks, Josh." They knocked the snow off of their boots and coats before entering the house.

Andrew and Isaac turned surprised faces towards Roman's appearance. They both stood and pushed their chairs away from the table.

Roman shook both their hands and said, "I'm sorry to bother you and your family like this. Hannah never came home yesterday and I am looking everywhere that I can think of."

"You know that you are always welcome here no matter the circumstance but I am afraid that I cannot help you," Andrew said before looking to his eldest son.

"What about you Isaac? Do you know anything?" Isaac was already heading for the door where all of the outerwear hung close by. He didn't even respond to his father's question. He could not think of anything except Hannah being out there somewhere, alone.

"Did you hear me Isaac?" Andrew spoke loudly this time. "You can't go off just half-cocked. You have to think. Do you know where she might have gone to after school?"

Isaac turned and said, "No, we haven't got to talk much lately."

Andrew knew his son was deeply upset. He had to calm him down. "Isaac, we must stop and think about what to do before we just go out. We must have a plan. Between all of us we will find her."

"You are right Dad. But we must not waste time." Isaac was visibly anxious. Bella and Katie walked into the room. Isaac asked, "Katie, did Hannah mention to you about going anywhere after school yesterday?"

"No." Katie answered. "But…"

"But what," Isaac asked his younger sister?

Katie looked at her father and swallowed nervously before continuing, "She gave me a note to give to Bella when I got home from school." They all focused their attention on Bella.

Bella shrugged her shoulders and said, "I never saw a note much less read one."

Andrew looked at his daughter sternly and said, "Katie could you please explain what is going on?"

Tears formed in Katie's eyes. "I never gave it to her. I lost it on my way home from school. It must have fallen out of my pocket." By this time Katie was crying uncontrollably.

"Don't blame yourself. It was an accident." Bella put her arm around Katie.

"Did you read the note? It is very important that you tell us. We will not be mad at you," Isaac asked trying to gain any information about Hannah's whereabouts that he could.

Katie hiccupped and said, "No. I didn't think any more about it until I changed my school dress for an old one."

Roman did not want to waste any more time. "The only thing that can be done now is to search every place that we can think of. She could be anywhere now." Roman's voice sounding his disappointment.

Bella cleared her throat. "You might want to check with Seth Johnson. They have been spending a good amount of time together lately," she said while sneaking a peak at Isaac through her long eyelashes.

Isaac's face had turned red with anger. He turned and started to prepare for the search. Andrew told Josh to help while he stayed with the women folk. It took them several minutes to saddle up the horses. Roman told Isaac and Josh that they should split up to cover more territory.

Roman struck out on his own while Isaac and Josh went to the Johnson farm. The snow had let up enough for them to see a fair distance but the landscape was as pure white as they had ever seen it. Isaac sure hoped that Seth knew what might have happened to Hannah or where she could be. He also didn't want to think about what that implicated concerning Hannah and Seth's relationship. He thought that his and Hannah's love was strong but lately he felt like Hannah was starting to draw away from him. Maybe Bella was right.

The going was difficult. The snow drifts were several feet in places. The horses were tiring out easily. They had finally reached the Johnson's place after stopping at two more neighboring farms on the way. He was getting a little bored with Josh's incessant jabbering. Dismounting, Isaac and Josh knocked on Ruth Johnson's door.

Ruth opened the door with a welcoming smile. "Come in. What brings you all the way out here?" Ruth stepped aside to allow them entrance into the warm house.

"We can't stay long. We are looking for Hannah. She never came home last night. We thought that Seth might know something." Isaac asked as he looked in a house that did not appear to have any other occupants.

"I'm sorry dear but Seth is not here. He left to check on some horses for his father. I don't expect him back for a day or two. I wish that I could help you more."

"Well then we should be on our way. We need your prayers for Hannah's safe return," Josh said as they hurried to be on their way.

"I don't see any reason why we should look further down the road. We will continue to look along the edge of the forest as we travel back to the house to change horses," Isaac instructed his brother.

"Don't worry Isaac. We will find her," Josh tried encouraging his brother.

"I am beginning to wonder if she even wants to be found."

Josh laughed. "That's ridiculous!" He looked at his brother's expression and said, "You are not serious, are you?"

"I don't know Josh. I just don't know anymore." It was way up in the afternoon before they reached home again. Their father informed them that no one else had been by so they knew there was no new news.

℘

Andrew went to switch their horses out while his sons went inside to grab a bite to eat. They sat at the table while Bella and Katie placed before them some piping hot beef stew and some biscuits. There was also some old fashioned stack cake for dessert. Although everything was delicious, Isaac barely tasted anything that he ate.

Bella sat down at the table and nibbled on a biscuit. She knew that it was highly likely that Hannah was the one who took the diary from her bedroom. Alice had told her that she had sent Hannah in there to fetch a quilt. She could have kicked herself for leaving it out like that.

"I am sorry that you did not find Hannah as of yet. I am sure that she is alright," Bella said. Then Bella placed her hand upon her chest as if the thought just came to her. "Do you think that she and Seth could be together? Maybe she went with him to Deadwood," Bella watched as her words began to sink in.

Josh looked irritated when he said, "What makes you say such a thing Bella?"

"Well I heard you tell your father how your search went and it just seems too coincidental for them both to be gone at the same time."

"You shouldn't assume such things about Hannah. And Isaac, you should be the one defending Hannah, not me." Josh pushed his chair back away from the table and said, "I'll be outside when you are ready Isaac."

Isaac sat still for several minutes before rising to leave. He looked at Bella and said, "I am not sure what time we will be back so don't hold supper."

"Of course," returned Bella.

Josh had the fresh horses saddled and ready when Isaac came outside. They decided to take the road back towards the Jamison farm. They weren't sure where Roman was searching but they were bound to run into him or Luke.

℘

The snow had stopped but it was still bitterly cold. It would not be long until the sun set. They would not be able to see into the dense trees. Isaac's thoughts troubled him. He could see no reason why Hannah would have strayed far from the road. It was becoming more and more apparent to him that Hannah and Seth were together. On the other hand, he had a difficult time believing that he could have been such a bad judge of character, more than that, a fool.

How could his heart have betrayed him into falling for someone so obviously not meant for him and hadn't Bella pointed out how they had been seeing Seth and Hannah in each other's company? Somewhere deep inside him a voice told him that things weren't as they seemed. But how could he ignore the facts.

"Isaac, I think that I see someone up ahead. It looks like Luke. Maybe he has some good news," Josh said.

"I hope so Josh, I really do hope so," said Isaac in an unoptimistic voice.

As Luke came closer, they could see by his expression that he had not found Hannah. "I am sorry boys. I have been everywhere that I know to look. It will soon be dark."

Isaac wondered if somehow Hannah had made it home while her father and everyone else had been out looking for her. "Do you know if Roman has been home in case she showed up there while he was gone?"

"Yes. I met up with Roman a couple of hours ago. She has not been there. He is going to search until dark and begin again in the morning," Luke informed them.

Luke looked uncomfortable as he glanced back and forth between Isaac and Josh. "Do you think that it's possible that foul play could be involved here?"

"I guess that I didn't want to imagine such a thing happening to Hannah," Isaac said with pain in his voice. "It would be easier knowing that she was with someone else than to think of any harm coming to her."

Josh spoke up, "Now just a minute, we can't go jumping to conclusions. We will meet up with Roman in the morning and decide on a plan of action if Hannah hasn't showed up by then." Josh turned sympathetic eyes on his brother and said, "Isaac you are not thinking rationally. Things will work out, you'll see."

Luke turned his horse back in the direction towards town. "I am going to head on back to town and ask around about strangers passing through over the past couple of days. Usually if there is anyone new in town, I see them come in the store. It wouldn't hurt to ask to make sure."

"Take care of yourself, Luke. We will see you tomorrow," Isaac bade farewell as he and Josh made their way home as well.

§

The next morning, Isaac and Josh rose well before dawn. They wanted to catch Roman before he left home to search. It had been well over twenty-four hours since Hannah went missing. Time was of the essence. They rode into Roman's yard just as he and Jacob were saddling up their horses. Jacob saw them first and let Roman know of their approach. Roman looked as if he hadn't slept any since the search began.

Roman spoke in a weary voice, "I wish that I had some news or at least something to go on but I'm afraid I don't even have a plan of action at this point. Any advice would be appreciated."

Jacob said, "We have pretty much ruled out foul play. I have talked with our new neighbors, the Chesterfields, and checked with pretty much everyone else that you haven't already talked to. It's like she has vanished. There has got to be something that we are missing."

Roman cleared his throat before saying, "There is something that I haven't mentioned to anyone." Roman paused to take a deep breath. "Recently Hannah was feeling like someone was watching her. A couple of weeks or so ago, Hannah was out to the barn and it caught on fire. The lantern had somehow fallen from its hook and I think someone may have purposely done it," Roman said letting his words sink in.

"Why didn't she tell me this was happening? I can't believe that she didn't confide in me." Isaac's words were full of hurt.

Roman put his hand upon Isaac's broad shoulder in understanding. "Hannah would probably be upset with me for saying this but she was feeling quite left out where you were concerned. Oh she didn't say anything to her mother or me but we could tell."

Isaac was taken by surprise at Roman's words. "I have just been occupied at home trying to help Dad and get things in order so that he could spend more time with Mom. I thought Hannah trusted me."

"Yeah, like you've been so obviously trusting her," Josh's comment struck a nerve.

Jacob cut in before more was said. "Let us all just calm down here. We won't get anywhere like this. Now the question is, who would dare to cause harm to Hannah?"

"Josh has Mandy confided anything to you that Hannah might have told her?" Roman asked.

"Mandy mentioned something about Bella always being with Isaac. She said she knew it bothered Hannah. That is about all that she has told me," Josh replied.

"Hannah knew that Bella was there only as my mother's nursemaid and nothing else," Isaac retuned in defense.

Josh rubbed his stubbly face before saying, "I wonder why Hannah sent a note to Bella the day before the storm."

Roman's shoulders sagged as though a heavy weight had been laid upon them. He said, "Evidently there was something going on that my daughter felt she could not reveal to us."

CHAPTER 24

Hannah's mind kept trying to push through the veil that hung between the safety of unawareness and the reality of consciousness. Her instinctive senses were starting to react to her surroundings before she was ready to emerge from her oblivious state. She tried in vain to remain aloof of the present world. The pain eventually won out. Her head throbbed and her shoulder felt like it had a knife in it. Still afraid to open her eyes just yet, she wondered why she felt such warmth along the length of her body. Hannah struggled to open her eyes in an effort to analyze her situation. Hannah was so startled that she would have sat upright if she did not hurt so much and if she wasn't pressed so tightly against what felt like a rock behind her.

Very soon she realized that the large warmth lying beside her was Spirit. The beautiful dog that was part wolf had saved her life. He was such a large creature that his body warmth had shielded her from the storm. Complete thankfulness enveloped Hannah's very soul. With great effort, she raised her good arm and placed it over Spirit's neck. She knew without a doubt that this animal was placed by God's hand in her life. She also knew that whatever was to take place from this point forward, her faith was sufficient to see her through. This time she closed her eyes in peace.

Seth couldn't believe the storm that caught him unaware. If it had not been for the kindly old couple that had offered him shelter during his trip home, he would have been stranded. He was finally coming close to home after struggling through snow drifts and removing broken limbs from his path. There were also several fallen trees that would need taken care of once the weather cleared. The journey home had been a rough one to say the least. He hoped his grandmother had gotten along well through it all. If it hadn't been for her he would have waited a little longer to return.

A horse's neigh got his attention. He turned his ear to the right and there it was again. He looked carefully through the trees and then he saw the horse. As he steered his big horse through the woods, he saw Goldie. "It's Hannah's horse. How did she come to be here?" Seth spoke the words aloud. He quickly scanned the area for Hannah. She was nowhere in sight. He swung down from his horse and loosed Goldie's reigns that were caught by some branches. He patted her neck in an effort to sooth the distraught horse. By the looks of things, the horse had been stuck here for a while. Taking one last survey of his surroundings, Seth led Goldie and his horse out of the woods. "Where could Hannah be?" Seth wondered aloud. He knew something was wrong. He would drop his horse off at his grandmother's since he was almost there. He would get a fresh horse if he needed to search.

Soon Seth was back on the road trying to think of where Hannah might be. His grandmother had told him that Hannah was indeed missing. He decided to search where it looked like no one had been yet. He would be able to tell by their tracks coming and going, thanks to the snow. He kept telling himself as he searched that maybe Hannah was home, safe and sound. He kept that hope alive until he ran into Luke and was informed that she was still missing.

He knew deep down that something wasn't right. Hannah had talked herself into believing that she was just making too much of things. Everyone around her had let her down, including himself. Seth had come upon the small untraveled road that led to the small shed that he had spotted while out hunting and exploring a couple of weeks ago. He thought that he may as well check it out and leave no stone unturned. The old line shack was not far but he had to dodge fallen limbs and those that drooped over with heavy snow. When he reached the time- stricken structure, he saw no signs.

He dismounted and pushed the door open and walked inside. A lot of snow had blown in from the wide cracks in the boards but there was evidence of activity in the dirt strewn floor. Someone had kicked the dirt and straw around very recently. He went outside and yelled Hannah's name over and over again. He walked a short distance in every direction from the shed. Looking up to gauge the position of the sun, Seth guessed it to be around three in the afternoon. There was not a lot of daylight left.

Hannah stirred at the sound of her name breaching the edge of her consciousness. She fought to regain wakefulness. A sudden shock of cold met her entire body. She knew her protector had left. Her eyes refused to open and allow the light to intensify the throbbing in her head. In an attempt to take in her surroundings, she concentrated on the sounds around her. She could hear the wind high in the trees. Very little wildlife seemed to be stirring close by. "There it was again." Hannah could hear her name being called in the distance.

Hannah had not let her mind begin to dwell on her reason for being there in the first place. She must first get home. She had no clue as to how long she had lain there amongst the elements. Her heavy wool blanket was still wrapped around her even after falling from her horse. Even as the outside forces worked against her, she took comfort in the small miracles that worked for the good. The true meaning of the scripture, "If the Lord be for you, who can be against you," took hold in her heart. Hannah mustered strength that she did not know she possessed and raised upon her elbow and opened her eyes. Her mouth was so dry that she could not speak. The brilliant white snow made it difficult to see. She focused on some movement in the distance. She closed her eyes and opened them again. Yes, someone was out there. Out ahead of the rider, Hannah could see Spirit guiding them closer to her. Spirit stopped right beside her and licked her on the cheek. Hannah wanted to talk to the animal but could not. She leaned her head against his front legs instead. Her tears wetted his fur.

Hannah's tears turned to sobs when she recognized Seth on his horse. He also had Goldie with him. Seth had a complete look of dismay on his face when he saw her lying there.

"Good gosh, Hannah, how in the world did this happen? Are you hurt?" Seth rushed to Hannah's aid. As soon as he saw her parched lips, he went and fetched his water jug and gave her a small sip at a time. When she had drunk enough, he laid the jug aside and reached to help her sit up.

He kept a close eye on the large beast that would not leave Hannah's side, even to allow him room to reach between them. He heard Hannah wince in pain as she slowly sat up. He carefully felt for any broken bones. It was possible that her collar bone was broken due to its purplish and greenish colors. Hannah took short breaths for it hurt to breathe normally.

She looked at Seth and managed a smile before saying, "I bet you are wondering how I got myself into such a mess."

Seth honored her with one of his crooked smiles and replied, "Well the thought had crossed my mind. But before you explain it, it would be best if I got you home first. Everyone is terribly worried."

"That sounds wonderful to me."

"Do you think that you can stand for a second and I will place you on my horse?" Seth stood to walk his horse closer to Hannah.

Hannah managed to rise on shaking limbs with Seth's help. Spirit moved close to her side. Hannah patted him on the head and said, "I won't leave Spirit behind. He saved my life."

Seth looked amazed at them and said, "I've never seen anything like it. You act as if you already know him."

"He is my friend," Hannah replied with a fresh batch of tears filling her eyes. Seth gathered Hannah into his arms and set her upon his horse before climbing up behind her. Spirit needed no encouragement to follow. He stayed by their side the whole way home. Hannah knew that she would have a lot of explaining to do, the worry that she must be putting her mother through now. The truth needed to come out. The way that things have been going can only lead to more misery. Hannah relaxed against Seth and prayed the whole way home.

CHAPTER 25

Isaac and Josh had ridden back to the Jamison place in hopes that Hannah had been found. They saw Roman dismounting from his horse near the barn door. They rode up straining to see the expression on his face for any clue of encouragement. They were soon disappointed.

Roman turned after securing the horse's reigns on the corral fence and said, "I take it you boys had no luck either."

"No sir," Isaac replied as he slid from his horse.

Josh kicked a rock with his booted foot. "We don't know of anywhere else to look. It will be dark before long."

"Jacob brought Mom over to stay with Sophie this morning. He searched all day as well," Roman informed them.

Roman raised his head and looked past Isaac and Josh to tell them of his plans for the next day's search. He caught movement coming over the rise in the road leading to their farm.

Stepping around the two large horses, Roman looked again before speaking. He continued to wait a little longer for fear that he might be seeing things. "Dear Lord, I think it's Hannah!" Roman's voice was almost a whisper.

"What?" Isaac and Josh turned in unison to take a look. The most glorious sight Roman was to ever behold. Seth held Hannah safely against him upon his large horse with Goldie tied on behind. The most magnificent animal that he had ever laid eyes on walked beside them. His beautiful daughter was safe and she was home.

Roman fell to his knees and knelt there upon the ground and thanked God with all that was in him. Isaac and Josh were completely shocked. As Seth and Hannah drew closer, they could see that Hannah might be injured. Isaac quickly handed Josh his horse's reigns and Josh laid a staying hand on his brother's shoulder.

Josh could see the raw emotion threatening to override common sense. "Isaac, you must let them explain. You cannot let anger cloud your reasoning." Isaac could not believe what he was seeing. He had all but given up on finding Hannah and all along she was riding in with Seth.

"Isn't it exactly as Bella had said? Was it true after all?" Isaac said in a low inaudible voice. It was all Isaac could do to keep from running up and punching Seth as soon as Roman gathered his daughter into his grateful arms.

As Roman carried an obviously injured Hannah towards the house, Isaac was torn between confronting Seth and following the woman he loved. Love won. He ran to catch up and open the door for them. He heard the shatter of glass as it hit the floor.

A mother's cry filled the room at the sight of her child. Roman placed Hannah upon her bed. There was no doubt that she had been through a horrific ordeal but he had never seen such a light shine in his daughter's eyes before. He stepped away to allow Sophie and his mother room to attend to Hannah but almost stumbled when he bumped into Isaac who was directly behind him. Sophie and Grandma Rose were there ready to take care of their girl.

Roman chuckled, "I guess I had better be getting out of the way, as if I had any choice in the matter." The room was barely big enough for two large men let alone anyone else.

Isaac stepped aside to allow Roman room to pass. He knelt beside Hannah's bed and placed her hand in his. "Oh Hannah, you scared me to death. I thought I had lost you."

When Hannah started to speak through dry, cracked lips, Isaac placed his finger over them gently to stop her. "We will talk later. You must first recover for a while."

"Yes darling, your grandmother and I will see to your injuries and then you must rest. There will be plenty of time to talk later," Sophie said as she went about her tasks almost blinded by tears. Hannah only nodded her head.

Grandma Rose entered the room again after acquiring the things needed to attend Hannah with. She first made Hannah drink some warm milk for strength. Barking orders and shooing Isaac out of the room were some of the last words Hannah heard before sinking back into a healing sleep.

Sophie and Grandma Rose were taken aback by Hannah's overall condition. While bathing her body with warm water, they saw how bruised her body was along one side. There appeared to be no other broken bones except for the collar bone. Her feet were very close to being frost bitten, so they carefully warmed them slowly. Sophie smoothed Hannah's hair back and found a rather large lump that was crusted with blood.

While Sophie finished dressing her daughter, Grandma Rose went to warm a couple of blankets by the fire. They tucked her in and left her to rest. The many questions that plagued everyone's mind would just have to wait until Hannah was able to explain.

Isaac and Josh saw that it was getting very late and there was no sign that Hannah was going to wake up any time soon. Roman invited them to stay but Josh declined telling him that his folks would worry without any word from them. Isaac was glad to accept for he had no intentions of leaving Hannah's side.

Roman extended his hand to Josh and said, "Thanks, Josh. You don't know how much we appreciated your help. Seth told me when he left that he would let Jacob know that Hannah is home safe."

Isaac heard Seth's name mentioned and he couldn't believe that he had forgotten all about him. Isaac's thoughts raced. He wondered if Seth had mentioned anything to Roman about what happened to Hannah.

Isaac bid his brother goodbye and turned to Roman and asked, "Did Seth say anything to you before he left?"

"No, he didn't. He just said that he needed to get back and check on his grandmother. He seemed in a bit of a hurry."

Grandma Rose spoke up. "Well, if you ask me, you should have had the boy come in and warm up a bit and offered him something warm to drink." They all shrunk under the elderly woman's reprimand.

"You are right, mother. I just wasn't thinking." Roman shook his head back and forth scolding himself.

Isaac felt a little guilty himself. He wondered if he could be seeing everything all wrong concerning Hannah and Seth. He wasn't sure about anything right now. He needed answers. It was past bedtime and there continued to be no sign that Hannah would awaken soon. Isaac made himself a pallet on the floor when everyone took to their beds. They were all very exhausted from the stress of the last few days. There would be many thankful prayers sent up this night.

℘

Hannah awoke while it was still dark outside. The house was still very quiet except for the crackling of the fire. She did not look forward to leaving her warm safe haven. Attempting to rise up, her whole body screamed in resistance. Hannah quietly groaned under her breath as she came to a sitting position. Startled at the movement beside her bed, Hannah was taken by surprise when she realized that it was Spirit right there in her room. The creature looked at her with such devotion. He was a part of her now. Hannah still could not believe all of the events that had unfolded over the past few days. All of the confusion that had shrouded her had only been a prelude to the time that all things should be revealed. Even Spirit was a part of that purpose.

Hannah gritted her teeth and rose up further into a sitting position with her legs over the side of the bed. The cold air was a shock to her as she pulled the covers back. Moving very slowly, she donned her housecoat and slipped on her slippers before trying to stand. Hannah heard someone stir in the kitchen. A lamp was lit, spilling light into her room. Footsteps sounded from the kitchen and continued until they stopped at her door. It was her father.

Roman poked his head slowly inside and said, "Good morning, sweetheart. I wasn't sure if you would be awake yet. How are you feeling?"

Hannah smiled at her father and said softly, "Like I have been run over by a herd of buffalo."

Roman chuckled, "I see you still have your sense of humor." He motioned his hand towards Spirit and said, "I let your dog in. He was not about to let us keep him from your side."

"Thank you. His name is Spirit. He is the one that I told you and mom about here a while back."

"Yes, I remember. It seems that I was mistaken where he was concerned. I think everyone else is starting to stir. There hasn't been much sleep around here lately." Roman's dark eyebrows rose questioningly.

"I am sorry. I know that I have a lot of explaining to do. I would like to talk to everyone after breakfast if that is ok with you," Hannah said. She hoped that she chose her words wisely and gently for her mother's sake.

"Sure that will be fine." Soon her mother and Grandma Rose were up fussing over her.

❧

When she was ready, Isaac came and helped her to the table for breakfast. Hannah was starved. Grandma Rose kept plying her with gravy and biscuits. Everyone talked about everything but what was really on their minds. Isaac kept giving Hannah an encouraging glance from time to time to show her his support. Sophie gathered everyone's plates and raked all of the leftovers into one plate and set it before Spirit. The dog had been patiently waiting beside Hannah. He slowly sniffed the food before eating it. He was used to providing his own meals and this was very different for him.

Hannah pulled the blanket more tightly about her. She knew they were all waiting on her to explain. She didn't know how to begin or where to begin. She only knew that it had to be done. It had to be done for her mother's sake. Her mother needed the help that only the truth set free could give. The truth would give her peace. Hannah sighed within herself. *"The truth would give me peace."*

Hannah folded her hands on the table in front of her. She looked at everyone's expectant faces gathered around the table. With a deep breath she began. "I know that for the past few weeks or months that I haven't exactly been myself. There have been so many things happening that I cannot explain and things that I have seen, that I didn't know the reasons for. I was beginning to think that I was just crazy or being paranoid."

Isaac placed one of his hands over hers and said, "I had no idea what you had been going through. I have been so absorbed in getting my family taken care of that I have been completely neglectful of you."

Hannah nodded her understanding but she must stay focused. "Before I go into further detail, I need to know if you found my saddle bags on Goldie when Seth brought me in."

Roman was confused but answered, "Yes, I took them off of her and laid them in the barn. Do you want them?"

"Yes, please. There is a small book in the smallest bag. I will need it." Hannah could see that she had their interest now. She knew that she would have to start with the journal or they would not understand the prior incidences, just as she hadn't.

Roman reentered and closed the door quickly behind him. It was frigidly cold outside. He placed his coat back on its hook and handed Hannah the small book.

The strangled cry that was torn from her mother's throat broke Hannah's heart. Hannah spoke apologetically to her. "Mama, I am sorry to bring this to you and Dad without warning but I didn't know of any other way. I feel this is best for everyone involved. Please trust me."

Hannah looked at her mother and could see the young, vulnerable girl that she had been reading about. Sophie looked at her daughter and nodded her acceptance. Roman reached over and placed a strong comforting hand over his wife's. Hannah knew in that instance that her mother had not kept her past a secret from her father. The love and understanding that passed between their gaze was undeniable.

Hannah untied the diary and opened it to show her mother's name written inside the time worn cover. Hannah began to tell them of the tragic event that was part of her mother's life years ago.

"I will not read to you every thought that lies within these pages. But I will tell you of a terrible thing that happened to an innocent and brave young woman." Grandma Rose scooted her chair closer to Sophie. The jester was an act of love. Hannah could already feel the liberty that would be granted to this family. Hannah couldn't help but look up and smile into the heavens.

"When Mama was sixteen years old, she had been walking home in the small town which she grew up in. The walk was not far for she and her parents lived just on the outskirts of town and she had done so countless of times before. As she was passing the stables, someone called out for help. Mama stopped and listened and the call came again. She looked around for someone close by but there was no one near. She walked around to the back of the building unsure of who was there, her concern overriding caution."

Hannah paused before continuing. She hated having to bring the memories so fresh before her again. With a deep breath Hannah went on. "As soon as she rounded the corner, a man grabbed her. She tried to scream but he covered her mouth. She fought back but he was a very large man. She did not give up fighting until he hit her so hard that she was knocked unconscious but not before he had utterly violated her."

Hannah looked at her mother who now sat with a distant stare. "After Mama came to, she made her way home, being sure to stay out of sight. When her parents found out what had happened to her, they did all they could to sweep the grave offense under the rug. This left a young girl feeling like it was her fault and she felt isolated from her parents.

Weeks went by and all appeared well until one evening she was forced to tell her parents that she was with child."

Grandma Rose took hold of Sophie's free hand and said, "Oh you dear child. How you must have needed someone to talk to."

Hannah waited until Grandma Rose finished blowing her nose before continuing. "When Mama started showing, her parents told her that they were going to stay with her aunt in Ohio until the baby was born. They said they were supposed to have better doctors there. Mama knew the real reason was that they were embarrassed.

Everything was normal with the pregnancy and when the time came, labor started on schedule. This was the last entry that you wrote in the diary," Hannah said looking at her mother. "Why did you stop writing after the baby was born?"

Sophie looked at Roman who encouraged her to answer. With a shaking voice Sophie said, "My baby girl was born dead."

"I am so sorry, Mama. Why couldn't you tell us? We would have been able to comfort you and helped you to grieve all of these years."

Sophie wiped her eyes. "I have never really been able to forgive myself. I have always felt it was my fault that my little Isabella died. That I didn't want her enough."

Grandma Rose spoke up in an authoritative and rebuking tone. "That's nonsense and you know it. As a young girl you may have convinced yourself that was the case but now you are an adult and a God fearing one at that. You know better. You know that you don't possess that kind of power. You cannot control who lives and who dies. Furthermore, would you even want to?"

Hannah and Isaac looked at each other, afraid that the words were too harsh for Sophie's current state of mind.

Sophie turned to face more towards her wise and always blunt mother-in-law. Hannah watched and held her breath for her mother's next words. "I know that you are right Rose. This year has especially made me realize exactly what you have said is true. With our dear Toby's passing, I have struggled more than ever with my past. I just didn't know how to tell my family. I am so sorry. Roman, I am especially sorry for all that I have put you through."

Sophie turned to find eyes that were full of love. Not love that is shared at the beginning of a marriage but a love that has matured into what God himself decrees between a man and a woman. Isaac squeezed Hannah's hand with his own large one. Hannah could see that though the truth hurt very much, it was never wrong. The time for healing was long in coming for a reason unknown to Hannah. Although there were many questions yet to be answered, there was one mystery solved for Hannah. All of those times that her mother seemed to be lost in another world they finally made sense to her. How her mother must have suffered over the loss of two children.

Sophie interrupted her daughter's thoughts by saying, "However did you come across my diary? I thought that I had lost it all those years ago. The last day I ever saw it was the day my baby died."

A perplexed look came over Hannah's face. "Well, you will never believe where I found it." Hannah paused for a second. "Do you remember when we went to visit Alice several days ago?"

Sophie's thick, black eyebrows raised in recollection as she said, "Yes but what has that got to do with it?"

Roman patted his wife's hand and said, "Let her explain."

Hannah continued. "When I went into Bella's room to retrieve the blanket that Alice asked for, that's when I found it. It fell out of the chair onto the floor when I picked the blanket up."

"Why would Bella have your mother's journal in her possession?" Isaac voiced the question that was on the tip of everyone's tongue.

They all turned in Sophie's direction. "I'm sure I have no idea. I am as puzzled as the rest of you."

"I thought that might be the case. So that is why I planned a meeting with Bella, to get to the bottom of this. I needed answers." Hannah's desperation was showing itself just below the surface.

She took a calming breath and said, "The day of the blizzard I had arranged a meeting with Bella at the old shack just out of town."

Isaac looked surprised. "Is that where Seth found you, the old shack that we passed when we all went out for your birthday?"

"Yes, Seth found me a little way away from there, thanks to Spirit." Hannah reached down and patted the dog's head lovingly.

Roman said, "That is probably the only place that we did not think to look. We had no reason to believe you would have gone there."

Hannah said, "It was no one's fault but my own. I didn't tell anyone where I was going. I simply sent a note home with Katie to give to Bella but she never showed up."

"We don't think Bella ever received the note. Katie somehow misplaced it or more likely lost it on her way home from school," Isaac explained.

Grandma Rose questioned curiously, "But why did you involve Bella before coming to us about the diary? Maybe she just found it somewhere."

"It's possible that she may have done just that but deep in my heart I feel that there is much more to it."

Hannah paused to gather strength before going further. It was hard to reveal the things that she had been harboring for so long. Doubt was there ready to spring forth attempting to squelch the rising truth that lies within.

"I have no factual basis for the things that have disturbed me for the past several months. Most of the incidences that have occurred could have happened innocently. Like the barn catching fire or my falling over the water fall the night of my birthday."

Isaac hurriedly cut in, "When did the barn catch fire? Why didn't you tell me?"

Hannah felt it was time to be completely honest. "A few weeks ago and to answer your second question I haven't felt like I could talk to you about what has been bothering me."

"I don't understand," Isaac said in a confused manner.

"That is part of what I am about to tell you, to tell you all. It's about Bella. I get this awful feeling that she really dislikes me. She gives me these looks when no one else can see her and I feel that she is trying to come between Isaac and me. Seth has even noticed this at times. He has been a great friend to me. I was so afraid of saying anything to any of you for fear that I was wrong. I still hope that I am wrong but for some reason I know there is more."

Isaac's tone was full of remorse when he said, "Can you ever forgive me for being so neglectful. I have taken you and our relationship for granted."

"Of course I forgive you, Isaac." Isaac held Hannah and it felt like it did when they first knew each other, pure again, without the pollution of mistrust.

Sophie blew her nose and gained their attention before saying, "So how did you plan on confronting Bella with the diary?"

"I believe that she already knows that I have it. Alice would probably have told her that I had been in her room that day. I was planning on just coming right out and asking her about it. Why she had it in her possession? I was also going to find out why she was treating me the way that she was and just hope that she would tell the truth about both things."

Roman pushed back from the table and stood and stretched before suggesting his opinion. "I think that although she might confess the truth to you, that doesn't necessarily mean that she will own it before all of us."

"I do agree son; it must be done in front of two or three witnesses. Since she only seems to reveal her true self to Hannah then whoever goes with her must stay out of sight until she confesses," Grandma Rose proposed.

Everyone looked at each other and nodded their agreement. They also decided that Roman and Sophie would be the ones to accompany their daughter. A moment of silence then swept the room as they all took in what had just transpired over the past few days. Surely, surely there was a purpose.

CHAPTER 26

Hannah spent the next few days recuperating. Grandma Rose had brought a relentless Mandy to visit her. There was no way Mandy was going to let them keep her from seeing to Hannah. The visit did much to lift Hannah's spirits. Sarah came along and the family drew close, allowing Sophie to soften her worries over her past. Hannah was nervous about confronting Bella. The longer she waited the more doubt crept in. Isaac was planning on bringing Bella over for a visit in a short while. She invited herself along which worked out perfectly.

Isaac had ridden over yesterday to let them know so that they would be prepared. Isaac would excuse himself and tell Bella and Hannah that he wanted to finish a gift that he had been working on out in the barn for his father. Hopefully Bella would feel free to speak truly. The next day, Hannah was walking the floors all morning. Roman and Sophie knew that such a task was not in their daughter's nature.

℘

Just after noon, they heard the rattling of a wagon pulling up out front. Roman and Sophie immediately disappeared into their bedroom, leaving the door slightly ajar. They sat in chairs next to the door to quietly listen. A wrap at the door sounded and Hannah went to answer it. As always, Bella's beauty was almost overly stunning. Her sleek black hair and emerald eyes seemed unreal. Drawing her eyes away, she looked at Isaac who stood behind Bella with a gentle prodding look in his eyes.

"Do come in out of the cold! It is so nice to see you." Hannah took Bella's gloves and scarf while Isaac helped her with her coat.

"Something does smell wonderful. I hope you haven't gone out of your way on my account." Bella twirled around in her full skirt, taking in her surroundings.

"Just some warm apple cider and cinnamon bread. Would you care for some?" Hannah offered.

"None for me just yet, thank you. What about you Isaac?" Bella asked him before Hannah could.

"No thanks. If you ladies don't mind, I would like to go out and finish working on my father's gift while I am here."

Hannah spoke first, "Go ahead, Bella and I have not had a chance to talk for quite some time, if that is ok with you Bella?"

Bella was visibly disappointed because she obviously had an agenda of her own. She looked at Isaac and then to Hannah and said, "That sounds lovely." Isaac turned and left the house.

For a few seconds, you could have heard a pen drop. It was as if each of them was waiting on the other to bring up the diary first. Hannah noticed that Bella was looking at all of the doors and rooms of the house which were not many. Hannah initiated one of the thoughts that were on Bella's mind.

"My parents will be sorry they missed you. They left not long before you got here."

"Oh."

"Is there something on your mind Bella?" Hannah hoped that she would be the first to ask about the diary.

Bella turned back to face Hannah, the sweet look gone from her expression now. Bella said, "I think that you know exactly what is on my mind. I would like for you to give me back my journal."

"You must be mistaken. The journal or diary that I found belongs to someone else and you know it," Hannah returned with a confidence she did not know she had.

Bella walked straight up to Hannah, nose to beautiful nose. "That journal rightfully belongs to me. It was given to me!"

"That doesn't make any sense. Why should I believe you? You have made it no secret to me that you dislike me for some reason that I cannot fathom," Hannah stood her ground.

Bella waved her hand in the air. "Oh right! Perfect Hannah, no one could dislike her. She does no wrong!"

"What's wrong with you? Where is all of this coming from?" Hannah's confusion was evident in her facial expression and tone of voice.

"Don't worry about it! Just give me back my journal, Hannah!" Bella's eyes were full of emotion.

"No! Not until you tell me what is going on," Hannah replied back.

"I see you think to take that from me also just like you have everything else."

Hannah said as calmly as possible, "I am not taking anything from you. It is my mother's journal."

Bella lay angry, tear filled eyes upon Hannah and said, "And it's my mother's journal." They stared at each other for several seconds, their hearts pounding and their minds trying to comprehend the implication of the words now spoken.

Across the room, the same words were being analyzed by Roman and Sophie. Roman placed a staying hand on his wife's arm. They must wait a little longer.

"I don't understand." Hannah's shaking body sought a chair and sunk down in it.

"It is not hard to figure out. I was the baby your mother had. The baby your mother didn't want. She just gave me away as if I was nothing," Bella said bitterly.

"That's not true. The baby my mother had died at birth. She never gave her away," Hannah said in defense of her mother.

Bella heard footsteps behind her. She turned and saw Roman and Sophie standing directly behind her. She locked eyes with Sophie and they tried to uncover the truth that had been buried for so many years. A flicker of hope was kindled deep in their hearts.

Roman took charge. "Come, let us all sit down and sort this out slowly," he said leading Sophie and Bella to a seat opposite each other at the kitchen table. He then took a seat beside his wife.

Sophie knew that she must choose her words very carefully. She did not want to make the mistake of losing her daughter for a second time. She could see that Bella was on the edge, refusing to listen and clinging to everything that she had always believed for so long.

"Bella, would you care to tell me how the journal came to be in your possession?" Sophie asked gently.

Bella's eyes went from Roman, to Hannah and then back to Sophie. "The woman who claimed to be my mother all my life passed away a few months before I came here to stay with Cousin Katherine. Her name was Beatrice. She was a widow lady and never had any children of her own."

Hannah chose not to join in for the moment. It seemed the only thing that she managed to do was anger Bella even more. She had many questions that she wanted answered but she would trust her parents to handle the important ones.

Sophie inquired, "Is she the one that gave you the journal?"

Bella shook her head no. "No. She confessed that she was not my real mother and told me that her brother, John, and his wife, Dianne, brought me to her."

Sophie's face went ashen. Her mother's sister was involved. The heavy feeling in Sophie's chest told her that what she was about to hear would devastate her.

"Please go on," Roman urged softly.

"I don't really know what Dianne told my mother, "Beatrice", but she told me that Dianne would have the information that I was looking for. So after a short amount of time, I went to see John and Dianne. They did not know that Beatrice had passed away. I demanded to know who my real parents were and that is when they gave me the journal. After I had read it, Dianne said that you and your parents did not want me," Bella said this with a bluntness that was meant to hurt.

"That's not true, Bella. I wanted you very much. My parents, for some selfish and horrible reason, told me you had died. They gave me a lock of your hair and what you were wearing and never allowed me to mention you again."

Sophie could not believe that her parents had been so cruel. She must find a way to convince Bella, her daughter, that she loved her, had always loved her. Sophie then thought of the small chest out in the barn.

"Hannah?" Sophie beckoned her daughter with the light of hope illuminating her face.

"Yes?"

"Will you please go out into the barn and look for a small, worn chest that is tucked away in the back corner of the tool room?" Sophie asked.

"Sure Mama," Hannah answered. Hannah didn't say that she knew exactly what her mother was talking about. Some things weren't necessary to mention, especially now.

As soon as Hannah was out the door, she let out the pent up breath that she had been holding unconsciously. She couldn't believe it. Bella was her sister. She could hear Isaac inside the barn. The ringing of the hammer drowned out the sound of her entrance. She waited until he stopped before walking up beside him. His smile had a calming effect on her rattled nerves.

"How did things go? Did everything get straightened out?" Isaac asked as he surveyed his handiwork.

"I am not sure. You won't believe what I just found out." Hannah's words had his full attention now.

"Go on."

"I just found out that Bella is most probably my sister. She is the baby girl that Mama had all those years ago."

Isaac's face transformed into a look of absolute disbelief. "How can that be? Why would she lie about this for so long?" Isaac stepped closer to Hannah and placed both of her hands in his. "I feel like such a fool for believing anything that she said."

"If it makes you feel any better you weren't the only one. I just don't know why she seems to dislike me so much. She has so much anger inside. We are going to need another miracle."

"Things will work out, you'll see." Isaac pulled her close to comfort her.

After a moment, Hannah went to get the small chest. There were so many clues right under her nose and she never knew it. Isaac chose to stay outside. Hannah knew he was there for her. From now on he would make sure that she always knew it. Isaac promised as he watched Hannah make her way back to the house.

Sophie and Bella both turned and looked her way when she reentered the house. Hannah was taken aback by the resemblance between them. She wondered why she had never seen it before. She handed the chest to her father and he placed it on the table before Sophie. Tears fell as Sophie opened the small ornate chest. She reached inside with trembling hands and withdrew a lock of dark hair. She also brought forth the tiny gown that had been hidden away but never forgotten. Then Hannah saw her mother reach in a side pocket that she herself had missed that day, in such a hurry to put the chest back in its place. Sophie pulled out an envelope with a small slip of paper.

She raised shining eyes to Bella and said, "Bella I wrote down your name and the day you were born on this paper. Would you mind telling me your birthday?"

Bella shifted in her seat. She fingered the infant articles and replied, "I was born on May the fifteenth, 1858." Sophie just bowed her head for a space of time and when she looked up, she had the most beautiful smile upon her face. She laid the paper in front of Bella. It said, Isabella Hope was born on May the fifteenth, 1858. Gone but never forgotten.

Sophie took a chance and reached over the table and placed her hand over her daughter's. Bella was not quite sure how to respond so she just kept still. It was a start.

Sophie softly said, "In time I hope that you can forgive me for believing my parents. I hope that we can move beyond the wrong that has been done." Sophie paused to look into Bella's confused eyes and told her, "Pray to God to give you a forgiving heart and He will grant you one, if you are sincere."

UNDER HEAVEN ❧ Karen McDavid

CHAPTER 27

Overwhelmed by the revelations of yesterday's encounter, Hannah lay in bed analyzing every notable moment since Bella, her sister, came amongst them. The word "sister" seemed so foreign to her mind and tongue but yet it was a reality. Bella had come here thinking that she was unwanted. Hannah could tell that she had obviously not grown up in a Christian home. Hannah was beginning to understand why Bella behaved as she had.

So many things had been brought to light. Hannah could only imagine how astonished her mother must be. To have lost a son and gained a daughter was surely to be a great mystery only known to God. Hannah only knew that whatever the purpose for Bella's delayed entrance into their lives, it was now the time and season to embrace the blessing that God had bestowed upon them.

Deciding it was time to rise and face the day, she went to the kitchen to get a bite of breakfast. Roman and Sophie were at the table enjoying a cup of coffee together. They were no doubt having a wonderful and meaningful conversation as well.

"Good morning," her parents said in unison.

"Good morning. How did you both sleep?" Hannah asked.

"Very little but I suspect that you already guessed that," Sophie said with a smile.

"Speak for yourselves. I slept like a rock. I feel as though a mountain has been lifted off our chests," Roman responded with vigor. "Also I forgot to tell you that you will not be going in to teach since it is only a couple of days until Christmas. I posted a note on the door while you were recuperating."

"Thanks. We could use the time to prepare. Did Bella say when she was coming back?" Hannah asked anxiously.

Sophie spoke hopefully, "Your father is going to see if she will join the family for Christmas. I wanted her to have some time to think things over. She must have a lot of emotions to sort through."

Hannah only nodded her head. She was looking forward to the family gathering. They chose to have Christmas there instead of at the home place for Bella's sake.

She and her mother soon got busy making preparations. Sarah and Mandy would provide much of the food also. Spirit kept out of the way, accepting bits of food when offered.

ℰ

Later that day, Isaac and Seth stopped by and Hannah noticed the camaraderie between them that she had never seen before now, little had she known what good things the Lord had in store for her and her family. She was very humbled.

Seth was running his hand along Spirit's back as he said, I still cannot believe what a magnificent animal this is and how he took care of you."

Hannah agreed. "There is no doubt that he was placed in my life and has been watching over me, only at the time, I didn't realize it." Hannah watched how Spirit had greeted Seth and said, "I think he is especially fond of you because you found me that day. He is very loyal."

Isaac cleared his throat and looked at Seth before saying, "I hate to admit it but I was jealous that it was you who rescued Hannah. I can't apologize enough for treating you the way I did, Seth."

Seth casually waved his hand, "Forget about it. I might have even behaved the same way if it were my love being carried in by another." Hannah turned bright red. She should have known that Seth was always ready for any opportunity to embarrass her. Isaac and Seth got a good laugh out of it.

Sophie, who had been busily baking in the corner of the kitchen, grabbed a plate of homemade candy and set it before them. "Now you two behave yourselves. Hannah is not used to dealing with both of you at the same time," Sophie admonished with smiling eyes.

Isaac told Sophie that he would be bringing Bella on Christmas. He also informed them that she was moving back to town with Katherine. His mother was feeling much better now. Hannah could see the relief flow across her mother's face. They all had some reservations as to whether Bella would join them or not.

Christmas Eve was spent decorating the tree that Isaac and Seth had left by the front door as a surprise. By evening they all sat quietly before the fire contemplating the year's events.

Hannah thought about how her life had changed drastically in such a short period of time. In that period of time, she lost a brother and gained a sister. She had fell in love and fought with hate. But she knew God had been with her through it all. He was in all things. He had been in her dreams and most of all, in her heart. He had given her a heart to trust in Him to direct her paths.

Christmas morning dawned with a fresh layer of snow on the ground. Hannah felt like a child again. She arose from bed before daylight to get a head start for the anticipated day ahead. This year they had new loved ones to share the special day with. Grandma Rose did as she promised. She made sure that Ruth and Seth would be there. It was not long before she and her mother had everything prepared for dinner. The whole house smelt like Christmas. Hannah excused herself to go and dress while Roman and Sophie took a break to relax and just enjoy the peace that was now present in their lives.

Hannah's closet held several dresses that were suitable to wear but Hannah saw nothing that she knew would compare to whatever Bella had on. Hannah chided herself for such shallow thoughts. Bella could have the wardrobe of a queen and she would still be one of the poorest people she knew. She did not have what God could place in her heart. She would pray that Bella would seek God so that she could truly have a sister, both naturally and spiritually.

Pulling a deep red gown that was almost black in color from her closet, Hannah held it up to her in front of the mirrored dresser. It was not new but it was her favorite. She dressed and left her long hair flowing. She pulled a small amount back away from her face and secured it with the combs that Isaac had given her for her birthday. The front door burst open when she had just stepped from her room. She could hear Mandy exclaiming over this or that.

Roman and Jacob had found a seat away from the kitchen and the chatter of the women. The table was already so full of savory dishes that they had to place some of them on the stove and hutch. This was going to be a Christmas to remember, one to treasure.

Mandy asked, "Hannah what do you think about everything that has happened? I just couldn't believe it! Bella is your sister!"

Hannah always felt better when Mandy was around. Her honest forwardness was as familiar as the four seasons. You can always count on them both.

Hannah sat down beside Mandy and said, "To tell you the truth, I am very thankful for how God brought her into our lives. Through it all, I have learned patience and my faith has strengthened."

"Amen!" said Grandma Rose.

At that moment there was a knock at the door and Seth entered with Ruth on his arm. Ruth hugged everyone and took a chair next to Grandma Rose. "Oh Rose, isn't everything just lovely! Thank you all so much for having me." Ruth declared as she admired the humbly decorated house. Seth joined the men and left the ladies to their own company.

Everyone had arrived except for Isaac, Josh and Bella. Sophie kept an eye on the mantle clock.

Grandma Rose noticed that Sophie seemed to be bit nervous. "Don't worry Sophie, Bella will come. God wouldn't have worked this all out for nothing." This seemed to calm Sophie and she took a seat for a much needed break.

They all joined in on the small talk and when Mandy caught sight of Spirit lying in the corner, she hopped up and went over to admire him. The large animal seemed to know that he had to put up with the attention Mandy showered on him. The movement outside their window drew their gaze to the door. It was Bella. Roman and Sophie went to answer the door together. Isaac entered first, his eyes automatically seeking out Hannah, then Josh who was followed by a slightly different Bella. Even the slightest change in Bella was noticeable. It was as a faint flicker of light that could be seen in the darkness by all.

This was a Bella who struggled with what she had known or thought to be true all of her life with the real truth that had presented itself. It had manifested itself through the humble lives of those around her, a beckoning that had breached her resistance ever so softly. Sophie very cautiously put her arms around her eldest daughter. Fear of rejection strongly plagued her thoughts. When Sophie felt no response, she started to back away. Then Bella, ever so hesitantly, raised her arms into an unfamiliar gesture of love.

Roman's voice was hoarse when he spoke, "Welcome, Bella. We are so very glad you came." Bella saw only sincerity in Roman's eyes.

"Thank you. I wasn't sure what to do. I did not want to impose."

"Not at all, we were anxiously awaiting your arrival," Roman assured her. After Roman took her coat, Sophie led Bella into the kitchen where all of the women folk were gathered. Of course the men were close by. They were just across the open room next to the fireplace.

Hannah patted the chair next to her. "Come sit here, Bella," Hannah smiled welcomingly to her new sister. " We usually do presents but this year since everything was kind of different, we decided to skip it and just enjoy each other."

Bella looked at them and said, "I am kind of relieved since I didn't bring anything."

Grandma Rose shook her head back and forth before saying, "For lands sake, don't you all know that the gifts have already been provided for us, the greatest being salvation through Jesus Christ. He also provided this family with another gift this year and that is the return of our beautiful Isabella Hope." Bella looked around at everyone with tears shining in their eyes.

She was not used to such displays of emotion let alone be the cause of it. The past few months she had often wondered what manner of people are these? She found herself feeling bad for the things that she had done wrong against them.

Bella took a deep breath and said, "I want to thank you all for being so kind even though I don't deserve it. Especially you Hannah, you probably already know that it was me that tried to harm you, first with the smoke in the schoolhouse and again by the waterfall. I even went so far as to catch the barn on fire. I don't think that deep down I really wanted to hurt you but I was just consumed with so much jealousy. I am so sorry and I hope that you can find it in your heart to forgive me." Bella was sobbing uncontrollably by the time she had finished confessing.

Hannah just gathered her sister in her arms and told her that she loved her. The house was peacefully quiet for a spell. Hannah felt as if she held a small child in her arms. Bella had not seen God's light shine in those around her as she grew up. Hannah prayed that with God's help, they could be that light. Therefore, when the gentle beckoning came, Bella would heed the call.

As the special day continued through into the evening, they all sat around telling stories of the past. This helped Bella learn much more about the family and become more intimately a part of them.

Hannah watched as Seth stared curiously at Bella. It was as though he was seeing her for the first time. Hannah's eyes caught Isaac's from across the room. He stood and came to stand next to her. Hannah looked up at him and he extended his hand and helped her to her feet. She had been sitting on the floor for a lack of chairs. She questioned him with her eyes and he only smiled.

Isaac grabbed their coats and they quietly stepped outside into the clear, starlit night sky. Isaac's large hand was warm as it clasped her small one. He led her out back to her path down to her special rock. Spirit cut out in front of them and led the way. Hannah had not even noticed that he had slipped out of the house with them. Tears stung her eyes. How much he meant to her. Isaac squeezed her hand. He looked at her and read her thoughts.

"A miracle for sure," Isaac whispered. They continued on until they stopped upon the large rock, the light of the full moon touching the rippling water. Hannah could feel that something was on Isaac's mind. He had been rather quiet all evening. Perhaps he was wishing that he was home for Christmas instead of being here for the whole day.

"Hannah."

"Isaac." They both said at the same time.

Hannah waited for Isaac to go first. He looked very serious. She hoped nothing was wrong.

"Hannah, I have been trying to wait for the perfect time to talk to you. I have tried to get everything in order but instead I am going to listen to my heart," Isaac said and swallowed nervously before continuing. "I have prayed about it and I want to make you my wife."

Hannah's heart leaped with joy. The tears flowed freely. She was given her heart's desire.

Isaac lifted her chin with his finger and said, "What I mean to say is, will you marry me?"

Hannah stared into his eyes and said without hesitation, "Yes! I will marry you!"

Isaac reached into his pocket and withdrew a gold ring with a ruby adorning the top. It was simple. It was perfect. They sealed their promise with a kiss.

As they walked back to join the rest of the family, Isaac suddenly stopped to ask, "When shall we say that we are getting married?" Hannah just looked up into the heavens and smiled as she said, "At the time of the singing of the birds".

Ⅎ

While Hannah Jamison's trials and purpose eventually become clear, there may yet be another season for the unfolding of God's plan amongst His treasured children of the Black Hills.

Ⅎ